ANGEL'S SMOKE

A PARANORMAL ANGEL ROMANCE

ELEMENTAL ANGELS

AIMEE ROBINSON

AMR PUBLISHING LLC

Angel's Smoke

Copyright © 2025 by Aimee Robinson

Cover by Angela Haddon Book Cover Design

Edited by Sara Burgess at Telltail Editing

All rights reserved.

No part of this book may be reproduced in any form or by any electronic or mechanical means, including information storage and retrieval systems, without written permission from the author, except for the use of brief quotations in a book review.

To the readers.
Thanks for loving these angels as much as I do.

ELEMENTAL ANGELS

Angel's Target

Angel's Duty

Angel's Devotion

Angel's Light

Angel's Temper

Angel's Conquest

Angel's Vengeance

Angel's Smoke

CHAPTER 1

Iron had known a fair amount of temptation in his day but never the sort that had chosen to visit him on the whispers of butterfly wings. Or were they moths? No . . . Skippers? Those insects with the patterned wings but with those cute anime eyes that always took in far more than their size should allow?

Fuck. Did it matter what kind of horse his dream girl rode in on each night if he could never truly see her? Iron kicked out in frustration against the tangle of flannel sheets anchoring him to his bed in the waking world while the more vulnerable cerebral parts of him sank further into his dream space.

Every night for the past three months, he'd crawl into bed, resigning himself to the tantalizing show his worse-for-wear mind would conjure up. And every night, like clockwork, his feverish thoughts would manifest *her*. Well, parts of her, at any rate.

It began when Iron had officially taken over as foreman for building the new homestead for his brother Rhode, the former seraphim commander of the Empyrean's legion of spying angels, and his brother's soul bond, Neela. And by taken over, he meant thrown himself into a project that would mentally and physically exhaust him to the point that his body had no choice but to tune out the hard truths of his reality and thoroughly pummel his tired ass into the mattress. Okay, so perhaps he wasn't *exactly* following the tenets of avoidance coping, but one didn't get to be an immortal angel as old as him without learning how to break the rules that needed breaking.

Too bad fate, like always, was a fickle bitch and would sooner yank the spark plug out of his car just so he could learn how to get himself back on the road rather than road flare that journey for him.

Suffice it to say, Iron needed the life lessons and reminders of his solemn circumstances about as much as mortals needed juice cleanses and food detoxes. Last he checked, humans still possessed livers and kidneys, but far be it for him to point out the functions of their own goddamn anatomy when he could barely keep his head straight.

Every single one of his warrior sentinel brothers had become mated. Not just mated but soul bound. Anointed with their other halves and inseparable regardless of the reasons that had landed all the angels in this mortal prison in the first place. Fortunately for them, when the road ahead blasted a firehose of eternal uncertainty at you, it was always a mite easier to stomach the stuff if you had someone worth braving the unknown for to lose yourself in each night.

Iron's limbs slowly stilled, finally giving over to that familiar heaviness that urged his muscles into their nightly repose beneath the sheets. The elemental magic of the minerals and metals within the great mountain he slept beneath had begun its ministrations, unstitching the day's tension to allow Iron's celestial powers to recharge.

A feat he was now also alone in, as the soul bond connection had finally unleashed his brothers' full celestial powers after eons of magically imposed limitations while his own were still on a tight tether of daily depletion and necessary renewal.

Fan-fucking-tastic.

The reminder kicked around his skull with rattling recognition. It was always there. The stark otherness of his circumstances while the ones he loved the most healed and grew into the full family of warriors they'd always meant to become.

It was a vision he'd long ago abandoned for himself, no matter how comforting the appeal felt wrapped around his most private thoughts, where he permitted, on the rarest of occasions, his mind's indulgence in fantasies.

Had he known what was coming for him, however, he'd have locked his mental palace up good and tight, as one would when faced with any sort of torture.

The first time the woman visited Iron's dreams, he'd done what instinct had him do against any intruder: fight. His mind had always been a safe space, regardless of the terrors his psyche would choose to visit upon him. At least, if he had to relive the past, the elements of his torment would be familiar. The players, the souls, the demon charmers. It was a dreamscape crafted from battlefields both celestial and terrestrial, from blood and magic to more sinister parts of his existence. But it was always his, and it was always familiar in some way. After all, outside of a few notable exceptions spawning from chain restaurants, even bad pizza was still good, to a degree. He was content to exist, even if the existence came with a toll. It was a toll he knew, however, and one he'd grown accustomed to paying.

Until the night after their most recent battle with Cyro, the demon ruler. That was when *she* had appeared.

The first glimpses of her were always the same, and that was how he knew that nothing of the dream girl visiting him was by chance.

Fate, as usual, had its grimy hands under his hood.

Even now, as the heaviness of the dreamworld shifted in its

opacity to reveal the spun silk of her hair that always seemed to reach for him before floating away, a new emotion rose to the surface: impatience. By the mages, even in his dreams, he was brimming with the stuff. Though he had no idea how, his body, both within the dream and without, still reacted to just the mere suggestion of her. Every muscle and tendon was strung tight, his shoulders tense, the coarse hairs of his beard scratching against his neck as his jaw clenched into a position his molars would curse him for later.

And then he felt it. That deliciously soft hair grazing across the inside of his reaching forearms, pulling up every single goose bump in its wake. Among the swirling white misty landscape of his mind, the delicate curtain of golden copper would always pool in the cruxes of his elbows, tempting him to twist his wrists so that the strands might sift through his fingers. But he couldn't. He'd learned that lesson the first dozen or so times he'd tried, which was how he knew she was no ordinary dream girl and this was no ordinary dream sequence. Every time he tried to grasp the vexing creature, something would yank her away from him and dissolve her back into the ether of his mind.

It was a new type of aggravation, one he regrettably couldn't smash into submission with his mace or disintegrate with the flames of his angel fire.

So he waited and waited as he did every time, until the female finally crept closer and grazed the skin of his arms with a brush of hair so soft and tantalizing, his breath caught.

Holy shit.

For the first time since she'd begun visiting him in his dreams, an outline of her form had begun to take shape.

Mages, she was so . . . slight, with her head barely tall enough to clear his rib cage, even if he allowed himself to stand at his full height around her, which he never did because, even in dreams, he knew how imposing his form could be to a woman. The mists around her steadily compressed into one slender arm, then another as small hands with dainty fingers rested on the outside of his elbows. The sensation of her ethereal touch against his skin was as odd as it was fleeting. A shiver of awareness thrummed through his body, coiling down his spine and stroking the secret part of him where his full celestial power had dwelled once upon an eternity.

And damn if he didn't feel that caress brush across every nerve ending. Iron's back teeth met again, and not for the first time, he wished he didn't sleep naked. Which was more than a little bit ridiculous, right? We existed in dreams as our mind saw us. But right now, as her soft feminine curves coalesced before him, he sure as shit regretted the image he was presenting to her: that of a bulky and very nude heavily muscled male with a sleep-tousled rat's nest of a mane brushing his shoulders, a beard a few days past a decent trim, and the most painful erection that refused to point anywhere other than at the dream woman before him.

Jesus fucking Christ. He looked like some goddamn NFL nose tackle who'd just wrestled a bear, sacked the starting *and* backup quarterbacks for half a dozen plays, and then had somehow stumbled into the women's locker room.

Iron exhaled through his nose and started to curl his fingers into his palms in frustration, but the woman let out a soft gasp and floated away, dissolving some of the form she'd begun to take.

"No!" he rushed out, knowing full well his plea would go unanswered, as his words always did. Iron tried to reach for her but caught only air. "I'm sorry. I'm so sorry. I didn't mean—"

"Who are you?"

Iron froze. All the moving parts knocking around in his cerebral space just locked everything up tight. His limbs, his muscles, his mouth.

Had she just . . . spoken?

The wisps of white ether merely continued to dance before

him, like a puppy playing keep-away, once more cradling the sheet of copper hair that was the only defining feature he'd ever been able to make out. Until just a moment ago, when he'd heard her voice for the first time.

A deeply resonant alto with a hint of annoyance that was so hurried, it seemed she barely had the patience to get the question out. He replayed those three little words in his mind and couldn't help but smile at the realization that tightened around his quickening heart. Her *you* had been spoken softly, barely even audible, but was still delivered with an air of indignation that he hadn't yet answered her question even before she finished speaking it.

The corner of his lips ticked up slowly. "You're a New Englander. From New Hampshire, if I had to guess."

Her silence was the confirmation he was shocked to discover his soul craved. Shocked on a few accounts. The first, because in all the months of their now-you-see-me-now-you-don't dance, he'd never once heard her voice. And the second being the literal gut punch of power blasting him behind his sternum that almost brought him to his knees once he'd heard her speak. But the blast was just as fleeting as the hope that had begun to flare in his chest.

His power. His full celestial power was there, knocking at his basement door like a boxed-away relic, and then it was gone just as quickly.

"How do you know where I live?" she asked, her words breathy and worried.

More indignation. More sass. But all of it was veiled under a blanket of uncertainty. And fear, if he had to guess.

Rattling breaths bellowed out of his lungs, which was a crying shame, because the poor things had yet to resume maximum capacity as far as the whole oxygen-intake thing was concerned. Iron squeezed his eyes shut and sank into the three-seconds-ago memory of what his body knew to be true. Yes, that roaring resonance within him was his angel fire. His *full* angel fire. A power he'd not known since he and his brothers had fallen from the Empyrean, Heaven's highest realm, way back before mortals had even been a thought.

Iron flattened his palm against his chest, his grip losing purchase against the sheen of sweat that had bloomed across his skin. Desperately, he scrambled to reach for it again. The door, the lock, whatever sort of fucking key would fit in the lock. Something that would grant him access to the very powers that would once again make him whole. When he came away with nothing, he gritted out a curse and opened his eyes.

The white ether had settled around slim shoulders now sadly hunched. Angled creases formed among the mist, sketching an elegant neck and softly rounded face beneath a mass of red hair. Iron sucked in a breath as more parts of his dream girl began to take shape. Pert nose. Dainty ears with adorable detached earlobes. A lower lip slightly fuller than the top. And then the wispy waves of his dream pulled his eyes lower, outlining her breasts, slightly rounded belly, and flaring hips.

Her eyes were the punch he didn't see coming. Vibrant jade orbs blazed amid the swirling ether as they stared right at him, quieting his rising panic and replacing it with an entirely new preoccupation.

"I'll say this again," she said. "Who are you?"

A tremulous wonder finally illuminated what he'd been searching for: the key to his basement door. By all the mother-fucking mages he'd sworn had abandoned him long ago, there she stood, as real as his secrets and as haunting as the future he'd never thought possible.

It had all been delivered in the form of a green-eyed goddess born of the fears in his mind. The answer to his fate. The solution to his bleak existence.

Iron straightened his spine, curled his hand into a fist, and dropped to his knee before her. In his periphery, the dream-scape moved slightly, pulling her farther back away from him, but he didn't care. Now that he knew who she was, *what* she was, there was nowhere she could go that he would not find her.

The weight of his discovery sank heavily onto the back of his neck as he bowed his head. With equal parts fear and determination, he smiled as he closed his eyes and mentally stepped closer toward the precipice he'd been set upon.

Fate had chosen a path for him once before, and it had nearly destroyed him. He would not allow the mages to condemn him so again.

"I am yours."

Anna Malone shot out of bed with all the grace of a startled scarlet-bootied baboon, complete with a wild mane and absolutely zero sense of what the hell had just happened.

No, that wasn't entirely true. She still had a sense of some things. That man, for starters.

That man . . .

A surging heat pricked her skin, which was a dozen kinds of unnecessary, really, given how often she sweated through her sheets after a visit from him. Any woman, or man for that matter, would have to be dead for a solid century, at minimum, not to appreciate the finest specimen of brawn and beauty ever breathing. And for some reason, which she honestly saw no pressing reason to uncover, her stressed-out brain continued to give her the gift of his imaginary company each night.

Anna itched the back of her dewy neck, frustrated that she still had to sleep with the heat on this close to spring, and tried to shake out why this particular dream felt a little . . . off. He was there, like usual, but good lawdy, that was where the thread of commonality ended. There was nothing usual about what had just happened, and that was saying a boat load given how often her REM sleep cycle served up the same images every night on repeat. She'd never been much into the psychological study of dreams, but she'd read enough Stephen King to know that reruns weren't normal.

Once her heart rate fell back into generally life-sustaining levels, she pinched the bridge of her nose and sighed. Oh, who the hell was she kidding? Did she even know what normal was anymore? The past few months had been such a tumultuous ride of unexpected marvels, painful disappointments, far too many you-should-be-happys, and a buttload of doubt that it was no wonder she needed to fantasize about some bearded hottie just to make it through the night sans the depression that perpetually trailed behind her during the day.

Then, like frickin' clockwork, her mother's old words came flaring up, as they were wont to do whenever Anna was at peak exhaustion or stress, which, these days, thanks to her present condition, was all the damn time.

You should be grateful, Anna.

"Nope. Not doing this right now." She grabbed the pillow next to her, still warm from sleep, and tried to smother out the ever-loving aggravation that always heated her skin further whenever her psychosomatic system was inclined to leap to her aid. "Ugh, just . . . no," she mumbled into the pillow, wincing as the polyester scratched her cheek, before promptly falling back and burying herself beneath the covers again. "Too early for this." Against her better judgment, Anna cracked an eye open. Yup, huge mistake. Numbers that had no business dangling an AM after their digits glared back at her in a muted red that, while somehow soothing during daylight hours, were far too forward and abrasive before the sun was up.

Wait, *was* the sun even up?

Anna peeled back the comforter just enough so she could see around her nightstand, because no way was she moving more of her body than she needed to again, and groaned. *Damn.* While no cheerful golden rays crept through the slats of her bedroom's Venetian blinds just yet, a pale color *was* beginning to lighten the sky, suggesting that said sun would be up within the hour.

Lovely. No way she would be falling back to sleep.

Enacting the only form of protest still available for the time being, Anna twisted her body so her face was squarely pressed into the pillow. "Should I be grateful for sleep deprivation, too?" she asked into the cushion.

When proper breathing became more of a requirement, she shifted her head away from the pillow, yanked the sweaty strands of hair out of her mouth, and, begrudgingly resigned to her totally unfair fate, swung the covers off and got to her feet.

The sigh that left her lips was the only thing she could bring herself to acknowledge true gratitude for.

"Oh, sweet, sweet equilibrium. How I've missed thee." The first three months of her pregnancy had dealt her the most horrific case of vertigo, which had resulted in more than a few unsightly gashes and scuffs now pockmarking her once passably clean walls. But now that she'd crept into the sixteen-week mark and was solidly into her second trimester, Anna was finally starting to get comfortable in her body again. Well, as comfortable as one could get with a genetically similar parasite setting up shop in the same rent-controlled apartment her vital organs had enjoyed roommate-free for the past thirty-four years.

Despite her early-morning ire, an inevitable smile teased her face at the thought of her tiny homespun hanger-on. Anna's fingers immediately unclenched and drifted over the roundest part of her belly, which had begun to take that unmistakable pregnancy shape. "Little squatter. When all this is over, you better be the cutest thing on the planet. For both our sakes. That's all I'm saying."

Unfortunately, despite her vertigo being blessedly behind

her, no amount of comfort in her pre-dawn shuffle toward the bathroom would ever shake the jitters of what she'd just woken up from or who.

Without bothering to turn on the Big Light, as she thought of it, she did her business by the soft glow of her Christmas Mickey Mouse night-light. The ancient thing was still perched in the bathroom after she'd neglected to put it away with the rest of the holiday decorations because when one woke up every two hours to pee and was also inconveniently blind as a bat without their glasses, one was not picky about where her meager five watts of light came from.

After shivering through a hand-washing cycle that was far too short to convince the water heater to get its ass in gear, Anna dried her hands, lifted her tired gaze to the mirror, and immediately wished she hadn't.

In the sepia-toned haze of her small bathroom, the shadows somehow pulled her attention to her eyes, but recast as they were in the reddish-brown glow of the night-light, all she could see, even without her glasses, wasn't the soft green of her glance but a starkly two-toned gaze. One hazel eye, one brown. Both belonged to a mystery man she still hadn't figured out how she'd conjured up. Though, bonus points to her pregnancy brain for giving her dream fella a decent set of muscles to go along with the mystery.

Yay for small wins.

Those early months when she'd somehow manifested him in her dreams were, in her best estimation, nothing short of a trauma response. She'd just peed on the stick that morning and, after doing her level best not to act like an emotional wreck with the handful of telehealth nutrition clients she'd had scheduled that day, had finally given her body an outlet for the flurry of crazy wreaking havoc on her brain. With her higher reasoning held hostage, she'd quickly run to the grocery store on her lunch break, used the last of her and her boyfriend Travis's grocery budget for the month to splurge on two steaks and all the trimmings, and settled in to thoroughly blow his mind with the news once he got home.

Instead, what she'd gotten had been a shocking panicked play of man-baby emotional insecurity that she didn't have the tools to deal with and never saw coming.

She and Travis had been together for six years and met when she was twenty-eight and he was twenty-four. The age gap hadn't seemed so big at the time, and she'd grown to love him regardless. His entrepreneurial spirit, the way he lit up a room and could pull a crowd of gatherers into his orbit as easily as a city street performer, all of it was as intoxicating as it was incendiary. And when he'd trained his charm on her and spoke of his dreams to open up a life coaching business—sorry, personal empowerment business—large enough to rival that of Tony Robbins's empire, she'd only been too happy to support him, even if it meant upping her own client workload to help fund his mastermind retreats and private coaching sessions with mentors. Dreams, he'd argued, rarely came with upfront investors, and yes, he'd say, coaches did need coaching themselves.

That was when her mother—whose experience with men was limited to a revolving door of Daves during Anna's childhood and adolescence after Anna's father, the first Dave, left when she was three—had sat her down and laid some impossibly hard truths on the table.

"Anna, you're not getting any younger. Travis is taking great initiative and a lot of risk to start his own company, and how wonderful is it that he's promised you a high-level role in his business once it gets off the ground and becomes the success you and I both know he's capable of? He's giving you a future, Anna. For both of you, for your family, for whatever dreams you desire to pursue. You should be grateful, honey. Not everyone takes their partners with them when

they finally find a road they can cruise down without all those bumps and potholes."

It was a testament to Anna's warped upbringing that, despite her mild success as a registered dietician, she still let her mother's words carve out such a sizable chunk of real estate in her mind.

What could she say? Childhood trauma was the gift that kept on giving. Even after two rounds of therapy, that trauma still had fucking claws.

In the end, the promise of a real family with Travis had been too enticing of a dream to let go, regardless of her career aspirations. But despite being together for six years and Anna being only one year shy of what her OB/GYN referred to as *advanced maternal age*, it hadn't made a difference. Her gratitude had been thrown back at her when, after she'd finally shared with him that they were pregnant, every lit feature on his usually exuberant and joyful face had plummeted as fast as their savings.

For some reason, the decibels of his shouting had been more alarming than the words. Things like "Can't be saddled with a kid right now" and "How could you let this happen? I'm still in my twenties. I thought you were on the pill" and "Can't record my new podcast with a baby crying in the background" had become the soundtrack of her new hellish life.

A life that had ultimately ended when Travis realized California was where he needed to be. The operative word being *he*, with Anna's sole consolation prize consisting of their small New Hampshire mountain cabin that he'd claimed wasn't so much of a house as an insect trap. No surprise he'd had zero problems signing that over to her. Or ghosting the debt she'd taken on over their years together so they could start their lives and help his career grow while growing a family of their own.

The triggering memory raked nails along her skin, and she

couldn't hold back the shudder, even while refusing to look away from the mirror.

The night Travis left was the first night she'd dreamed of her mystery man, and it had simultaneously been the most enticing and frustrating experience of her life. She didn't know his name, didn't know what part of her psyche had dreamed him up. Hell, she didn't even know what he looked or sounded like. Not really. Whatever dreamy world she'd conjured up never quite carved out a clear enough picture. Within the white fog of her mind, the outline of his presence was the best she could grasp. Literal heads taller than her, he always stood as though he were bracing for something. Around him, the mist would float and fall along his form, stopping to rest where his body began, peppering the stark outline of sturdy shoulders, arms, and a chest that looked as solidly formed as the White Mountains around her.

But it was always just the essence of him, the impression of his size and strength, never more. Occasionally, if she'd stayed up too late scrolling on her phone and struggled to fall asleep, the vision of him almost seemed to reflect that. His hair, which fell to his shoulders in tousled waves of ruddy auburn and was usually the only feature she could ever make out along with his beard and eyes, would be more mussed and unkempt. Almost . . . manic. Like his bicolored stare whenever he'd capture hers.

Anna smiled at the secret memory as she finger combed a tangle out of her hair. Why were those moments always the most comforting? That if she'd had a shitty night's sleep, her imaginary hero did as well?

Then she squeezed her eyes shut and held tight until little floating stars danced across the backs of her eyelids. When she finally popped those babies open, all she was met with was her ragged pale complexion that was only slightly sweatier than the one she'd gone to bed with. And just like that, the ghost of his gaze fled the scene almost as quickly as she'd summoned it.

To make room for other memories, ones that were new to the nightly lineup but were also the very things that sent her scrambling from sleep moments ago.

He had been naked. Very naked. Naked with a body she doubted even her pregnancy brain could have filled out properly. Not only that but he was naked and *speaking.* As in, saying real live words directly from his mouth to her ears. Words she would never consciously put in her dream. Words he expected her to respond to.

"Gah!"

Anna swiped a hand in front of the mirror, padded back to her room, and snatched her glasses off her nightstand, intending to do something so incredibly productive that it would kick all that free-thinking nonsense right out of her noggin. Squinting at the time again, she took a deep breath, threw her shoulders back, and put her hands on her regrettably larger hips. She had a few hours before her first telehealth client, and she wasn't about to spend it analyzing why her heart wouldn't calm the heck down after replaying the dulcet timbre of his voice, or how he knew she lived in New Hampshire, or what the hell she'd done to deserve a veritable Greek god kneeling naked before her feet and spouting words of ownership.

I'm yours.

Oh, she'd caught that little diddy, all right. Caught it and became so sick with it that the very notion of another man, even one she'd made up, holding any kind of possessive sway over her—and, by extension, her baby—was enough to catapult her out of the few hours of rest her traitorous body had finally let her have.

Anna stormed over to her dresser, not even bothering with the light, and searched around by feel for her workout clothes. If Captain Dream Muffin was going to start getting real, then so was she.

Nothing like an extra-long session of prenatal yoga, followed by a double dose of guided meditation and a cup of decaf French vanilla coffee to get her mind back in the game.

Yoga. Coffee. Clients. Throw some food at the problem. More clients. More food. Rest. Repeat. *That* was the routine she needed.

Nowhere did she have room for the haunting eyes she couldn't stop imagining. Eyes that somehow made her chest feel lighter in the same way that her motion detection lights would as they'd fire up and illuminate her steps when she'd take out the garbage before she'd even realized she needed the light.

Eyes that seemed to follow her everywhere she went.

CHAPTER 3

The weight of dawn's impending presence bore down on the granite walls of the den's great room. Despite the angels' underground haven being nestled cozily beneath New Hampshire's White Mountains, the rocks cocooning their home always managed to alert its residents to the rising sun. Or, at least, they'd used to back when each of the sentinels was more attuned to their metals at that hour, instead of their mates.

Iron smoothed out the first of several architectural drawings along the farmhouse table—a table that had been the centerpiece to so many battle plans and breakfasts—and, with his palms pressed to the paper, closed his eyes and just let the energy of the mountain ground him for a moment. Mages knew he needed whatever magic was available to get his head on straight after the night he'd had.

The granite and shale he and his brothers had long ago carved their home into had always been a source of comfort and security, and yeah, he'd go so far as to say solidarity as well. While all the mortals were barely rubbing the morning crust out of their eyes, Iron and the other angels were being softly sung to by the burgeoning and resonating warmth of sun on stones. The metallic powers each of them commanded were literally rocked awake each morning by the minerals' subtle infusions of magic into their celestial makeup. For some reason he'd never been able to parse out, the morning sun always seemed to take a liking to his small, stranded family and showed its favor accordingly.

It was a lovely gesture. Truly. Except when you'd been fortunate enough to find your soul bond and regain full use of your long-lost celestial powers as a result. Once that happened, all of that becoming-one-with-the-dawn crap? About as obsolete as a mortal's appendix. For everyone except him. Half the time, the other angels skipped out on sunrises altogether in favor of more leisurely ways to spend their morning.

After last night, could he blame them?

Then those jade eyes, which had yet to grant him a moment's peace in the two hours he'd tried and failed to find sleep again, swam to the forefront of his mind and all but dolphin kicked away any hopes he'd had of trying to be productive.

She was in New Hampshire. Fucking New Hampshire. In the eons he'd spent waddling around the mortal plane he'd been stuck on, all this time, she was here. *Here.* Not even near him so much as right under his goddamn nose. Hell, she could have brushed his shoulder walking past him on the sidewalk or been working at the front desk of the barbershop he went to once a month for a beard trim and that hot lather lineup his barber, Charlie, was so good at.

Before the dreams, he could have been staring into her face every day for who knew how long and not even known it.

Iron exhaled every last bit of air from his lungs and forced the tension in his muscles to get gone. A few more slow inhales, followed by agonizingly long exhales, was a trick Rhode had taught him. Breath work, he'd called it. Well, whatever it was, it sure as shit didn't fix his problems, but it definitely helped shift perspective on his priorities a bit. When he opened his eyes again, the array of building sketches, utility layouts, and property zoning maps pulled him back to the present.

Rhode and Neela's homestead. With any luck, the ground would thaw out shortly and they'd be able to make headway on some of the foundational work. Fine by him. The sooner, the better in his book. When Rhode first floated the idea of building the property, Iron had not only thrown himself into the project but practically elbowed anyone else out of the way who offered to help him.

Of all the other sentinels, he was the most analytical, so the solitude and schematics soothed him, and it gave him a refreshing purpose that didn't involve smashing his knuckles into charmer cheekbones. Besides, when the den would grow quiet and his brothers tended to their soul bonds behind closed doors, the building project was the only thing that managed to keep Iron's head on even remotely straight while the rest of his sour senses were doing their damnedest to spin wildly out of control.

But as Iron slid over a few of the stainless steel demitasse cups he'd grabbed from the kitchen and plunked them down on the corners of the sheets so the drawings would lay flat, his knuckles bumped against something else. Glass, not metal.

A hazy veil swept over his vision. Odd. He didn't even remember carrying the shard around with him anymore. For so long, the small test tube containing the long bony bit had sat nestled within his flannel shirt pocket, warming his skin through the fabric with the smooth reminder of the other weight bearing down upon him: returning home.

But it wasn't in his pocket this time. When the hell had he taken it out?

The vial spun a lazy dance as it rolled, its stoppered end arcing cleanly across the proposed electrical map while its bulbous tip stayed still, like a drawing compass determined to chart out Iron's options for him. As if he didn't already have a fucking clue that the severed shard from the Empyrean relic, which they'd managed to swipe from Cyro, had about as much magic in it as the proverbial white tip of a birthday-party-circuit magician's wand.

Iron and the other sentinels had learned that the bone-like bit broken off from the relic, the rest of which was still in Cyro's possession, was so prized by the demon ruler because the relic was also a fragment, one carved from the Empyrean's gates and thus believed to still hold the celestial power of the Empyrean. A power that Cyro had attempted to corrupt so he might finally enter Heaven's highest realm and lay waste to the light that had resulted in him—the first charmer—and all other full-blooded charmers after him being relegated to the darkness.

Iron's interest in the relic had taken on a similar obsession, though for entirely different reasons. If he could harness the relic's dormant celestial power, maybe, just maybe, he could find a way for him and his brothers to finally make it back home.

But that hope had been ignited months ago and had since been burning way too hot for far too long. If this tiny sliver of the Empyrean's gates had any juice in it left to give, it certainly wasn't interested in letting Iron know about it. No matter that he'd pored over every tome in their library, all written in various languages, or gassed himself to exhaustion trying any combination of magic and angel fire he could come up with. In the end, the tiny needle-like vestige did what it always did for him: hit him with its infamous sorry-not-sorry pearlescent wink before rolling over to give him the cold shoulder.

This time, however, Iron met the shard with a glare, though

it was more at his annoyance for not grabbing his overshirt before he left his suite. Therefore, the shard had to hitch a ride in his fist instead of his flannel.

Because, of fucking course, Iron wasn't about to be without the thing, goddammit, no matter how annoying it was. The very paralyzing thought of it somehow burping up answers when he was showering or it finally hope-casting its secrets at the exact moment he wasn't around to hear them kept him awake at night. So, yeah, no wonder the damn thing was rolling around under his nose. He'd freaking put it there.

With thumb and middle finger cocked and ready, Iron hefted any amount of deftness he might have had against the mocking little mystery and let loose his annoyance, flicking the thing into its spin cycle. On gentle, of course. Contrary to his brother Chrome's loudmouthed opinion, Iron wasn't so moody as to send a relic of Heaven shattering across the dining room floor, no matter how hard he wanted to. He wasn't *that* stupid.

"You still fondling that thing?" Titan's question preceded his commanding presence into the great room, followed closely by the air and faintly smug swagger of any male who'd enjoyed the company of his soul bond for far too many fortunate hours. Which begged the question Iron in no way needed to ask but would anyway because he didn't want his pissy mood pissing off others . . .

"Where's Rose?"

The sentinels' second-in-command grabbed a mug of coffee and joined Iron on the bench seat across from him. Despite the male's meaty fists cupping the sides of that fifteen-ouncer and creeping up over the rim to conceal the liquid within, they couldn't stop the pungently artificial perfume from wafting through the air and sawing off what remained of Iron's regularly trimmed nose hairs.

Peppermint mocha creamer. Motherfucker. Et tu, Titan? Damn.

"Still sleeping." Titan took a bracing sip, careful not to let—

Jesus Christ, was that whipped cream?—too much of the drink decorate the hair on his upper lip.

"No one's going to kill you for liking that crap, you know. There's no need to hide the bottle of creamer in the back of the fridge. Just don't park it next to the steaks or anything. Wouldn't want the cows knowing what you turned their milk into."

A smooth smile carved out a knowing look of compassion on Titan's face, one that said, in no uncertain terms, *I'm whipped, and I like it.* "It's dairy-free."

"Of course it is," Iron muttered.

"And Rose likes it. I've gotta say, it's not so terrible on occasion. The whipped cream is fun, too."

"Agree to disagree, my brother. I prefer to eat my ice cream, not drink it." Then he scratched the back of his neck, because his nerve endings just *loved* small talk. "But, yeah, I get it. Make her happy."

"Wouldn't dream of doing anything otherwise." Titan's smile slipped, and his tone glided into the one he often donned when he preferred to use his words as weapons.

Shit. Here it comes.

"It'll happen for you as well, if that's what's been bothering you lately. Your soul bond, your other half, I know they're out there for you. I refuse to believe the prime mages have granted us all this joy, even among the sorrow we've seen, yet would not—"

Iron's hand flew up. "Save the pretty speech, all right? It's too early in the morning for pity."

"It's not pity. It's encouragement and hope." Then Titan leaned in closer. "Look, I know it's on your mind. We all do."

Aaand that's just great. Fan-fucking-tastic.

"You don't have a fucking clue what's on my mind," Iron gritted out, no longer giving a shit about breaking the seal on his soul's secret anger.

Titan wanted to talk? Wanted him to open up and spill shit like his back was flat on some therapist's couch and his heels were kicked back instead of making headway? Fine, he had no problem playing along.

"Or have you all forgotten that we had a home once, and newsflash, this ain't it?" Iron spread his arms wide to encompass all the granite around them that had begun to grow colder with each passing minute. "I've got all the goddamn pieces to get us back to the Empyrean, back to where we had duty and a purpose, back to where we fucking belonged. And for the life of me, I can't get any of these pieces to fit where they should." Hot rage singed his throat as he let the words that had been haunting him these past few months fly free. "You and the others have a choice, Titan. You have Rose. Tung has Tammy. Everyone has a reason to make a considered choice, and it's the giant elephant in the fucking room that no one wants to talk about."

It was Iron's turn to lean closer, and it was a testament to Titan's long-held calm honed on the battlefield that the angel didn't flinch.

"Are you staying or going? That's the million-dollar question none of you want to acknowledge is hanging over your heads. If I crack this relic and she gives up her secrets of how to finally get home, then you all have a choice to make. But as long as I stay stuck on this puzzle, you and the others get to live out your happy mortal dreams with your soul bonds, while I just stay stuck. Never mind the fact that Cyro's behind-the-scenes scheming is the ass ache none of us need, but as long as that bastard stays quiet, you can all pretend that life with your woman in your arms is how it always will be. Well, I don't have that luxury," he said, jamming a finger into his chest. "I can't pretend that I'm not losing my fucking mind watching you all act like the wonderful bubbles you float around in aren't about to burst at any moment."

Iron stood from the table and dragged his tense hands over his beard, stopping just short of yanking the thing off his face entirely. "I've . . . I've seen someone." And goddamn, did he hate the ring of torture and tension enveloping his words.

Titan straightened his shoulders but wisely stayed put. "You have?"

"Yeah. Been dreaming about her. For months. Never saw much of her face or heard her voice, though. Not until last night."

A knot of concern wrinkled Titan's brow. "What happened? Where? What's her name? Who is she?"

"All excellent questions, and hell if I know the answer to any of them. The only thing I do know is when I'm so dead tired after racking my brain all day trying to figure out the key to getting this relic's magic to fire up, she's there at the end of it to rattle my brain even further." Then Iron scoffed and shook his head. "It's almost like she *wants* me to be exhausted, to ensure I'm so tired that I won't ever have the energy to find a way back home."

The silence between them stretched on, until he was pretty sure Titan kept quiet on purpose to draw out the tension of Iron's shitty circumstances into a rope just long enough to fit snugly around Iron's thick neck.

But Titan didn't pull that rope. Instead, he looked into his coffee cup for answers, pensive but for the briefly stricken expression that skittered across his features. Finally, he spoke, his words thick with a subtle sadness. "Why do you think you don't have a choice, brother?"

Iron didn't miss the fact that the angel dodged the original subject by firing it back at him or how the second-in-command's features smoothly slipped into a mask of indifference.

So he *did* know what was coming. Interesting.

Iron lifted his head to the arched ceiling, scanning the

granite for the specific specs of mica that, sometimes, if he squinted hard enough, resembled a constellation or two. His only access to any sort of night sky when he was forced to remain belowground and recharge his angel fire. Unlike the others. "Because something tells me these dreams, this fantasy woman, aren't just dreams but visions—visions that are leading me toward figuring out how to get this relic to finally release its magic." Iron started to pace in stride to the hammering of his heart as he finally let his crackpot theory run wild. "What if I'm meant to find her and, in doing so, at last discover how to return to the Empyrean and stop Cyro for good? What if I regain my full powers? What if I force you all to choose between the lives you've fought so long for versus the lives you live now? Who the hell am I to force any one of you to make that decision? But this woman . . ."

"What about her?" Titan asked baldly.

The abruptness, both of the tone and the question, drew Iron to a halt. Just laid the brakes on whatever force was pushing him to crave the restless sleep that had begun to rub him raw for a reason he'd been too afraid to analyze.

"I think she's hurting," he confessed softly.

At that, Titan sat up straighter. "Hurting?"

"I don't know the how or why of it, but whenever I dream of her, I also dream of . . . sadness. Suffering, maybe. The encounters we've had of late, if you can even call them that, have changed. Her spirit or aura or whatever the hell it is that visits me each night has gotten increasingly . . . yeah, I'm going to say strained, if that's even possible. Over the months she's held my mind captive, she's been becoming more and more skittish, darting away from me when I reach for her, even though she must know I'm no threat by now. I wasn't certain of it at first, but after last night, when I heard her speak for the first time, her words were hurled at me with such defiance, such fear masked with ferocity, that once I found out she was from New

Hampshire, I swear I thought it was just more of that typical New England grit.

"But what if I was wrong? What if she acted that way as a form of defense because she was feeling attacked and is no stranger to suffering? What if I'm the cause of it somehow? What if she's been right here all along and I could have helped her, but I didn't, and she's still out there somewhere hurting? Or what if I find her but then dragging her into my life only ruins all of yours? Or, worse, hers?"

The three shots of espresso Iron downed earlier had finally offered up their concentrated caffeine, effectively shooting his already panicked mind into overdrive.

Titan rose from his seat but still stayed clear of the path Iron was doing a damn good job of wearing into the granite floor. "Easy, now. You're getting yourself worked up. There's no use agonizing over hypotheticals here. You're a data man. Work with the facts. Let's start there."

"Facts," Iron parroted, only mildly less flustered. "Facts. Okay."

"Yes, facts. I'll ask you one *factual* question. Only you can answer it, and it's a yes or no choice. Super simple. You ready?"

Iron finally put the brakes on his pacing and fisted his hands at his sides. "Shoot."

Titan nodded knowingly. "If you could stop her pain, would you?"

"What the hell kind of a question is that?"

"I'll ask it again. If you believe this woman is in pain and it was within your power to stop it, would you?"

"Yes. Always. A thousand times over. Without question. I wouldn't let her suffer."

"Good. Now, question two." Titan flicked his gaze toward the test tube containing the severed shard of the Empyrean's relic.

A shard that was now glowing with a jumpstart of celestial magic Iron had been trying to unlock for months.

A shard that was pointing directly toward Iron's chest, where the core of his tethered angel fire lived.

An overwhelming panic seized Iron's lungs as Titan's final question solidified his resolve. "What the hell are you still doing here?"

CHAPTER 4

There were certain behaviors that never truly got old, no matter how much Anna wished they'd go the way of the dodo or, at the very least, the way of electric seat belts. Could the residents of Aurora, townsfolk and tourists alike, come together and agree that hoarding bread and bottled water before a snowstorm wasn't the action New Englanders needed to take when their town was only two and a half hours from Boston and had every major East Coast highway running through it? The boonies, it was not. Did they think one of the statistically snowiest regions in the country would truly see its residents stranded to the point of endless peanut butter sandwiches or—and she'd tried so hard to understand this one, she really did—frozen milk?

The small grocery store's overhead lights buzzed a soft hum of disapproval, mimicking the mildly stern judgment of a tenured college teacher who hadn't had to change their teaching methods in thirty years because their contract included a parking spot.

God, she hated this and was mentally kicking herself for not prioritizing appropriately. Without realizing it, she'd turned herself into one of *those* people. The bread-and-milk-ers.

Lovely.

"This is your own fault, Anna. You really should have known better." The verbal lancing she gave herself wasn't enough to quell her frustration, however, or bring back the past three hours of her booked-solid afternoon when it would have been smarter, though similarly impossible, to run to the store to stock up.

Through the miracle of scheduling and the desperate need to pay her mortgage this month, she'd stacked clients as close as virtually possible. Unfortunately, by the time five o'clock rolled around and she was finally able to shut her laptop and check her phone, it left zero time to analyze weather alerts or figure out what she needed to stock her house with before eighteen to twenty-four inches of heavy, wet white stuff started blanketing the area during the overnight hours.

Thank you, higher elevations.

Oh, her pregnancy-induced sciatica was going to *love* shoveling that out.

Anna tucked the shopping basket more securely into the crook of her elbow and stood as flush as possible against the bags of chips while a few straggling shoppers plucked two loaves of pumpernickel from the otherwise barren bread shelves. Along the empty stainless steel rows, a few price tags had begun to peel off. Several had already fallen to the linoleum floor, their sad presence having been plastered to the faux tile beneath the earlier afternoon's most likely stampeding footsteps.

Every single one of the newly adhered tags was for a higher price. *Fucking figures.*

"I swear, I thought the local businesses saved their price gouging for the tourists." But then, when had that ever stopped anyone with the appropriate resources from gaining anything they wanted anyway? Right on cue, Travis's smug face came to mind. His charming smile and affable demeanor had been the very virtues that enabled the bastard's vices, hadn't they?

Anna squeezed her eyes shut. "Nope. We're not going down that road. Not again and certainly not right now."

Before her mental wherewithal could course-correct her even further, a flat feminine voice bellowed through the tinny PA system. "The store will be closing in fifteen minutes."

God. What the hell was she even doing? To hell with the bread. Anna made a beeline for the things that had always taken up the highest places on her survival pedestal: high-fiber cereal, evaporated milk, trail mix, and an extra bag of M&Ms to go into the trail mix because the meager amount it inevitably came with wouldn't cut it on a good day. And honestly, if her body was already moving on autopilot through a familiar circumstance in a familiar setting, that meant her mind had fewer opportunities to chew over the fact that she hadn't dreamed about her mystery man in three nights.

Three nights. Three whole nights that, for the first time in months, had gifted her with a few hours of precious uninterrupted sleep.

And the most unnerving sense of disappointment.

The few remnants of customers shuffled past her on their way to the registers, just as eager to get back to their wherevers as she was. Except, their wherevers most likely included other people or, at the very least, a cat or a gerbil or something. Did people still have gerbils for pets?

Lost in a brain fog of Swamp of Sadness proportions, Anna filled her meager basket with whatever her fingers happened to graze on her way over to the candy aisle.

What the hell was his name?

Of all the lingering questions trying their hardest to make sure her now sleep*ful* nights were otherwise as unfulfilling as possible, that one took the cake. She'd never gotten his name.

Oh, she knew he wasn't real. Couldn't be. That was why she had no problem spouting off at the mouth and aiming every ounce of sass befitting her hair color at his smug face.

But it hadn't been smug, had it?

Her fingertips tossed another package of something or other into the basket. Ah. Chocolate tea biscuits. Sure. Why not?

"What if I forget him?" she whispered into an empty aisle. Already, the imagery of what little she'd been able to glean from his features seemed fuzzier than it had been, and she'd only ever really gotten that much of an eyeful—literally—the one time. What if the rest of him would soon be lost to other far more mundane but ultimately pressing thought cycles now that he no longer took up space in her sleep?

And then there was the ten-million-dollar question: why did she care?

A gnawing worry propelled her woodenly toward the only self-checkout register still open. When she finally took stock of what she'd collected in her wee basket, the true consequences of her fantasy man's inexplicable absence from her dreams stared back at her. A few hours away from the largest late-winter storm to hit the White Mountains in fifteen years and all she had to show for supplies were two boxes of Fruit Loops that were very much sans fiber, chocolate tea biscuits, two bags of M&Ms—one peanut butter, one plain—a bag of grapes, four cans of what she thought were evaporated milk but two of which turned out to be sweetened condensed milk, and—she groaned—a pack of random cupcake liners that were usually stocked next to her favorite just-add-water protein pancake mix.

A pancake mix that, despite Anna's best intentions, was noticeably absent from her grocery haul.

The PA system's rusty crackle only added to her rising tension. "The store will be closing in five minutes. Please take your final items to the registers. Stay safe, everyone."

"Wonderful. Just . . . yeah. Perfect way to top off my Friday night. Truly."

Before she could officially work up a good wallow, her phone pinged with an incoming text.

622622: This is a reminder that you have an appointment with Dr. Michelle Abramowitz on March 14, at 10 a.m. Please press C to confirm or call the office to reschedule.

Few things had the power to bring her back to reality quite like the very real and very little child currently stretching out her abdomen, discretionary allowances, and calendar availability.

Anna ticked off the days in her mind, surprised she'd forgotten all about her next OB/GYN appointment. But yeah, it was time. Sixteen-week checkup and such. It didn't matter that, despite choosing the smallest practitioner in the area for the very specific reason of being around fewer clientele, Anna still always wound up in a waiting room full of glowing pregnant women with doting partners.

Partners who'd already taken care of the bill and insurance arrangements while the appointment was happening. Partners who had their thumbs on their vehicle's automatic start button as soon as the appointment was over. Partners who'd made the post-ultrasound lunch plans the week before and happily took off work to spend the rest of the day beaming over Bolognese and baby talk.

It was a lot to come to terms with, no matter how hard she tried to punch through the reality of her situation, one that had become so different from the one her heart had begun decorating with ornamental trappings after that positive pregnancy test months ago.

Doing her best to shake off the chill of a reality gone cold, Anna tapped out a *C* to confirm her appointment and caught the eye of the grocery employee standing at the door, ushering everyone out with no small amount of *let's go, people* energy.

Anna had just plunked the last of her items into her shopping tote before the employee skewered her with an exasperated stare as though Anna had just used full-volume vocals during quiet time at the library. The woman tucked her elbow-length highlighted hair farther into her Red Sox cap and used her inch-long acrylics to direct the last of the pedestrian traffic, sans Anna, out of her store.

Because of course it was *her* store, judging by the prominent *Manager* taking up the majority of her name tag's real estate.

Then she bobbed her chin in Anna's direction. "You finished, hon? We're cl—"

"Closing. Yeah, I got that. Just bagging the last of my items."

"You'd bag things faster if you weren't on your phone."

Anna paid for her items, tucked the tote under her arm, and didn't even have it in her to belabor the point. Much. "You know," she said as she somehow managed to propel her exhausted body toward the exit, "it's just snow. We'll be shoveled out an hour after it stops falling. This is New Hampshire, not Florida. We have plows and road brine vehicles, and last I checked, Aurora's municipal budget had plenty of overtime allocated to the Department of Public Works for snow removal. It'll all be okay. This isn't our first rodeo."

The woman curled her nose and wiped it with the back of her hand. The gesture didn't need sound effects for Anna's first-trimester nausea muscle memory to fire right up. It also didn't need the look of abhorrent disdain sweeping back and forth beneath eyelashes the length of a mascara brush and currently sizing up Anna's paltry purchases.

And, like, *really* unfairly judging her, too, it was important to note.

"Well, it sure looks like *your* first rodeo."

"I'm not a tourist," Anna fired back. "I know my way around snow."

A perfectly plucked eyebrow inched toward the ballcap's

brim. "Honey, I don't care if you know your way around a Zamboni and carve chainsaw ice sculptures in your spare time. The store's closing in"—she squinted at the clock above the customer service desk—"a minute and a half. Some of us have our own families to get back to, you know. We don't just take care of the town's needs. Look, I'm glad you got your, uh, baking supplies, but the forecast isn't getting any friendlier."

Yeah, neither are you, lady.

"The storm isn't supposed to start until after midnight."

The woman narrowed her gaze. "Oh, what? Are you a meteorologist?"

"Obviously not. I just know that there's no snow on the ground right now."

"And I'd like to get home while that's still the case."

Out of gas and interest, Anna nodded her defeat and ambled past the woman. "Understood. Have a good evening."

That was the thing with small tourist-town grocers who were stuck between the financial slog of winter commerce and the shiny spring promise of new vacationer dollars. Stress was pretty much the only thing holding them together until the short-term rentals began filling up over spring break and the money started flowing again.

Anna's stark circumstances were more than a glowing testament to that particular plight, so could she blame the store manager for wanting to hightail it back to who or whatever was waiting for her?

Once Anna managed to tuck herself into her car and *not* snag her coat in the door, she punched the ignition, tore into the most easily accessible bag of M&Ms (peanut), and let the satisfaction of mass-produced chocolate cascade over thoughts that had grown far too punishing in their perpetuity.

As she chugged along through Aurora's picturesque downtown, a vague awareness of blue and red emergency lights strobing out several streets in front of her did their best to impress their urgency. But her maneuvers were more rote than reactive at that point, with her foot automatically easing off the gas in response to the braking lights of the car in front of her. Soon, her brakes were firmly applied, and her Subaru became just another car in a long line of lemmings inching toward the precipice of whatever cliff life had intended them to dive off.

"Traffic. Of course. Again, I should have known."

What she couldn't have known was how, when she reached into the shopping bag to snatch up another fistful of M&Ms, the orange and brown bags snuggled side by side would completely erase any blue and red hues that should have been at the forefront of her mind given the emergency vehicle presence up ahead.

Instead, brown and orange melded together in her thoughts, replacing the sharp primary colors in front of her with the rich brindled gaze of a man who wasn't real and never would be.

CHAPTER 5

The biting cold followed Iron around through the no-business-being-this-bustling streets of Aurora, until it settled over the back of his neck like an enemy's icy breath. On some level, he supposed that was what it was. Time. Failure. The absence of achieving his goals while the world continued to buzz around him in a kaleidoscope of taunting confusion.

A storm was coming, and that was enough of a wrench in Iron's plans not only to sidetrack his pursuit of the woman from his dreams but make it so every fucking mortal establishment he'd relied on for answers was effectively shutting down for the time being.

Three days. For three days, he'd neither dreamed of her nor anything but her. He'd never been much of a fairness guy. Kind of hard to believe in the stuff when he'd gotten the shit end of the stick for more years than trees existed, but if he had to argue a point, it sure as hell would have been along the lines of addiction logic.

Why would the universe rob him of his months-long nightly

thoughts, only for them to consume his every waking moment since and offer up no hope of ever finding her?

The harsh wind picked up to a relentless degree, a lovely side effect of Aurora being built close to the valleys long ago carved out from the White Mountains. Wind tunnels were common enough, but coupled with unseasonably low temperatures and late-winter precipitation that the downtown businesses had hoped was behind them and misery was always the result.

Regardless, his bad mood followed him around like a shroud of despondency for the damned and did nothing to counteract the cheerful scenes of the soon-to-be-dawning spring that some mortals had already adorned their businesses with.

Aurora held all the trappings of a tourist town ready to peel off its winter layer, unwrap its synthetic spring flora (because in New England, true spring was a far cry from Gregorian calendar spring), and welcome customers with the promise of pastels, new merchandise, and seasonal eats. Storefront window displays, which had upheld their commitments to comfort and coziness only a week ago, now boasted products of vibrant colors pledging vibes of rebirth and renewal. The popular boutiques offered boots with noticeably shorter calf lengths while the sports and recreation outlet across from the municipal park had swapped out its skis and winter wear for freaking pickleball rackets and eco-friendly water bottles that could make water taste like lemons or grapefruit or whatever just by adding some calorie-free powders to the water (for an additional charge, of course).

As if squeezing an actual fucking lemon wouldn't do the same thing, but dead horses and whatnot.

While the shops sat pregnant with spring supplies and sales, the rest of the streets were a clogged congestion of mortals snuffling up last-minute items before everything shut down for the immediate future and the weather decided to make itself known. On any other night, Iron would have applauded the mortals' efforts for putting forethought into their safety. Tonight, however, his skin itched with the overstimulation of it all: the speedy shuffling of feet on concrete, the air perfumed with the impatience of traffic exhaust, the twitchy honks of drivers both enraged and eager to move two inches from where they'd been a moment ago.

It grated on nerves that Iron had been certain had no nerve endings left to grate down.

Yet more proof that the universe was full of surprises.

Over the past three days, Iron, an immortal sentinel warrior and guardian of the Empyrean, had been forced to resort to combat of the keyboard variety. His investigation into his mystery woman had started with any low-hanging fruit he could find. With Chrome's help, they'd been able to tap into a multitude of mortal state and municipal databases, but having no idea where to go from there, Iron had started with the ones that included photo entries for each registrant. Though his female's features were still mostly hazy in his mind, he figured he'd be able to at least pinpoint someone who matched a basic description and start from there.

Yeah . . . no. After days of staring bleary-eyed at image after image, Iron had pushed the laptop away and pinched the bridge of his nose. Had her hair been a bright strawberry red or more of a darker auburn? Or perhaps it hadn't been red at all and it was a trick of his mind? Shades of brown were similar to red, as he well knew given his hair color. Or what if she'd dyed her hair or had grown it out from the time a potential photo could have been taken?

He could very well be staring at a picture of her from five years ago where she sported a blond pixie cut, nose piercing, and goth eye makeup, and he'd have no idea who the hell he was looking at.

The shrill honk of several cars choking the street next to him drew his thoughts away from the dark path he was heading down and instead painted his landscape in garish hues of red and blue. Up ahead, some vehicle had made the unfortunate decision to give up the ghost in the middle of an intersection, effectively congesting every artery in town into individual wells of despair.

He could *so* relate.

Iron let the cold prickle his ears as he barreled down the sidewalk with a mountain-sized chip on his shoulder.

Despair . . . that was certainly a concept his conversation with Titan a few days ago had scratched at. Iron had referred to it as suffering when he'd recounted his worry of not finding this dream woman in a timely manner, but perhaps that had been the wrong approach. Then he froze, digging his heels into the concrete.

Tired. She'd seemed so damn tired. There was a tightness to the edges around her eyes that he hadn't bothered to think too closely about before. Was she a teacher? Or a member of another overworked profession?

"A teacher. Hmm . . ."

Iron pulled out his phone and began typing out a text to Chrome about checking the different education rosters of all the New Hampshire school districts. It would take more than a hot minute, but if he could recruit his brothers in the search, perhaps—

The resounding screech of brakes set Iron's back teeth on edge and slowed the harried steps of everyone around him.

"Jeez, lady. Drive much?" The tallest mortal in a teenage gaggle of women in front of him looked up from her phone just long enough for the rest of her party to cast their attention toward the line of standstill cars next to them. Before the urge to care about a stranger took too strong of a hold among the women, the siren song of social media pulled the group back into the numb safety of their screens.

The disruption was minimal. To a mortal. To Iron, it was the Freightliner he didn't see coming.

Boxed into the far-right lane was an unassuming Subaru of lower-middle-class proportions spotlit by alternating beams of headlights mixed with shadows of pedestrians weaving through the thrall. The car's bumper would have all but given the Jeep in front of it a proctology exam if the driver hadn't slammed on the brakes when they did. Even so, there was barely a centimeter's worth of breathing room between those bad boys. Impressive for a near-miss love tap.

On any other night, Iron would have dismissed it. Just shoved his hands into his pockets and kept right on walking away from yet another mortal mess. He had exactly fuck all to do with congestion best practices and even less interest in being first on scene to an almost oopsie.

But the flash of the driver's rust-hued copper hair pulled any remaining acts of self-preservation from his mind and chucked them toward far more useful endeavors.

All that remained was the shocked resonance of recognition as, through a foggy window, his enhanced nighttime vision had him staring into the soft jade eyes of the woman from his dreams. The one he'd been looking for.

His feet were moving before he could think better of it and then sped way the hell up once he realized what must have happened. Despite the wall-to-wall traffic, she must have stepped on the gas by mistake and then stopped short before she hit the vehicle in front of her.

Iron ignored the honking around him as he weaved through the stalled cars and went over to her window. Gently, he tapped his knuckle on the glass. "Miss, are you all right?"

The defroster's poor performance did nothing to prevent his celestial senses from picking up what he needed to through the pane's haziness. And when the glass finally lowered, revealing the woman inside, he was . . . amused.

The woman pushed a pair of clear-framed glasses higher up her nose and then went to work lifting and lifting and *lifting* sections of long hair into some sort of complicated top knot situation. Like nearly rear-ending cars was all in a day's work and she was about to go on lunch. "Yeah, yeah, I'm okay. Just got a little too trigger-happy there. I didn't hit him, did I?"

"Uh, no. No, you stopped in time."

Iron took a step back when she moved to lean her head out the driver's side window and wave at the car in front of her. When no one waved back—or even noticed, though something told him he shouldn't point that out—she just sank back into her seat, her features twisting into despondency. Was she . . . *unhappy* that she hadn't hit the Jeep? Then she fished around into the shopping tote next to her and pulled out a handful of M&Ms. Peanut, judging by the smell.

Oddly enough, only *after* she popped a few into her mouth did she start talking. "I don't know what happened to me there. It's not like I didn't know we were in gridlock. I was just thinking about something, and then I had a sort of shitty experience at Nature's Value Market. Which, newsflash, don't go to that place on a night like tonight. Or ever, really. Pretty sure the owner has me on a list now. Anyway, they didn't have the cereal I wanted, or maybe they did, but I couldn't find it, and then I forgot to get the pancake mix. But then the M&Ms looked good. They always look good, don't they?" A wistful sort of acceptance curved her mouth into a sad, small smile, immediately disarming him of whatever line of questioning he'd been preparing to throw at her.

"I prefer mint M&Ms myself. The peanut ones are okay, too."

Mint M&Ms? What the fuck, Iron? *Mint* M&Ms?

He was about to retract his prior statement for something more appropriate, like whether she needed help, when her shoulders shook with a sharp laugh, and she looked up at him.

Whatever haze had clouded his thoughts around her

thinned. With one hard shake of his mental snow globe, the blurred edges of what he'd dreamed she might have looked like crisped up with all due haste and purpose. There was no mistaking her eyes, gems of rich sea glass floating in a jade lagoon, or the softness of her features he thought had fled his memories for good. But it was all there, the pert nose and resolute lower lip that she seemed to push out without realizing it. The hair, even the tension that pulled her shoulders higher beneath her ears while her chin aimed at whatever threat was in front of her.

It was her. *Her.* The woman who could potentially help them all get back to the Empyrean again. And she was . . .

Looking at him as though he'd give her a UTI from eye contact alone.

Iron's mouth went dry, and a sharp recoil of magic began to pulse within his core. "I won't hurt you," he rushed out.

"Are you sure?" she challenged. "Because you just said you like mint M&Ms, and I'm pretty sure there are no fewer than several dozen varieties of chocolate mint candies that would reliably rank higher in double-blind taste tests. I'm not exactly certain you're of sound mind at the moment."

"Well, I also didn't just get into a fender bender."

"*Almost* got into a fender bender. You verified that one yourself."

"Yes, and as you so astutely pointed out, my judgment is under scrutiny at the moment."

Watching ten kinds of thoughts shimmy behind her eyes was enough to keep him glued to the asphalt indefinitely. There was a fascination to it that had begun tugging at achingly tired parts of him, parts that hadn't just rusted over long ago but had made headway in the ten-thousand-year fossilization process.

As if he needed yet another reminder that he was a war-torn relic of another time, and she was a modern-day woman by herself who was being cornered by a creep in a coat with an apparently brand-new dissociative complex.

Juuust fucking great.

Iron worked to free the frog in his throat and took a healthy step back from her door. Blocks ahead, a scratchy "Scene's clear" worked its way through to his celestial senses from a police officer's radio. Fast on those heels was the growling rumble of a tow truck pulling away. Another minute or two and the traffic would start to move again.

"What's your—"

"Anyway, thanks for checking—"

Their collision of words was met with the same awkward half-laugh common among prepubescent boys asking out a girl for the first time. At least that was the case for him. For her? Nothing but that gracious smile again, which he was quickly coming to realize he'd commit no small number of murders to see.

Body counts had never bothered him.

A lock of hair that somehow hadn't been secured well to begin with—impossible, given the perceived tensile strength of that thick-ass elastic band, but what did he know?—fell free and, like a falcon diving for its catch, was snatched up by her deft fingers that had so swiftly put both hair and him back into place.

"You're sure I didn't hit him?" she asked again, even though they both knew she hadn't. But there was something there, something she clearly wasn't willing to let go so easily either.

At least, that was what he hoped.

"Positive."

She nodded and stared out through the windshield. With her hand on the steering wheel, she gestured a finger up ahead. "Looks like traffic's moving."

It sure is, goddammit.

"Yeah." Then before she could get the genius idea to take her foot off the brake and drag herself farther away from him, he plopped his hand on her door, covering the pocket of her still-down window, and said, "Your brakes sound rough. Like, really rough."

There were any number of things he expected her to do when faced with a large male pressing into her open window. She could scream, hit the gas, grab the butt end of her phone and slam it down on his fingers. At the very least, choice words with no shortage of expletives would have been a good place to start. Any of the above was fair game, really.

To his never-ending surprise and perhaps delight, she did none of those things. Instead, she just looked at him and nodded, nodded as if the weight of the world had left a few things off its grocery list and decided to add them to her shoulders before it, too, skedaddled back inside to take cover before the storm.

It broke his fucking heart.

"I'm painfully aware, thank you. They're on the list."

"That list really big?" he couldn't help but ask.

She pursed her lips. "Big enough. But whose isn't?"

Already, some of the cars in front of her had begun to move up inch by inch. "You live far?"

"Does anyone in this traffic jam live far?"

"You always answer a question with a question?"

Then those jade eyes narrowed, and that earlier fire returned. The fire he'd last seen in his dream and had been chasing the warmth of ever since. "Listen, buddy. If you're in the market for a Good Samaritan badge, you might want to check with the Aurora Police Department. I hear they still give them out to Boy Scout troops and when they teach school kids about K-9 units. As you can see, traffic's moving again, and I'd like to get home before the sky opens up. So, yeah, thanks for . . . whatever it is you think you did."

"Give me your phone."

"Yeah, that's a big old no on that one."

"Wasn't asking." In the red haze of the brake lights only two cars ahead of them, Iron ducked into her open window and snatched her phone from the pocket in her center console.

"Hey, what the hell do you think you're—"

It was the work of a moment to program his details into her contacts and, yeah, favorite that shit at the tippy top. Might as well. "You need anything, you call me. Name's Iron. I'm local. Your brakes sound like shit, and I don't need to tell you that storms this time of year are unpredictable. Or maybe I do need to tell you that." He smiled, then eyed her paltry provisions as she grabbed her phone out of his hand and threw it in her bag.

"You can't take people's stuff."

"Didn't take anything I didn't give back."

"Do you always do this?" she said, mimicking his tone from earlier, though with a heavy bend toward the obnoxious.

"Do what?"

"Act out what I suspect is your warped code of integrity?"

He smiled at that. Smiled big and wide.

She had no fucking idea.

Iron raised two fingers to his temple and saluted her off before ambling back to the sidewalk. Her window was up and sealed a moment later. And as he watched her drive off with the moving line of cars, he pulled out his phone to finish making those notes to himself from earlier.

Except this time, they'd have nothing to do with scanning school district rosters and everything to do with running her license plate.

CHAPTER 6

As Anna tucked her newly acquired and equally laughable snowstorm rations into the pantry, minus the open bag of M&Ms, which had already been slotted for that evening's dinner and dessert, the dormant analytical part of her brain took over, as it so often did in times of stress.

Numbers. Macros, calories, grams, fiber, protein, all of it boiling down to a tidy numeral that was neither positive nor negative. Numbers had no feelings, no preferences over the outcomes they projected. And they certainly didn't play odds or favorites. They just . . . were.

Anna plunked her handbag down on her small kitchen table and leaned into her method of emotional dismantling.

Because, oh boy, did she need it.

Forty-five minutes. That was how long it had taken her to finally get home after she'd left the grocery store. About thirty minutes longer than it should have taken. The traffic had been the problem there, though. Traffic and . . .

Twenty-three sentences spoken by a stranger through an open car window after she'd narrowly avoided rearranging the front end of her slightly-less-reliable-than-it-used-to-be Subaru.

Like the tide called back to its master, shadowed images of frosty oceans parting overtook the quaint cabinetry of her kitchen and pulled her into the moment she hadn't stopped reliving for forty-five turns of the minute hand.

Twenty-three sentences articulated in urgent rumbles that set her skin to scorching. Of those soul-searing sentences, the majority of them had been only a smattering of words and had still managed to flood humbler parts of her with more oxytocin than her starved brain could handle. If she took those words and divided them into the modicum of minutes she and the man had actually conversed for, the result would give each word far more power than they had any right to have over her. And that had only just been the tip of the proverbial iceberg.

Anna's mind reeled over yet more numbers it called forth from her jumble of an evening.

The number of digits he'd tapped onto her phone's screen, which included no screen protector whatsoever and therefore had still held every drop of oil from the stranger's skin? Ten.

Ten, plus the bonus four. I-R-O-N. Each letter stamped into his contact card in her phone may as well have been carved into the side of her car for all the shock it still left her with.

The guy's name was Iron? Iron, as in he who pumps a lot of it at the gym and therefore must be known by it?

The need for security floated Anna's hand down to her stomach, the gesture having become an anchor when her world started to spiral out of control, while her other hand, in need of something to judge, had its ever-indignant finger pointed in the air.

"This is a good thing," she told herself. "The only men with names like that are either in biker gangs or have YouTube channels where they spout off the benefits of chemically processed protein supplements while eschewing the need for vegetables and dietary fiber." That last one was a particular pet peeve of hers. And if any positive thing could be said for her time with Travis, it was her ability to see the red flags whipping across her nose and *not* diving straight toward them like a bull in a ring.

Progress and all that.

Anna hung up her coat, toed out of her boots and, as was her nightly habit before bed, turned the living room TV onto the home shopping channel, hit the mute button, and scampered her way toward the bathroom. There was no passing Go, no collecting two hundred dollars. Not when her feet and thoughts were frozen from an encounter that had as much of a chokehold on her mind as another number.

Not a number, really, but a concept, one as boundless and intimidating as anything her usually adaptable brain could wrap its synapses around.

Infinity. Despite all the numbers that scrolled through Anna's mental ticker tape reel, that one—which wasn't really a number but kept standing out in the bunch regardless—was the one she didn't want to examine too closely when engaging in her earlier stress-reduction tactic.

To be infinite was to know no limits. This would be particularly applicable in, say, the unlimited number of inappropriate thoughts Anna had also had about a stranger who just happened to fit the lingering vibe of her mystery man.

She closed the bathroom door, not even stopping to stare into the mirror this time, and instead made straight for the bathtub. Once the water was cranked to just hot enough to where her obstetrician wouldn't yell at her for soaking in it too long, she reached for her super-secret basket of contraband beneath the sink. The things she'd kept private from Travis because the only risk he'd ever been willing to overlook (no shocker there) was his career being financed by someone else. If he'd known the aging septic system on the cabin would take a hit every time Anna indulged in one of her few comforts, he'd have literally thrown these babies out with her bathwater.

There, nestled within its wicker bassinet, was Anna's version of *in case of emergency, break glass*. Her hand-curated spa kit, complete with her French clay facial mask, cold-process all-natural artisanal soap made from coconut oil, vegan bath salts, lavender essential oils, and her favorite brandy-and-marshmallow-scented small-batch soy candle with the perfect edge-to-edge burn circumference. A daily plumbing indulgence of such a high salt and fat diet would set her poor septic system on a path her homeowner's insurance would never come back from, so she reserved these private primping moments for very choice occasions.

And, oh boy, was this a doozy of an occasion.

By the time she kicked her toes free of her fleece-lined leggings, the water had reached optimal body-to-water-displacement height. Anna quickly killed the tap, hiked a leg over the rim, and slowly sank into the only respite the outside hadn't figured out how to take from her yet.

"Oooh, god*damn*, that's wonderful." The water lapped over her chilled skin, drawing out the wrinkles of tension that had seemed to so firmly implant themselves in every pore of her body. The buoyancy had taken on a new air of enjoyment since she'd become pregnant. Her belly was only slightly rounder than it had been a month ago, since she'd finally started putting on some weight once the daily puking ended, but it was her breasts that had really been through the ringer.

Anna rested her neck against the lip of the tub and let her long hair ride the current of the water. In some sort of bodily symbiosis she'd never thought about too closely but was oddly grateful for, her hair always chose to pool around her breasts instead of directly across them, as if even her hair knew to stay away from her aching nipples. The damn things had been pulled to tender peaks for most of the day, and the only relief was letting the water handle some of her body weight so she could finally spend time *not* thinking about her pregnancy. Or her clients. Or her bills.

Or the man whose name and number were currently taking up more space in her mind than they had any right to.

Because that man, Iron, had tap-danced across her psyche and sent reverberations that were way too similar to another man she also couldn't stop thinking about.

"Stop. You're connecting dots that aren't there." She groaned into the gathering cloud of steam.

But were they? Her fingers drew lazy figure eights on the surface of the water while she tried to untangle the threads of just what in the hell had bothered her so much about the man who'd saved her from the fate her Subaru nearly suffered. Sort of.

She hadn't even gotten a good look at the guy. Not really, anyway. It'd been dark, and beyond him having an equally dark beard, a smoky voice like warm whisky, and the wherewithal to jump into crowded traffic to referee an almost-accident, she didn't have a lot to go on about him.

"Still, things were . . . similar." Anna closed her eyes and rested her other hand on her slightly rounded stomach, curling her toes as a new thought entered her mind.

Would it be so bad to *pretend* to know someone like him? Someone strong, brave, caring. Someone thoughtful and kind, who looked after others when they were too stubborn to look after themselves. In a hypothetical situation, where eyes of brown and hazel could live on the face and body of a man like Iron and she could quell her surliness and mistrust long enough to let someone like him know her in return, would it *really* be so terrible?

Water droplets pattered along the tub's edge as Anna lifted her arm out and reached for her basket of goodies. With two fingers, she hooked the edge of the wicker and drew the items closer.

"He'd be strong. That's an obvious one. Probably the type of guy to get your oil changed for you before you realized you needed to—and do it himself in his garage or change the smoke detector batteries twice a year on daylight savings." She rooted around in the basket, bypassing all the soaps and oils she'd usually grab. On any other night, the bathroom would be heavily scented with lavender and her body so drowsy beneath aromatic clay and coconut oil soap that she wouldn't have had the energy to do much else.

But all it took was for her fingernail to graze along that curved smooth surface of silicone and her path forward was diverted toward a different course.

One she hadn't thought to travel in quite some time.

Anna retrieved her compact waterproof vibrator, also colored lavender, and glided it down into the water between her legs. While she cradled the thing in the safety of her palm, her fingers led the way for a fantasy that had no business existing and had every business turning her night around from the trajectory her day had started on.

On instinct, she tapped the button to her favorite setting and parted herself, searching out the needy pulse that pounded within the cove of her thighs. The moment her middle finger grazed her clitoris, she couldn't help but imagine that it was someone else's fingers touching her in slow circles, discovering her secret slickness. Fingers that were thick and strong and quick enough to place themselves over the edge of her car window to keep her attention or snatch a phone out from under her nose to anoint it with his name. Deftness was surely an underrated skill among such men.

Soft battery-powered pulses replaced her stroking finger, pumping erratic breaths and ill-timed bravery into her body. She'd never done this before, fantasized about a man as she took care of her needs. The two had always been mutually exclusive. And just like in her fantasies, they always ended with her landing back in the real world.

Until that unfortunate occurrence, she was content to ride the wave of whatever her small tub could contain. As she crested her peak and let loose a guttural orgasmic cry so powerful her throat burned, her stomach somersaulted over itself.

A tinkling laugh escaped Anna's lips as she killed the vibrator, dropped it in the water, and quickly brought both hands to her abdomen.

Her baby. Her future.

Her first flutters.

Born from the thoughts of a fantasy.

CHAPTER 7

The snowstorm began as most New England storms did when the temperature had been below freezing for a few days. It wasn't the pretty fat flakes that Hallmark would have its audience believe were regularly occurring in small towns. Nor were said small towns inhabited by entire populations of people who, for some reason, always wore their scarves outside their coat collars—coats that were never ever zipped up, mind you. Likewise, the snow didn't funnel at people from the side in gusty torrents, knocking toddlers and toy poodles over left and right.

Instead, it was more of a soft snow globe effect that Iron rather liked. The kind of snow that started out lightly dusting cars and concrete like powdered sugar over a chocolate torte. All that other shit, the wind and the accumulations piling up hand over fist so DPW workers couldn't get ahead of it? That always came later, once Mother Nature had worked up a good rage. But for now, as he sat atop the Aurora Rescue Squad's slanted roof and looked out over the newly frosted pond nestled at the center of the municipal park across the street, he was struck with a quiet and peaceful calm. It was always Iron's favorite place to slink off to when he needed to gather the storm clouds of his thoughts.

Kind of helped that the Rescue Squad was pretty much abandoned on days like this, as the rigs were always out running calls the moment a cloud farted out a snowflake. According to mortal logic—and he was using that last word *very* loosely—when snow started, *that* was when people magically realized they were sick and needed to go to the hospital right that goddamn minute because what if something happened and they couldn't get to their doctor in the snow? What if that callus on their knuckle that had formed when they were fifteen was actually a small tumor?

Mortal forethought was truly an art form sometimes. If only he could have their problems. So, yeah, he enjoyed the quiet, and it was a gift from the mages that he even had the wherewithal to park his ass on freezing roof shingles instead of flying off to the precise address of the woman he had a name for—a name, along with height, eye color, age, and a few other choice tidbits the Department of Motor Vehicles had offered up when he'd run a search on her license plate.

Anna Malone.

A woman heavy on sass, light on sense, if her grocery offerings the night before a snowstorm were anything to go by, and full of so many questions, Iron's mind couldn't spin through them fast enough.

Why the hell hadn't she prepared better?

When was the last time she'd had her brakes checked?

What was her plan for—

He sucked in a sharp, frustrated breath as another paralyzing thought occurred to him.

Fuck. What if Anna *was* like those mortals who might actually need emergency services during a storm because she was so ill-prepared? Or would she just ignore her welfare entirely and, fueled by fucking Fruit Loops, try to power through with spit, glue, and hope?

Iron thought back to her Subaru and its vocal protestations of its brake conditions . . . Of her overreliance on subpar chocolate to see her through the worst . . .

Shit. She was definitely one of those mortals.

Iron dragged his hand over his face, annoyed at himself because he knew damn well every single one of his questions about her had been superficial pokes at problems largely common to the mortal condition. They didn't come close to the real quandary that had been boring a hole into his brain matter for the better part of the new year.

"What *is* she to me?" Iron's back teeth met as he ground the words out, giving voice to a lament that had become as soul-deep as the honor he'd sworn to the celestial mages upon taking up the mantle of an Empyrean sentinel.

Determined to still make good choices because he wasn't a goddamn creep, Iron tamped down the urge to fly over the mountain district east of Aurora proper to check—just *check*—on the state of the roads leading to a certain cabin he had *not* memorized the address of. Instead, he tried to clap some heat back into his frigid palms and stilled.

A subtle warmth flowed from the breast pocket of his flannel shirt beneath his coat. The kind of heat well-loved in leather car seats but in no way should be coming from a dude's pec, least of all his.

Then a hollow realization weaseled into his brain.

"Don't fucking tell me . . ."

Iron unzipped his coat and dug around, already knowing—and fearing—what he'd find there. When he pulled out the test tube housing the small shard, it pulsed back at him with the same glowing-heat performance it'd put on in front of him and Titan a few days earlier.

At a loss for what any of it meant, Iron brought the thing

closer to his nose, gently rolling the glass vial between thumb and forefinger as if it were one of Chrome's Nicaraguan cigars. "What the hell am I missing? What do you want from me?"

Iron traced every action, thought, and conversation back to his time with Titan, what they'd been doing, where they'd been sitting, how much fucking whipped cream it took to ruin a perfectly good cup of coffee. It was all trivial shit. Nothing that seemed important or magical enough to miraculously jumpstart a shard of a long-dead celestial relic. Nothing he hadn't tried before. Nothing except . . .

Across the pond, the wind had begun to pick up, pushing the soft snowfall out of its steady pattern and scattering it into tiny clouds of chaos. It was only eleven in the evening, and the storm was already showing signs of ramping up, far sooner than the dense mortal meteorologists had predicted.

"Prediction," he mused, turning the word over on his tongue, trying to grasp at what he'd been missing. "A dense prediction. About me being wrong . . ." Then his hands flew to his hair. "Holy shit, I've been so wrong!"

When Iron had damn near lost his mind to Titan, rattling off every single thought about this woman, his family, the fight against Cyro, *everything* that had been keeping him up at night, he'd been a man of panicked inaction. Of indifference born of some bullshit higher purpose because the not doing was easier than the doing. It wasn't until Titan had called him on his bull-shit that Iron had been able to blow the rust off his rationale and see things clearly.

If you could stop her pain, would you?

Eight words had simultaneously magnified his foolishness while catapulting him into a realization that had literally—finally—jump-started the shard's celestial magic.

Iron slipped the glowing test tube back into his pocket as he untangled the jumble of threads that had tripped him up over the past few months and at last began piecing them together.

The moment he'd begun analyzing the relic's shard and keeping it close to him was also the same night he'd begun having dreams of her. Anna.

It was his physical proximity to a piece of the Empyrean's gates, a piece that still held traces of Empyrean magic like he suspected, that somehow must have been enough to light the celestial fire that would show him—

"My soul bond."

Every time, every *single* time Iron had decided to go in the opposite direction of the very mate who held the twin spark of his soul's flame, the relic's shard would light up like a damn Christmas tree and point its judgmental finger at just how fucking dense of an asshole Iron truly was.

Because he was refusing his destiny, his fate, his former power and ability to finally get him and his brothers back to the Empyrean and end Cyro's tyranny by connecting with his soul bond.

All so he could diddle over a puzzle he'd been holding the missing piece to all this time.

Iron's angel fire licked at his core, filling his limbs with celestial power that seemed to spread and search for what it couldn't find but yearned for regardless. Crouched low and deep, with his heart hammering in his ears, Iron prepared to unfurl his wings and take to the skies. The inaction was killing him. If he didn't at least get eyes on her property soon, assess the roads, check for frozen tree limbs in threat of falling, he was liable to pull his hair out.

He needed to know she was all right, even if he couldn't speak to her yet. He needed to know—

That tingling warmth patted his chest, emanating from his flannel's breast pocket again. Before he could grab the vial, however, the small tube twitched within the fabric, jostling and moving slightly until the shard's tip was angled toward his left hip where he kept his phone.

Then a soft vibration pulsed against the denim. When he slowly retrieved his phone and looked at the screen, the rest of his world fell away. A single text.

Unknown number: Hi, it's Anna. The Subaru lady with a braking problem.

A row of three dots appeared, then more text followed.

Unknown number: Just checking to see whether your warped code of integrity has any room for gratitude. I hope so. I hate owing people. That's how ghosts are made. And I never said thank you, though I'm still not entirely certain for what. Either way, thanks.

Three dots made an appearance again, then vanished, appeared, and vanished once more before her texting finally fell silent . . .

That wouldn't do.

CHAPTER 8

Anna didn't even wait for the remote possibility of a response. She just buried her phone beneath her pillow, flung her glasses back on her nightstand, and returned her ear to the divot it had occupied for the past hour.

Holy shit, she'd actually texted him. A complete stranger with a hero complex who had been running laps through her thoughts for the lion's share of the past five hours. Even her bath, which *always* helped her fall asleep, apparently decided to pile on the pressure instead of relieving it.

It didn't matter that she'd tucked herself into bed at nine thirty or made a very intentional choice not to consume any more media, written or watchable, in hopes she'd coax her mind into a pleasantly euphoric state of slumber.

Nope. Instead, she'd had to go and contract a bout of guilty conscience over how rude she'd been to the man who, for some reason that still failed to find her, had taken time out of his evening to ensure she was okay.

When she was still wide awake hours later, she typed out a message before she could call the words back. It was only after she'd realized what she'd done that true embarrassment prickled her cheeks. Before any dots could bubble up under his name in their nonexistent text string and possibly pepper her screen with encouragement, she cut the conversation off real quick.

"A small thank-you. Just a small thank-you. Nothing that needs a rejoinder."

Of course, these were the words of an irrational woman who had convinced herself that such a text likely wouldn't be responded to. For one thing, it was late. Far past acceptable communication windows. And surely, if he even felt compelled to respond, it wouldn't be with anything more than a simple thumbs-up reaction or a smiley face. For most people who were either sleeping or well on their way to getting there, the path of least resistance was often the most desirable. Why tap out a whole sentence when a simple emoji would suffice and get the point across quickly enough for them to both fall back to sleep?

Besides, if he *did* respond to her, was that even someone she wanted to be talking to in the first place? People who had conversations or intense thought processes this close to midnight were often very bothered people. She had more than enough clients who confessed to late-night snacks and work sessions being a significant part of their dietary undoing to know this.

Good decision-makers kept reasonable hours with reasonable boundaries, something she clearly needed to work on more herself. And no, she was *not* about to blame it on the pregnancy. After the night she'd had, any sane person would have wanted to show their gratitude. It was an act of goddamn integrity, really, a virtue they'd already established to be an area of concern between them. Doing what was right without the expectation of reciprocity. To volley back against her message would just be inconsiderate. What would he do, after all? Thank her for thanking him? And where would that cycle end? In madness, obviously.

Anna hitched the covers higher up over her shoulder to block out both the chill of the room and the frigid wind pelting the panes of her windows. Only once she settled more snuggly into her cocoon and tried to search out sleep again did a soft vibration tickle her cheek and ear.

Her eyes winged open. She scrambled for her glasses and dove for the phone beneath her pillow. Within the soft pale-blue glow of her screen sat a message, offered up like an oyster presenting its pearl. From Iron.

Iron: Is becoming a ghost a sizable worry for you?

More dots . . .

Iron: And no thanks needed.

Anna settled the pillow behind her head against the wall and tucked her knees close to her chest like she used to as a kid when reading before bed held far more interest than dreaming.

Anna: I wouldn't have made it this far in life without a healthy amount of worry.

Iron: Worrying borrows more trouble than you need.

Anna: I'm also very good at managing debt, so don't you *ahem* worry.

Iron: About as good as managing your vehicle's maintenance schedule?

Anna scoffed, read the words again, then dug her top teeth into her bottom lip and set her thumbs to typing.

Anna: Do not make me take back my gratitude, sir. I don't give it out lightly.

Iron: Wouldn't dream of it. Such an action would be outside my integrity.

He'd accented his point with a cartoon wink floating within the small lemon drop circle of an emoji. That little smiley face siphoned up every last bubble of hot air from within her sails, and any venomous retort she'd been readying died a quick and painful death.

Anna: Didn't figure you for an emoji guy.

Iron: Now, that has me curious. In the five minutes we've spent in each other's company, what did you figure me as?

Anna: Oh, I don't know. Someone who travels around the country looking for logs to flip at Highland game festivals. Maybe find a hot dog eating competition or two. Oh, I've got it! Someone who operates a crusher. You know those machines that compress cars down for recycling? I bet you'd be really great at running one of those.

Her exuberance once again got the better of her, and as she stared back at the term-paper-sized text she just fired off, her face pinched with embarrassment. Words were her thing, had always been. Clear communication was a hill she'd happily die on and was why she often let her nutrition appointments rattle on for an extra fifteen nonbillable minutes when she wanted to make sure the directions she was imparting were sinking in with the client the way they needed to. And yes, in her mostly solitary lifestyle, she'd learn to perfect the conveyance of her true self through written mediums, with perhaps an unhealthy reliance on adjectives.

But these were texts. Short-form messages. The realm of Ks, BRBs, and OMGs.

And she'd just lapsed into purple prose with a total stranger.

Her fingers flew fast and furious over the keys. *I didn't mean to type that much. I know texts are for—*

Iron interrupted her, answering her paragraph bubble with an impressively sized one of his own.

Iron: First, it's called the caber toss, and contrary to what you've assumed about my physique, I don't quite have calves athletic enough to pull off a kilt. Second, hot dogs give me indigestion. I'm more of an espresso and biscotti guy. And third, don't really care for hard hats.

Anna: Because of helmet hair?

She smiled, remembering that his hair had been long enough

to pull back into a hair tie, and then immensely relieved that he was playing along with her profuse chats.

Iron: Because hard hats aren't foolproof, and I like to look at the margins.

Anna: What the heck does that even mean?

Iron: It means that even the safest bets come with risk, and I'm risk averse.

Anna: Ah. Is that why you're so offended by my car's lack of brake pad thickness?

She'd meant it as a quip, a light shot across the bow that would keep this surprisingly buoyant conversation from swapping places with the mildly mounting worry over what she would do when this tête-à-tête eventually ended. Of the sleep that would ultimately claim her and spit her out into a dawn full of snow and uncertainty. But when Iron didn't immediately respond, a new concern shot ice water through her veins, shocking the vibrant enjoyment the universe had seen fit to give her into just another memory.

When his words returned, they forced her lungs to hold back her breath of relief.

Iron: Do you have anyone to help you?

The question cast a shadow of promises that had seemed as out of place in her cheerful bedroom as the man's presence.

Anna: I won't answer that.

Iron: Why not?

Anna: Safety.

She may have been slightly orgasm-addled from her earlier tub escapades, but that didn't mean her awareness of what it meant to live life as a thirty-four-year-old single pregnant woman just went by the wayside. And if the man didn't know that, he wasn't as—

Iron: Good.

Her thoughts spun to a complete stop.

Anna: Good?

More dots wiggled across the screen while she waited for an explanation. She'd stared at the damn things so intensely that the little ellipses had begun skewering the corners of her vision. After she'd gnawed off the cuticle of one finger and had gotten to work on a second, she threw the covers off, wrapped them around her shoulders, and padded over to the window in search of something to fill the wait.

Outside, the snow had begun to pick up, falling to the mostly forested ground around her cabin in an even coating of winter's final regards. Three years ago, nestled among the blanket of blue spruce, sugar maple, and mighty American elm, at the end of a private road that could barely be called such, sat the two-bedroom cabin that had claimed Anna's heart and dreams. The charming structure, built in 1940, had just enough of its original wood-plank charm preserved, while leaving a reasonable number of starter-home renovations for her to sink her teeth into and make this place her own.

Far enough from nosy neighbors but no more than fifteen minutes away from anything she might need, and with the perfect dappling sunrise poking through verdant evergreens, the cabin had been a secure balm to the turbulent turnstiles of her childhood homes—plural. In the end, she'd begged, and Travis had caved, largely due to his indifference at the time about where he slept, since the Internet buttered their communal bread anyway.

Slowly, over those three years, Travis had had no choice but to acquiesce to her indulgences: butcher block counters, specially mounted shelves to display her cast-iron cookware, and a large picture window overlooking the sloping mountainside that spat her out into civilization whenever she needed it.

A civilization that lately, not to put too fine a point on it, had required far too much of her participation and nowhere near enough grace in return.

The wind howled an echo of loneliness through the trees

that mirrored her own, even as she stared down at the phone clenched tightly in her hands. Still no response.

Anna's teeth met with the snap of every twig succumbing to the storm. It was even more jarring of a hit to realize that her conversation had distracted her entirely from what was happening outside her window. Now that she was in a holding cell, waiting for clarification on a single word from a man she'd barely talked to for five minutes, she was beginning to question her earlier notion of safety.

A booming *thud* shook the forest around her, shaking free the loose snowfall that had already begun to collect on some of the thicker branches. Anna's heart leaped into her throat, and her uterus's tiny tenant performed its own symbiotic dance.

"Crap."

Anna adjusted her glasses and tapped out what her very cells needed another living organism to hear.

Anna: Something just happened.

The three dots disappeared, and Iron's response flared hot on the heels of her own.

Iron: Explain. You okay?

Anna: Yeah. I mean, just jittery. A really loud bang sounded outside my property. Shook a bunch of trees around my house. Wind's picking up. Got a little spooked.

Another pause, and just when she thought he was going to ghost her response again, more of his words filled her small screen.

Iron: If someone, a male who you don't know well, for instance, but who, so far, has a perfect track record for inquiring after your well-being, would like to inquire further, how might he do that so as not to appear . . .

She smiled, instantly seeing where his thoughts were going.

Anna: Like a multiconvicted felon on his way to his fifth parole hearing for charges of repeated sexual assaults and that one time he tried to fuck a cored pineapple at a Fourth of July barbecue in front of the kiddos?

Iron: That was . . . oddly specific.

Anna: What can I say? I have a very vivid imagination. I'm also pretty sure I'm the only millennial who still watches Dateline.

Iron: A woman who loves her murder shows. Noted.

That and home shopping. I like to keep it on when— Another crack farther down the mountain sent a shudder through the cabin, stalling her response. The small night-light she kept plugged into her hallway outlet dipped before reigniting with the more muted glow from the thing's puny battery backup. Around her, the dinosaur oil heat furnace wound down, churning to a standstill and taking the heat along with it.

Anna: Shit. Power just went out.

Her text screen vanished, then was filled with Iron's name, practically amplifying the force of her phone's meager vibrating ringtone.

She answered before the first ring had ended. "Hi."

"Tree went down?"

"I guess so. I lose power a bunch where I am. I have a generator. Once the sun's up, I'll head back to the . . ."

The string of curses flitted through Anna's mind as she realized just where the hell her generator was stored and how her very pregnant and sciatica-prone body would *not* be able to safely drag that thing from the shed to her house where she could connect it to the transfer switch, let alone hobble back in the snow to get the can of gasoline.

Crap. She was supposed to check the oil levels in the generator after the last storm they had. That was . . . mid-February? Was that when one of her neighbors much farther down the mountain had helped her haul the thing to her house and set it up? No, there had been a storm since then, right? But then why didn't she remember when she filled up the gas can last?

"You okay? Anna?"

"Yeah, I just had to readjust some things in my head, that's all."

"What the hell does that mean?"

"It means that, given the snow, I don't think it'll really be worth it to lug the generator out. Besides, Aurora's so well-prepared. I'm sure the power will be back on by the morning anyway. I could just—"

"Where's your generator?"

"It's . . . on property."

"This isn't fucking Disney World, Anna. The storm's about to get a shit ton worse before it gets better. Can you access your generator or not?"

"At the moment? Not."

A long hard pause plunged their conversation into a fathomless silence. Finally, Iron said, "Please, tell me where you are. I can get to you, get you hooked up and comfortable before things get really bad."

"I'm not sure that's such a good—"

"Please, Anna." A painful angst hardened the edges of his words, and it caught her off guard, but then the lightness she imagined coating his earlier texts returned. "Hey, perfect track record, remember?"

Oh, she remembered.

Anna shook her head and looked to the stormy sky for answers, but the damn thing was too busy causing problems.

With a shaky sigh that did a piss-poor job of hiding her trepidation, she told him where she lived.

And hoped like hell she hadn't just made the biggest mistake of her life.

CHAPTER 9

An hour. It took Iron an entire goddamn hour to make the ten-mile trip from his family's parking garage in Aurora proper up the road toward Anna's house. What had started as annoying fluff quickly turned into two inches. At that rate of snowfall, it wouldn't take long for the roads to become impassable, and while he would have loved nothing more than to take to the skies and bypass this whole mess in ten minutes, exposing himself that way wasn't a good idea. Not yet, at any rate. He'd *just* gotten her to tell him her name, and even that trusting courtesy didn't yet extend to surnames.

So, the F-150 it was.

His snow chains crunched like popcorn through the winding road's unplowed terrain until the truck's headlights passed across the roadside mailbox with the number he was looking for. Already, the thing had a healthy funnel of snow growing around its base. Set back from the road was a modest cabin with a quaint sloping roof, obligatory fenced-in porch, and flashlight beams darting from behind its prominent picture window.

Anna's house.

Iron grabbed his phone, sent a quick text, and backed his truck into the driveway.

Iron: Here.

His boots barely hit the snow before the cabin's front door opened a crack, and Anna poked her head out.

"Thanks for coming," she yelled as her words caught on the wind and traveled closer to him.

He stalked up her porch steps but found himself stalled out on the coir doormat.

Anna stood there, wrapped in a comforter of insanely floofy proportions, with one hand gripping a phone while the other fisted a Maglite. A soft corona of flickering light from the candles lit in the room behind her haloed her hair in a gentle embrace. And damn if his angel fire didn't stir within his core, pulsing in time to the ambient glow that wisely chose the perfect subject to illuminate.

But there was something else he saw there that he'd missed earlier.

Shadows. Ashen smudges that, through the veneer of her glasses, still pulled at the lower lids of her eyes, spotlighting an exhaustion that seemed to swallow her almost as much as the comforter around her shoulders.

"Where's your generator?" he asked, determined to get her warm and rested as soon as possible. They both knew it was unwise to run the thing while she was sleeping, but he could at least make sure it was ready to go come morning.

"It's in the shed behind the house. The hookup is next to the electrical meter on the right side, where the oil tank is. The generator should already be on a little rolling dolly, and there's a rack in the shed where the gas can should be."

"Got it. You stay inside while I get this squared away."

Iron didn't want to linger on her front steps because he knew the nature of mortals. The longer he stood there, the longer she'd feel compelled to keep hanging her head out in the elements. The only way she'd hurry her butt inside was if he gave her something to observe through the window, so he threw his hood up and did exactly that.

The shed was an eight-by-ten metal number that sat crookedly on a concrete slab, which was sporting cracks in more than a few spots, not to mention overgrowths of moss. He was about to yank open the doors when the unfastened combination lock hooked through the loop that was *supposed* to be holding the two doors together stopped him.

Iron simply stared at it, then blinked. Yup, the thing was definitely unlocked. He was about to mutter some choice words to no one in particular when a gust of biting wind whipped across his face, pressing its urgency into his actions.

"Later," he ground out, yanking the stiff doors open while eyeing the rust that had built up on the doors' track, wondering just how in the hell Anna expected to open this thing on a good day, let alone during a snowstorm. Once he blinked back the musty tang of algae that coated damn near everything, the generator wasn't hard to find. It sat in the back corner like a sleeping metal giant, slightly rusted and worse for wear, but with all its knobs and pull cords intact, thank the mages.

Working quickly, he took care of the fluids as best he could, then lugged the thing through the gathering snow, leaving the dolly and its fucking office chair wheel casters behind. After he'd found the plug, secured the generator, and cranked that thing to life, he locked up the shed—properly this time—and trudged back to Anna's front door.

She was already there to greet him, still with phone and flashlight in hand.

Stomping the snow from his boots, he slid through her front door. "Where's your breaker box?"

"I can manage that, thanks."

"The same way you managed to lock up your shed?"

An icy mask of indignation carved hollow lines into features already stressed with exhaustion. "Hey, need I remind you that I didn't ask for your help? *Again?* And now's hardly the time to nitpick how I live my life. The shed is old, all right? Half the time, I can't even get the door holes to line up correctly to even slide the lock through in the first place, never mind going through the trouble of fastening it. I don't often have a reason to go in there, and it's not like I have super close next-door neighbors itching to steal from me. It's called seclusion for a reason, and one of the benefits is not having to worry about whether your groceries will be nabbed out of your trunk if you need to take more than one trip to get everything inside."

She let her eyes fall closed for a moment, took a deep breath, then opened them again. Her gaze landed on his face, but her attention was somewhere else. "Look, the shed's on the list, too." Her hand flew up to cut him off. "Yes, it's a long list. Yes, it'll all get handled eventually. But none of that is happening tonight."

Iron wanted to go to her, to push right past her excuses and follow the track his metallic powers were pulling him along that had already identified and located the metals and wires of the breaker box within her house. *Laundry room in the hallway to the right.* But as soon as he lifted his foot, he was reminded of his snow-laden boots . . . and of another problem entirely.

If he took his boots off, he was stating his intention to farther enter her home, which she had not invited him to do. If he stayed on the doormat, he was resigning her to an evening of more work, more exhaustion, more goddamn survival, and it was already after midnight.

The beaten-down bravado in her gaze ripped the sigh from his lungs. "Can I stay here, at least, while you flip on the breakers? Just to ensure the generator's working properly and you'll be able to fire it up easily come morning. I'm not sure how old the oil is in that thing, and the gas can was only half full."

Her eyes narrowed into slits, but there was no true fight in them. Thank the mages. "All right. Wait here."

A moment later, a few lights flickered, the furnace groaned out of its slumber, and the low hum of the refrigerator compressor began vibrating the wooden floorboards.

Anna returned. "Seems to be working. I can't run the entire house on the generator, so I have to pick and choose which amenities to fire up when. But it's better than nothing. At least I can run the water pump and septic when I need to. I'm a simple girl, but if you take away my indoor plumbing, I'm a bear to deal with."

"More so than usual?" Iron lifted a brow and waited . . . waited for her to jest with him again. He liked her fighting much more than freezing.

She hitched her comforter higher. "Yeah, but more like a giant panda or something."

"A giant panda? Not a grizzly?"

"Nah. I'm not physically violent, just really passive aggressive. I always got the sense that pandas were given the luxury of black masks so they could silently judge other animals and people."

"You know, I can't say that I find fault in your logic."

"Me neither." She smiled, and damn if he didn't enjoy the way her cheeks rose to meet the rims of her glasses, as if her joy was more than enough to support the rest of her.

"Go shut everything off, then get some sleep."

"Don't tell me what to do."

"I'm not telling. Just suggesting."

"Oh, like you were *suggesting* I take better care of my shed or my car's brakes?"

"Nope. Because those things are on your list, and you've made it very clear your list is your responsibility. I'm not privy to the list, so I can't comment on it. But I figured I was allowed to comment on the breakers since that's what I came to help with. The sleep thing just seemed like something you'd benefit from, being human and all."

Anna shook her head. "You're something else, you know that?"

Heat crept up the back of Iron's neck, a heat that was very much fueled by more than mere blood vessels. Inside, his fire was roiling in and around itself, pressing beneath his skin for release.

Iron swallowed, dipped his head, and offered a quick "You know how to reach me" before about-facing and getting his ass out the door. Fuck, he hadn't even touched her, and his fire was already reaching to claim that which it had never known but couldn't exist without.

And hell if he'd risk his uncontrollable angel fire coming out surrounded by a goddamn log cabin. No, he had to get out of there while his actions were still ruled by some form of higher reasoning.

There was time. He'd take his time with her, get to know her leisurely. Maybe even do what the mortals did and ask her out on a few dates. Then, slowly, he'd find a way to explain things, and they'd learn together, understand and answer questions in a calm and safe way.

He was Iron. He was a sentinel of the Empyrean. He was—

His boots skidded to a halt when he saw the rows of thick tree branches that had fallen in front of his truck, blocking him in.

He was about to tear off his glove, bring his power forth, and torch the suckers when something urged him to look back at the house. Sure enough, the corner of one gauzy curtain was peeled back and Anna's curious form was watching him through the window. Not even a hint of shyness there. Oh no. That girl wanted him to know she was keeping tabs on him.

Which also meant he couldn't use his celestial strength to pitch each of those logs into the woods, let alone scorch everything to cinders.

A sharp wrapping of knuckles on glass had him squinting

back at her. To his surprise, she lifted the stiff window, ducked her head out into the snowy wind, cupped her mouth, and yelled, "Caber toss!"

The comment would have been hilarious, if not for the unfortunate truth it highlighted about his circumstances—a truth he was painfully aware that Anna now knew as well.

Until the storm was over and the road could get cleared by more conventional means, Iron was going nowhere.

Unless he revealed the truth to her, and for a woman who could barely manage to keep her own life in order, he wasn't sure she'd be able to survive being dragged into his.

CHAPTER 10

Something about the words "You know how to reach me" being the last phrase Iron cast in Anna's direction set her insides to vibrating. Whether or not he actually meant the agitation was less of a concern than the final result.

Her cells, and her senses, weren't quite ready for him to leave just yet.

Padding over to the window, Anna drew back the curtain and watched as his broad back, hunched forward against the wind, traveled down her driveway. He navigated the mounting snow like a snow leopard, all grace and careful footing as his large boots seemed to distribute his weight evenly with each trudging strep. The figure he cut through the snow was an enthralling one, captivating her despite her weariness. Man, she still couldn't believe he'd shown up. And maybe that was what made it so hard to watch him walk away.

His hand had already gripped the driver's side door handle when he froze, and she followed his hooded head as it swiveled farther down the road leading to her house. A slew of not-so-insignificant tree branches had fallen, barricading the only way down the mountain in unorganized crosshatches. Nothing she'd entertain moving on her own even before her pregnancy, but she was not Iron. Iron was not her. And Iron, she instinctively knew, was not most men. No, he possessed the stature of a Roman gladiator who fought lions for warmups and obviously had a hang-up over obstacles in his way, be they literal or figurative.

He could move the branches. They weren't *that* unmanageable, at least from what she could see of them through the wind-whipped snow.

Anna bit her lip and snorted into the balled-up comforter still curled up around her hands. It was just too perfect.

She wouldn't . . .

She shouldn't . . .

The window was thrown open a second later. She encircled her hands around her mouth and yelled, "Caber toss!"

But when he looked back at her, he didn't offer a smile acknowledging a joke out of politeness. Instead, he adopted a downtrodden grimness that set his features into stone. That was when she realized something was wrong. He began walking back to her cabin, and she met him at the door. His boots had barely hit her porch welcome mat before the truth of their circumstances revealed themselves.

Those branches were far bigger than she'd thought.

"You're blocked in, aren't you? Like, for real?"

"Yeah."

"Oh."

On overly thick fuzzy socks—one of the few pairs that *hadn't* gotten snagged in the dryer—she shuffled in a circle, trying to take in her modest living space through the eyes of a perfect stranger. The worn leather couch with the rip in the armrest. The unfinished wooden coffee table mottled with heat rings from her mugs after too many near-misses with coasters. A kitchen sink weighed with cereal bowls and spoons that had yet to make their way into the dishwasher.

Not to mention the mess that was her linen closet/food pantry/place where old makeup went to die.

One didn't need to look too closely to see the cracks her living situation had carved out since Travis's departure. The runnels of grief had, over the past several months, eroded any semblance of order she may have enjoyed into gullies of chaos that were now the hallmarks of her life. That was all fine for Anna. She'd figure it out. Always did. But in no way was it fine for anyone else, especially a would-be rescuer who she'd already felt beholden to in some immeasurable way.

Anna's worries were shrugged off before she'd even had time to voice them as Iron turned from the porch and started to walk back to his truck.

"Where are you going?" she asked.

"Truck."

"But I thought you said you were blocked in."

"*You* said I was blocked in."

"And you confirmed it."

"Yes," he breathed, rubbing a gloved hand over his beard, which had already accumulated a fair amount of snow. "I did. But not because it should be your problem." He tossed his thumb at the vehicle. "I'll be in the truck tonight."

The absurdity of his words quickly swapped out her worry of hospitality for good old-fashioned humanity. "You are *not* sleeping in the truck."

"Wouldn't be the first time."

"Iron, no!" Anna stepped farther onto the porch, abandoning what little warmth remained in the cabin, and brought her socked foot down with mean old-school marm gravitas. "I have a spare bedroom."

"Anna, you don't know me."

"I know you're human and stuck on this mountain just like me until the storm stops and the roads are cleared. C'mon. I don't want to have this conversation out here. I'm beat, and chances are you are, too."

She let the storm door swing closed behind her but kept the main door open for him to follow. Footsteps didn't chase hers immediately, which she was okay with. It gave her time to run to the spare bedroom, shove everything she didn't want seen into the closet, and do a quick sniff check of the sheets. Due to an earlier quilting interest several years prior when her nutrition practice was still growing and time between tele-clients had been longer than she'd liked, she'd worked up a nice accumulation of sort-of-symmetrical quilts. They'd do for tonight. She was just grabbing two out of the closet when she heard the front door close, and a pair of heavy boots hit the floor next to her snow boots where she kept them by the door.

When she returned to her living room, Iron still hadn't moved from the mat, though his socked feet were a welcome sight, as was the knit hat he'd removed and now twisted in his hands.

"Here." She set the extra quilts on the armchair next to her. "The cabin's not too big, so you shouldn't have a huge problem finding things. The spare room is down the hall, across from mine. You'll pass the bathroom on your way there. You need anything, you can just knock."

Iron nodded but still stayed rooted to the spot. What little candlelight remained in the small living room seemed disinclined to illuminate much of anything, especially the shadows that had fallen over Iron like a shroud, lending their concealment for his intentions. With him standing within her cabin, she finally got the sense of just how large he was, and not just physically but his presence as a creature of the earth. Every movement of his body was a considered activity, as if he took no step without first weighing its cost on the floor beneath him.

He was just so . . . *much*. Far too much for her tiny home to accommodate.

Anna adjusted her glasses to try and conceal just how heavy her thoughts had become.

"I'll take the couch," he said.

"Why? I have a bed. It's a double bed, sure, but it's still a bed."

"I know," he said, smiling slightly and pulling his gloves off before shoving them into his pockets. "Get some sleep. We'll deal with tomorrow tomorrow." Then he walked toward her and took the quilts from where she'd placed them on the chair next to her.

"Okay," she said, not understanding but not having the energy to fight either. "You need anything else?"

"Yes."

"What's that?"

He stood silently for a minute, his eyes obscured by shadows she was coming to associate with him, being pulled around him like obedient servants. They brought their own sort of chill, one that spoke of possibilities more than precautions.

But when Iron's bare hands brushed the edges of the quilt and lingered where her fingers had been just a moment ago, her heartbeat struck a riot against her ribs.

"Never mind."

AN AGGRESSIVE YET FAMILIAR hum didn't so much tease Anna from sleep as slingshot her from it.

Her arm flew out blindly and quickly captured the glasses on her nightstand before they could clatter to the floor. Able to see, if not so willing to, Anna blinked to bring the numbers on her phone into focus.

Nine thirty a.m.

By the time cognition bestowed its awareness to her sleep-fogged brain, her bladder was already hammering out its SOS and likely had been for a good hour or two before then.

With a speed befitting quadruped hunters, Anna leaped from bed and bolted to the bathroom. Once her business was attended to, she simply stood in her hallway and let the sounds of her generator knit together the facts she couldn't help but accept.

Her generator was on. It was nine thirty in the morning, and her generator had already been turned on. Not only that but the breaker switches had been flipped correctly so that the septic and water pumps were usable, a fact she regretted not realizing earlier when she'd thoughtlessly flushed the toilet.

And if the generator was on, that meant the person who'd fired it up was also still in her house.

Then she remembered *why* it was on. Because someone must have gone back out in the middle of the night to shut everything down before they both fell asleep.

In *her* house.

Anna quickly grabbed a sweatshirt and walked out into the living room. Beyond the window, in the light of day, the storm was in full gear, landing punches against her cabin and conifers alike. The ghostly howls pulling their bellows through the trees sank their teeth into her skin, hauling up goose bumps and reminders of her current circumstances—and who she was sharing them with.

As if summoned from the mist of her mind, Iron walked into her cabin from the front door. "Morning," he said as he beat the snow off his boots.

"Um. Good morning. You were outside already?"

He shrugged out of his coat. "Had to see to a few things."

"A few things being the generator?"

"Yeah."

"And you figured out how to work the breakers?"

A smile curved his lips. "I'm good with electrical stuff."

"Clearly," she said, impressed. "Did you sleep okay last night?"

He nodded while keeping his eyes noticeably anywhere but on her face, a move she would have to unpack later. She didn't miss the way her quilts were folded exactly the way she'd left them but now rested on the couch instead of the armchair.

"So, what's the damage? Storm sounds like it's finally worked itself up to full bore."

"I checked the weather. Reports say it'll move out around Sunday evening."

Her heart sank. Damn. Sunday evening. That was decidedly not the *it'll be out of here in a couple of hours* answer she'd been hoping for. "Have the snow predictions changed much?"

"Well, there's about a foot out there now, so I'd say totals are moot at this point. The amount of exact tonnage is irrelevant when it's all a shit ton. The cleanup will be brutal regardless."

"Wonderful." The way Present Anna would have kicked Past Anna's ass up and down this mountain for not preparing better would have been some avalanche-worthy devastation in and of itself, for sure.

"Are you hungry? I brought some groceries in from my truck. I unpacked what I could in the kitchen. The rest are in a cooler on the porch under the overhang."

"I'm sorry. Groceries?"

"Here." Iron walked past her toward her piddling little kitchen, and damn if her quivering stomach didn't have nine kinds of thoughts to express on the subject. What she saw was an answer to her pregnancy prayers.

An assortment of fresh fruit was the focal point of the display, her wooden mixing bowl laden with apples, bananas, and oranges. Beyond that was a sea of cans, jars, bread, and dried goods: tuna, mayonnaise, beans, pasta, peanut butter, and the *good* strawberry jam, just to name a few. Stacked around it were individual servings of instant oatmeal in—her teeth sank into her lower lip—maple brown sugar *and* apple cinnamon varieties, along with assorted boxes of all her favorite and ruthlessly high-in-sugar breakfast cereals.

"Good thing about losing power in a snowstorm is you don't need to worry about refrigeration. Anything we open that's perishable, we can keep in my cooler out front. I've already got some milk and eggs in there. Besides, all the nonhibernating animals that would be interested in a snack are dealing with the same weather conditions as we are, so they're stuck, too."

"When and how did you go grocery shopping?"

"Didn't. Grabbed it from home before I left to come here. Also brought with me a few more gas cans and some fresh motor oil. Checked the pilot light on your stove, too. All good there."

A strained emotion worked its way into her throat that she had to swallow several times to dislodge. "I, um. This is all—"

Iron lifted the tea kettle from the stove and filled it with water, then pulled out a box of matches he'd also included with the goods and, while cranking the dial, lit the burner. Then he grabbed an apple, shined it on his flannel, and handed it to her before selecting an instant oatmeal variety from the tower he'd stacked.

"Apple cinnamon," she said, smiling. "How appropriate."

He returned her smile, winked at her, and then got to work pulling out two pieces of bread.

A cold chill whipped through Anna as she clutched the apple tighter to her chest. Woodenly, she walked back to the living room and sank into the first soft surface she could find.

Her tongue had gone as dry as desert sand, and new waves of tension froze her limbs.

In the light of the snowy morning, Anna had finally gotten a good look at Iron's face.

A face that stunned her with bicolored eyes, with its stark hazel one winking at her beside its brown fraternal twin.

CHAPTER 11

Anna's stomach cartwheeled at the prospect of realizing two very different things about herself that she'd previously not thought possible. The first was a newly discovered ability to wolf down three apples in a row, being sure to gnaw the juicy flesh from each core like a picked-over chicken wing. The second, and this one was a bit more disturbing, was grappling with the fact that key components of her dreams had somehow manifested into her very real and very untidy kitchen.

Scratch that. A *formerly* untidy kitchen, as the mountain of dishes that had been overflowing in her sink for an indiscriminate amount of time had miraculously disappeared.

Iron slid out of the small space holding two mugs whose handles were gripped together in one hand, along with a plate of various breakfast offerings in the other. He set the food and one mug down on the end table next to her armchair and took the remaining mug with him across the living room where he plopped down on the couch.

Coffee. The man had brought her coffee. And not the putrid decaf garbage she'd had to endure lately but, judging by the smoky chocolate notes singing their siren's song at her elbow, real honest-to-god *coffee*. Next to the mug and her battlefield of mutilated apple cores was a plate serving as an altar to her instant oatmeal topped with, hot damn, more apples and two slices of cinnamon toast.

"Didn't know how you took your coffee," he remarked, taking a careful sip of his own.

"I don't, usually. It's more of a special treat these days. Thank you."

The warm mug was in her hands and feeding its heat into her stiff fingers in searing waves. Anna brought it to her lips and used the curtain of steam fogging her glasses to piece together what she could about the man on her couch.

The light from the windows certainly took no time doting on the shocks of auburn that ran, woven and blended, through his russet hair, now pulled back tight into a bun at the back of his head. It would take no work at all to imagine those locks running wild and free around the bulges of his shoulders, capping off at his collarbones. The sharp blade of his nose twitched slightly before disappearing behind the mug, drawing Anna's attention to features previously obscured by the mists of her mind.

Anna charted a course across Iron's broad forehead before her eyes were pulled southward to slope around a jaw nestled beneath his thick beard. She knew that slope, knew the stony grimness it often took on. It perfectly matched the image of the mouth in her mind, one that had danced on the backs of her eyelids night after night as she'd tried to envision what those lips might look like forming words meant only for her.

That dangerous slope continued, carving out the strong shoulders and craggy cliffs of a frame that made her worn leather couch bow down in submission and crafted a true statue of a mountain man that, were it in a museum, would keep docents batting away women for decades.

Days without her nightly visitor could never erase the months she'd spent with him, but she wasn't willing to take that verifiably insane leap just yet.

Pregnancy brain. Just chalk this whole thing up to pregnancy brain, like the time you went looking for rubber bands in the refrigerator.

Anna swallowed another sip of unapologetically black coffee, relishing the burn for the distraction it offered.

Iron made a soft noise of approval. "You take it black. Wasn't sure."

"I take it any way I can get it." When Iron halted his mug's trajectory to his mouth, she quickly added, "Coffee, I mean."

His smile relieved just enough of her embarrassment to keep the burners currently firing up her heated cheeks to a low simmer.

Not wanting to risk an opportunity to put her foot into an otherwise vacant mouth, Anna got on right quick with the rambling. "Since we're stuck here for a bit, maybe we can backtrack on information usually shared between two strangers. We can start with full names, occupations, hobbies, you know, all the stuff that I probably should have asked you before I let you sleep in my house."

She'd hoped the shot at levity would calm her nerves since it never seemed to occur to them to decompress on their own, but the lack of even a soft chuckle from Iron kept her adrenaline right on spiking.

"You don't need to do that, you know."

"Do what?"

"Crack jokes when you otherwise wouldn't."

"Excuse me? I happen to adore humor. It always makes the best out of any situation, even the gloomy ones."

"Not when it costs you so much to say it."

"I don't know what you're talking about."

"It's in the eyes," he noted. "Yours seem to strain at the

corners when you're trying to make light of something, like you're forcing yourself to hold eye contact. Elevated cortisol levels, which can be brought on by stress, can add to eye strain. You don't need to do that with me. I'm not here for comedy."

Anna felt her jaw practically unhinge from her skull. "And what the hell *are* you here for, exactly? That has got to be the rudest thing anyone has ever said to me in my own—"

"You. Because you reached out to me."

The statement was delivered with the finality of the mountains around them, of rock standing still while time shuttled forth in inconsequential increments.

No one had ever summed up need in so few words, and it almost—*almost*—was enough to quell the apprehension stiffening her limbs ever since she'd parked her butt in that chair and fanned the flames of her memories, if dreams could even be called such.

Iron must have seen some glimmer of unease streak across her face because his features hardened, and he scooted forward on the couch cushion. "I'm sorry. Let me start over." He gentled his tone with a practiced precision that made her wonder how easily *he* could shift intonation when he otherwise wouldn't.

Grab your slingshot and pack that little nugget away for later.

"To answer your questions, I go by Iron. No surname. I've worked every gig under the sun but lately have taken on foreman duties at a construction job. I have a penchant for metallurgy, a moderately severe coffee addiction, and currently live with my brothers who I'm convinced keep me around because I'm the only one who knows the Wi-Fi password."

Her sharp giggle couldn't be helped, and he smiled at that, even as she tried to quickly put her unamused expression back in place.

"I also hate long walks on the beach, prefer winter to summer, have a deep love for Korean food, know my way around several forms of martial arts and other hand-to-hand combat, and, in a former life, dabbled as a Dungeon Master when my brothers were going through their Dungeons and Dragons phase."

"Wow."

His lips creased at the corner. "Wow?"

"Except for the coffee addiction and perhaps the construction job, I can't say I would have guessed much, if any, of that."

"Didn't know we were playing a guessing game."

Anna shook her head. "We weren't. I just didn't expect to hear such a colorful menagerie of accomplishments coming from . . ." She let the sentence die off as soon as she realized the picture it painted.

Far too late, however, Iron snagged those words and seemed to steer her ship toward the iceberg of regret faster than she could avoid it. "Coming from . . . who? Someone who looks like they bench-press semitrucks in their spare time, buys his clothes from the Army Navy surplus store, and hasn't let the sun hit his jawline since global warming became an actual thing and not just a cause to support with hashtags and protest signs?"

"That, sir, was completely and totally uncalled for," she snapped, then gentled her tone, the corner of her mouth ticking up a hair. "Last I checked, you needed at least three visible tattoos to even be eligible for the service member discount at most Army Navy stores. Otherwise, what's the point of shopping there? No one wants to pay full freight for tactical gear and paintball guns."

Iron's laughter was like a cathedral bell's peal, reverberating through her homely cabin with a magnetism that had her heart fluttering in time to its zeal.

"Well, you've figured me out, then," he said, leaning back and spreading his arms wide. "The clothes, the character. Whatever else you want to know, I'm all yours."

Though he said those words in jest, they filled Anna with anything but humor. Instead, shards of ice flooded her veins as her earlier worries rose to the surface, breaking free of the lighthearted barrier that had begun to form over them.

Images of that final dream pricked her eyes, shuttling to the forefront one very stark, very clear image of almost those exact words being spoken to her.

With a cold calm she in no way felt, Anna removed her glasses and made a show of rubbing at her eyes with her other hand. The glasses swung loosely from her fingers in a manner that no one who'd paid as much for her prescription and frames as she had would ever risk, but risk it she did.

She had to know, had to make sure.

The frames fell from her grasp and clattered to the floor, half on and half off the area rug near her feet. Still too far away.

"Whoops." When she reached down to grab them, with one hand still holding her mug, she bent awkwardly in her chair to hide the flick of her wrist that sent the glasses skittering across the floor to rest closer to Iron.

Not *too* close. Just close enough.

"I've got 'em."

Iron went down on a single knee, reached for the glasses, and held them in one hand to his chest before he rose to take his seat on the couch again. Anna's breath caught. With his head bowed, back arched, shoulders dipped beneath his ears, and her clear frames clutched in a fist hovering over his heart, she saw it all as plainly as she'd dreamed it in her mind.

As plainly as the last time she'd seen him on one knee before her.

Anna shot to her feet. "Who the fuck are you and how the hell did you get in my head?"

CHAPTER 12

When Iron thought of all the different ways of breaking the truth to Anna, not one of them had him on his knees. An error in judgment on his part, clearly, and one he feared would cost him far more than his honor if she got it in her mind to put some power into that right thigh of hers. Given how close her foot was to what he'd left unprotected between the goalposts of his bent legs, he wouldn't blame her.

He would, however, take the blame for the shimmering fear in her eyes, and that somehow brought him far lower than any bended knee ever could.

"Anna . . ."

"Nope. We're not doing that. I'm not in the mood to hear my name spoken in placating tones. And I'm *not* crazy. I know what I've seen."

Iron sighed, getting to his feet. "You're not—"

"Stay the hell away from me." She shot out her arm, palm up, and started circling toward the front door. Fear, blazing and brilliant, had struck an urgency into her movements, regardless of sense.

"You can't go outside, and I'm not here to hurt you."

"What are you here for, then? To brainwash me? Drug me? What the hell was in those apples, anyway?"

"Nothing! Anna, please. You're not—"

Her hand reached the doorknob behind her back. "You were in my head," she accused, trembling. "In my dreams. How the hell did you do that? How—"

"Anna, you're not crazy!" Iron threw the full force of his power into his words, and thank the mages, it worked. All at once, the alarm behind her eyes took a station break, signaling to the rest of her body to do the same. Only when some of the tension fled her fingers and her hand fell away from the knob did he finally breathe out the tension from his lungs. "Yes, I have been in your dreams, as you have been in mine."

Uncertainty cast her features in a pale light, and she must have seen the reciprocating emotion reflected in his, because her socked feet shuffled a step and a half away from the door.

Away from the exit but not nearer to him.

Instead, she skirted around the arm of the loveseat opposite the couch he was standing in front of and collapsed into the cushions. "What do you mean?" she pleaded in that way mortals often did when asking questions to beings they could not see but hoped were listening anyway. "How is any of this possible?"

Iron scratched the back of his head, then brought his fingers around to knead his eyes. He was doing this. He was actually going to do this. "I'm not mortal."

"What?" she whispered, shocked uncertainty plunging her eyes into a simmering haze.

"May I sit?" He took her stiff nod as a sign that he had the floor but only until her curiosity reached nuclear reactor meltdown levels, which was surely any goddamn moment. After that, all perceived stability and safety on her part would go out the window.

He had to work fast.

"I'm a sentinel angel, a fallen warrior who once served in the Empyrean, Heaven's highest realm, but has been trapped in the mortal plane for eons. In our quest to return home, my brothers and I—yes, they are like me, as well—obtained a relic of the Empyrean's gates from our enemy, Cyro, the demon ruler. That was several months ago. Once I began to examine the relic to try and unlock a dormant magic strong enough to destroy the demon charmers and reopen the gates we'd been sealed out of, I unlocked something . . . more. A different sort of discovery. One that led me to start dreaming." He held her frightened gaze. "Of you."

Anna's brows shot up, then she shook her head vehemently. "That's not a real explanation. Those aren't even real words actual people say. They're just things from, like, comic books or those fantasy shows you always have to pay extra to watch. They're not real."

But Iron knew that the moment her worried words left her lips, she didn't fully believe them. It was her poor mind trying to paint facts out of fiction, and the battle was a brutal one, judging by the toll it was taking on her furniture. Anna's trembling fingers had dug into the nearest throw pillow, some frilly number with enough fringe to at least keep her hands distracted so her mind could hopefully focus on what he was saying.

It was better than nothing and something he could work with. Perhaps starting with that much truth had been the wrong move. He needed to go simpler, to the root of the matter, and connect with something easier for her mortal mind to understand, at least conceptually.

"In the Empyrean, there exists an Eternal Flame, and every being's soul, mortal or otherwise, contains a spark of this flame. And when these twin sparks find each other, a soul bonding occurs. It is a link between two individuals that can never be severed."

Iron had no idea how to sugarcoat the facts or lessen the

blow that came with the heaviness of his words, so he stuck to the basics. There would be time for questions, and if he didn't cause Anna to scramble up the wall to get away from him, he'd welcome each question openly. But for now, he could only distill the choicest cuts of information into the words she needed to hear first.

Mages willing, her trust would come later.

"My brothers and I, when we were cast out of the Empyrean, the fall altered our powers, robbing us of some and gifting us with others. My celestial angel fire, the strongest magic and connection held to the Empyrean, was essentially put on notice once I landed here. I can call upon it and wield it as needed, but it drains from me each day. What was once as much an innate part of me as breathing now must be recharged each night while I sleep belowground, absorbing my metal's essence from the mountains and minerals around me."

A flash of recognition brightened her eyes, and he could clearly see relief softening her features at having connected some dots in the kaleidoscope of their conversation. Anna's mortal mind wasn't just adrift but near to drowning, yet despite all that, she still managed to grab the straw he'd offered.

Smart woman.

"Yes, my name was chosen due to the metal I command."

She still didn't say anything but slowly nodded. It was as close to an acknowledgment as he would get, and he took it. Because, boy, would he need it.

Iron exhaled slowly and shifted against the couch. "Eventually, it was discovered that, in finding and activating that soul bond connection, our full angel fire returned. There was no more need to recharge our powers belowground each night."

"But you didn't sleep underground last night," Anna added softly, yet another indication that she was at least following his story, if not believing some of it.

He smiled, hoping it hid the pang of worry over any conclusions she may be drawing. "No, I didn't."

Then she leaned forward, still clutching the pillow to her middle. "I don't believe any of what you're saying, okay? But if I did, what does all this have to do with me?"

Easy, Iron. Baby steps.

"The first night I started examining the relic, I kept it close. Like, against-my-heart close." He patted his flannel pocket where the vial sat comfortably. Then he plucked it out and set it on the coffee table in front of him. Anna's eyes bloomed in shock. "It's rarely left my side since, and every night after that, I dreamed of you. It was only a few days ago that this thing started firing up, showing its magic to me in a way I couldn't get it to do before. That was when my dreams stopped, and I found you."

Anna stood and walked over to the coffee table, pillow braced against her like a shield. Once she got within three feet of the shard, it began glowing and pointing at her, tapping out its eager message loud and clear against the wood.

"Every time I thought to go in the opposite direction of what my dreams were showing me, this thing got angry and chose to redirect my course."

Anna shook her head. "I'm not sure I follow."

"What I'm trying to tell you, and what this piece of the Empyrean is backing me up on, is that our soul's twin sparks have found each other. Our shared dreams were spawned from the celestial magic awakening to finally connect our two souls. And that magic is what brought us together and what will help me and my brothers destroy Cyro once and for all and return to the Empyrean."

Outside, the wind beat its desire to join the conversation, to pull attention and focus back on the destruction it sought to wreak outside, but its turmoil could never hope to match the unsteady storm brewing behind Anna's eyes.

They were impossibly wide, pulled round as they took in the glowing bone-like shard pointing its tip in her direction. For anyone else, he would have claimed it was a parlor trick. Some up-the-sleeve nonsense that mortal minds were more than happy to believe because recognizing the unknown had always been a fear far too terrifying to unlock fully.

But Iron couldn't bear to see that with Anna, couldn't bear to see what her refusal and dismissal would mean when it came to securing the only ticket home he could ever hope to offer his brothers.

Please keep an open mind, Anna. Remember our time in the dreamscape.

When she still didn't respond and kept flicking her gaze to the front door, he took a step around the coffee table and held the hand containing her glasses out to her. "Here."

Anna extended a shaky finger toward the relic's glowing shard. "It's pointing at me. It *moved.*"

"And it'll move toward you again if I'm going in the wrong direction. But here, please."

Thankfully, she heard the sincerity in his voice and gave her attention to what he was offering her.

"Put your glasses back on."

"I-I forgot about them."

"I know. You've had a lot to take in."

She shook her head, still stunned. "I didn't even realize I wasn't wearing them."

But when she reached forward, he pulled them back slightly. "There's something else I want to show you. It . . . it might be a lot."

"That thing is still following me. Why is it following me?" she said, eyeing the shard as it turned in her direction.

"I can answer that question, as well as every other question blowing through your mind right now. I'll tackle every last one and many you didn't know to ask, I promise. But first, I need to do one thing."

"What's that?"

Iron dropped her glasses into her hand and gestured for her to put them on. "I need to convince you that you're not crazy."

With that, he worked quickly, pushing every piece of furniture, rug, and living room adornment as far against the walls as they would go. Once he was satisfied that the center of the room was as bare as it was going to get, he offered his hand to Anna again, this time palm up.

"Take my hand."

"Why? What will happen if I do?"

"You mentioned I hadn't slept underground last night. That was very observant of you, very smart. So, no, my angel fire isn't strong right now and not up for doing the tricks I need it to do to convince you of all this on its own."

"This is real. This is all really happening. You're not kidding me, are you?"

"No. I'm not. And if you place your hand in mine, the contact will start the soul bond connection between us, pulling forth my full angel fire. But it'll be brief and burn out almost as fast as it'll take to flare to life. You won't be burned or harmed in any way. If we are truly soul bound, as I believe we are, only you could initiate my full fire after it's been dormant for so long. My flames couldn't harm you even if they wanted to."

"And if I'm not part of this . . . soul-bonded thing?" she hedged.

Iron lifted the corner of his lips. "Then nothing will happen except I'll finally get that handshake of thanks I've been clamoring after."

She blinked. It was a small crack spidering out from within her veneer of doubt. Then a slight chuckle bobbed her shoulders, and a tentative smile forced her open mouth into a grin. "More integrity jokes?"

"It's never a joke," he vowed. "Not when it comes to you."

They stood there for a moment, her huddled behind her meager pillow protection and him offering her a hand that was growing colder the longer she denied him the warmth of her trust.

But he knew it had to be her choice just as much as he knew he had to be the one to be tested in such a way.

Anna lifted her hand and held it above his, her fingers curling downward in a mimicked position of his uplifted ones. Then she speared him with a gaze sharper and more vulnerable than any razor-thin edge he'd ever honed on a blade. "I'm telling you right now, if you burn my house down with me inside it, I will haunt the living shit out of you for the rest of your life."

A mellow heat warmed the chilly thread of anticipation that had worked its way behind his breastbone, and he smiled, rewarding her for the fight she threw at him despite her fear. "I wouldn't dream of it."

"Oh, yes you fucking will." She smiled, too, a nervous grin that she'd plastered reluctantly so it might escort her over the threshold of whatever she'd told herself she could no longer ignore.

Then she placed her hand solidly in his.

Iron screamed, and the room erupted into blue flames.

CHAPTER 13

No sooner did Anna touch Iron than electric fire burst across his skin. Before her senses could parse out what was happening, she screamed. Then he flung her away from him, arched his back, and bellowed a great deafening roar. Though more than satisfied, if mildly stunned, to be huddled in the corner of her living room away from the small inferno, her brain hadn't gotten the message that fleeing was most definitely the course of action to take. She crouched there, mouth agape at the spectacle lighting up her tiny cabin.

Iron twisted his flaming body about, his deep chest rising and falling with far more than simple breaths. Snapping out of her stupor, Anna stood and finally started to creep toward the hallway, farther away from the inexplicable blaze before her. With her one shoulder blade already curved around the corner into the hallway, it would have been the work of a moment to run in the other direction, lock herself in her room, and call whatever emergency services specialized in dousing men who lit themselves on fire to impress women.

But her feet weren't moving. Despite the hammering of her heart and her brain's logic center screaming at her to get help, there was another warning, one that cast a veil over her worries and spoke softly to her mind that all was safe and right, which forced her to bear witness to what was happening before her.

The screaming had stopped, and she had to swallow several deep breaths to absorb the wonders that had taken center stage in her small living room. Iron stood on her hardwood floor like a warrior phoenix emboldened by its rebirth. True to his word, not a hair or patch of skin on either him or her had received a lick of heat, yet he still stood there, eyes closed, with blue flames swirling around his strength like the waves Poseidon would call to his side in service. His brows were drawn down his forehead in stern concentration, but his lower lip hung open in an expression of peace and rapture. There was no pain there, no tension in his muscles or any sort of bracing for the worst to come.

There was only tranquility. That and, if she read him right, a bit of bliss painting a face that she'd known to host a muted harshness, with only brief glimpses into soft-hearted humor.

Holy shit, he was right. This is all real.

The fire danced around his muscled arms, swaying in time to his subtle movements. Then, as fast as it appeared, it receded into his body, as if his heart had been the Bunsen burner responsible for igniting such a spectacle and it had just flicked off the gas. When the flames were all gone, not a hint of smoke fragranced the air. There was nothing to show any evidence that her cabin had just hosted a sort of mini nuclear reactor.

All that remained was Iron, who stood there with that same resigned expression, though now it was far more wistful than worried, and he had his eyes open.

Eyes that no longer held their bicolored charm but instead flashed a startling topaz.

"You don't need to be afraid of me, Anna." His voice was the same, if a bit raspier, as though he'd just completed a ten-mile hike.

"I . . . I think I know that." It was true. The fear receptors in her body, the ones that had initially spiked her pulse and urged her to seek out anything other than the flaming man in her living room, had since dissolved into whispered echoes. In their place was a pleasant warmth not unlike the sensations she'd used to feel upon waking from her dream encounters with . . .

Iron.

Anna's hand flew to her forehead, but she couldn't stop the smile that broke free. "Holy shit, you were really in my dreams. For months, it was actually you!" Then a distressing thought occurred to her. "Wait, I'm not dreaming now, am I?" Anna started tugging at her hair and pinching her skin.

"No, you're not dreaming. This is all real. Unbelievable," he admitted in a rush of breath, "but real."

"So, everything you just said is true, then? You're an angel? And we're connected somehow?"

Iron didn't say anything, because what else was there to say? He'd done the right thing by urging her to find out for herself, by showing her that bone-like shard thing and letting her witness the circumstances of a fire that there could truly be no earthly explanation for.

Anna stepped fully into the living room, admiring the quick redecorating job Iron had done in preparation for the only form of proof he knew would convince her she wasn't, as he'd firmly established, crazy. When her calf bumped her coffee table, the small curved shard—a piece of a celestial relic, he'd said—sat there nestled within its little innocuous test tube. The thing looked like no more than a small antler, similar to the ones she'd often seen shed by the deer around her house. It was no longer glowing and, strangely enough, didn't scare her, nor did it look entirely out of place, well, sans test tube, among the dark wood of her cabin. If she closed her eyes, she could almost imagine it was just that—a shed antler, a token brought home from a hiking trip. It could almost be . . . normal.

She was about to mention as much, as well as ask about the whole lack-of-wings thing, if he really was an angel, when a quivering unease tightened her abdomen. Like a bad penny that always returned, a familiar sensation crashed through her, and her mouth puckered in preparation.

Shit. I thought I was past this.

Iron scrutinized her, a worried expression pinching his features. He took a step toward her. "Are you all right? Did I hurt you?"

Anna shook her head, then brought one hand to her stomach and cupped the other over her mouth. All she could leave him with was a muffled "Excuse me" before she bolted to the bathroom. Her knees barely had time to hit the tile. Then a torrent of nausea squeezed everything out of her. Apples, coffee, the two bites of oatmeal she'd managed. It all came rushing forth in violent spasms.

Vaguely, she thought she heard footsteps, but even those weren't clearly defined. Thuds, echoes, poundings, they were all the same as another surge took control and flung her head farther into the toilet bowl. After two more rounds of that, she was bracing herself to take another hit when rough fingers brushed the sides of her neck and gathered her hair back from her face.

"It's okay. I've got you."

Iron's low voice in her ears dug its heels into her scrambled mind, anchoring her nerves against the waves of nausea. He kept collecting more pieces of her hair, gathering them loosely at her back. The rhythmic soft tugs straining gently against her scalp seemed to be the distraction her body needed. Like flicking the hair tie on her wrist during departure when she used to fly, the diversion worked. Soon, Anna was able to close the toilet lid, flush, and crawl to the vanity below the sink to pull out her mouthwash. Once Iron helped her to her feet, he stepped back out into the hallway, giving her the space she needed to defunkify herself.

"Sorry about that," she said after splashing water on her face. "Man, I thought I wouldn't have to go through that anymore, but I guess it can still linger."

"What could you possibly have to be sorry for?"

The towel she'd been drying her face with halted beneath her chin. Iron didn't just look confused but angry.

"Getting violently sick in front of someone isn't generally a good thing. My fault for not closing the bathroom door. Kind of ran out of time, though. It's been a few weeks since I've had to deal with this, so my reflexes aren't what they used to be."

"This happens often?"

"Well, not so much anymore, but it used to, yeah. It was pretty much a semi-daily occurrence for the better part of two months."

"Why? Are you ill?" Iron pelted her with that topaz gaze, the one that housed a host of swirling flames dancing through his irises, instead of the bicolored ones she'd grown used to. It was yet more proof of his wonderment and words. The effect would have been beautiful if not for the tension pulling his jaw into even harder lines.

Anna cleared her throat. "No, I'm not sick," she said, hoping to infuse some lightness into her response, if only so it could melt away some of whatever had just soured his mood.

"Then why—"

"I'm pregnant."

<hr>

IRON HADN'T MOVED from his post in front of the picture window since Anna had practically dropped a fucking football stadium on his head and politely dismissed him so she could shower and get dressed. The hot water was still pumping strongly thanks to the generator, though in another few hours, he'd have to go out and check on the fuel.

If Iron had learned one thing during his years in the mortal realm, it was that Mother Nature had a penchant for irony. A small snow squall had decided to move through, whipping its load around like a kid who'd just discovered packing peanuts and a box fan. Nothing devastating, since driving was out of the question, but definitely not something even he would brave, metallic armor or no. Thankfully, it would pass soon enough.

What wouldn't pass was the image of Anna on her knees, heaving up her breakfast, and the casualness with which she declared her condition.

Pregnant. She was pregnant. By another man. And alone.

Outside, the snow whipped through the trees with the force of a sea gale, peeling off chunks of bark and leaving behind frosty coatings that would build up and ice over throughout the rest of the storm.

In a way, it was a type of defense through endurance. Whichever trees were still standing despite the assault were the ones that saw another season. It was a monumental bet in arboreal evolution, a gamble that those trees would heal and thrive in time.

Was that what Anna was doing here? Iron shook his head and let the side of his forehead rest against the glass, rapping his knuckles on the window in time to the tumultuousness of his thoughts.

In the span of five minutes, he'd felt the full kiss of his powers again after innumerable ages without them. The second Anna placed her hand in his, a wellspring of angel fire had burst from his core, spreading throughout his frame and infusing his muscles with memories of strength and satiety. Knowing what to expect had been far different than the influx of magic and emotions he'd not been able to access since falling to the mortal realm. Overwhelmed and uncertain, he'd flung

Anna away from him just in case his fire didn't behave as it should have.

Had he known she was pregnant, he never would have been so reckless. He would have been more controlled, more—

A paralyzing thought gripped him, chilling his blood.

Did I hurt her? Her baby?

"Ah, much better." Anna walked into the living room, her long wet hair pulled back into a braid far more intricate than how he'd seen Chrome's mate, Drea, usually wear her hair. A French braid, he thought it was called. Otherwise, she was the picture of comfort. Lounge pants, sweatshirt, and thick cozy socks provided a far softer contrast to his usual ensemble of flannel and jeans.

Like the trees' bark, it was her sort of armor, one that also spoke of endurance and protection. Of defenses.

The sadness it called forth was a bitter pill on his tongue.

He walked around the coffee table, which he'd put back in place, along with the rest of the furniture. "Are you all right? Hurt at all? I pushed you back hard and saw you hit the wall."

"Yeah, I'm fine. Just a bit shaken up. It was only the fleshy part of my arm. My stomach's actually more worse for wear than anything else, but that's not from anything you did, and it's getting better." She hugged herself and plopped down into the armchair she'd claimed earlier.

Never on the couch. Always in the chair alone.

"Do you want me to make you some tea?"

She wrinkled her nose. "Honestly, I'm sick of tea. I've kind of been stuck with the herbal stuff because of my lowered caffeine allowances. Unfortunately, that crap tastes like whatever junk was left on the floor at the tea factories."

"Why are you alone?" He didn't mean for the question to be so abrupt, but he'd never been in the habit of dancing delicately through dialogue.

Anna's eyes widened, then darted to the living room window. "Poor choices, I suppose."

When she didn't elaborate further, Iron took a seat on the couch in front of the window, forcing her gaze to focus on him. Once it finally landed where he wanted, those soft green eyes had begun to mist over.

"My baby's father, Travis, and I were together for six years. I'm older than him by four years, but his dream was bigger. He wanted to be a life coach guru, and I wanted to be a nutritionist. My telehealth business was what kept us afloat for those early years, until it didn't, and I had to find new ways to get clients so he could attend mastermind retreats, rub elbows with the next promising someone or other, and bet on a life that would be better for both of us. And then I got pregnant."

Those pursed lips lifted into a small, sad smile that twisted his gut, even as she rested her hand on her stomach. "When I told him, he showed his hand." She shook her head. "It's funny, but my mother, when she was still in my life, always told me that when someone shows you who they really are, you should believe them. Turns out, the little life I was willing to bet on, the one we'd created together, didn't fit into his entrepreneurial risk assessment. In the end, I forced him to leave me with the cabin and a promise for him to stay in California. I wasted far too many of my good years on that asshole, and I'm not about to let him have any more."

Iron pushed back the rage threatening to coat his words. "How far along are you?"

"About sixteen weeks. I have my next checkup on Friday."

"Do you have any other family?"

Anna took a deep breath. "Yeah. This little pumpkin." She rubbed her stomach. "Though, I think it's technically the size of an avocado now. Otherwise, no one I really speak to."

"Anna," Iron said, unsure what the hell to say. He leaned forward and tried for all the world not to leap to his feet and get closer to her. Fuck, he could hear it. The small hurt in her words that she clearly had so much practice at keeping small or hidden.

"So, what happens now?" she asked, cutting him off while sinking farther into the chair, into herself, and curling her knees up in front of her.

The wind lashed its roaring blows against the picture window, which, on any other day, would have no doubt reflected back at Anna the beautiful solitude of her life in the mountains.

But it wasn't just *her* life. She would soon have a child to care for and raise. The comfort she'd crafted here wasn't so much a security blanket but a lie dressed in the trappings of hard work and hope.

He'd bonded with her, had been chasing after her for months in his own way, and now that he'd finally found her, he was less certain where to go from here.

She was pregnant, and he would sooner rip his wings off than risk Cyro and his demon charmers getting a hold of her, a prospect that only increased in likelihood if she became a part of his life.

He'd been down this road once before long ago and had spent countless years trying to forget the pain he still bore the mark of beneath his leather cuffs.

For now, though, Anna was safe, secluded behind the screen of the storm. And it was daylight. Even if they knew about her, charmers couldn't touch her and were just as susceptible to the elements as mortals were.

Iron exhaled slowly and adjusted his flannel sleeves lower over his wrists. "For now, we wait."

CHAPTER 14

"Remind me who the celestial mages are again?" Anna took a sip of her drink, a hot water, lemon, and ginger concoction that had seen her through many a rough gastrointestinal spell, and studied the man across from her as he scrutinized the game board and tiles on the coffee table between them.

"They're what you would call the Empyrean's governing bodies and spiritual guides."

"Ah. The top brass," Anna mused.

"Essentially."

"They always doled out your marching orders, I take it?"

Iron grunted, adjusted his position on the floor, and dropped two tiles onto the Scrabble board. "We serve at the pleasure of the mages."

Not knowing what to make of that statement, Anna let the subject drop and leaned over the coffee table. Her brows dipped low. "A double word score with *wyvern?* How long were you hanging onto that *w* and *y* for?"

"Since you played the word *uvula* several turns back." Iron took a swig of a beer he'd also brought with him.

"Bastard. I thought I was being so clever."

"You were. Just not clever enough."

A swath of rich brown leather peeked through the cuff of his flannel as he brought the bottle to his lips again, but Anna just chewed the inside of her cheek and went back to staring at her tiles. It was one of the few curiosities she had about him that he would always blatantly skirt around, and that was saying something given the Dateline-worthy interrogation she'd put him through all day.

Since the pyrotechnic display that morning and still with little in the way of proper power or provisions, she and Iron spent the entire afternoon unwrapping all things supernatural. She'd asked him questions about his brothers, the demon ruler Cyro, the war, how mortals played a part in it all, and then, to her ever-loving glee, they got to the demonstration portion of the lecture.

Wings. Metallic wings. Never in a million years would she have imagined the stunning beauty of Iron's wings or how they functioned. When he first showed her, she'd had to change into her *good* glasses, the ones with the most up-to-date prescription that she usually kept on her desk for work. She was convinced the grungy frames and lower-power lenses she usually wore when putzing around the house weren't doing justice to the single most breathtaking bit of actual magical realism—unrealism?—she'd ever seen.

When Iron had placed his hands on her shoulders and positioned her into the corner of her living room, she hadn't known what to make of it, until he backed up as far as he could and translucent skeins of energy rippled from behind his back. Once they consumed the room, they'd solidified into enormous sheets of charcoal-gray feathers.

Anna hugged her mug closer to her body, recalling how her eyes prickled at the sheer awesomeness of it all. Iron's presence, strength, power, they radiated off him in magnanimous currents that made sense of every action he'd ever bestowed on her, twisting the meanings of their interactions into something she wasn't entirely certain how to interpret.

So she leaned into the tactics that had always served her well: escape and evade.

It was her idea to bring out the board games. And as the afternoon light faded into the chill shade of night, with the storm showing no signs of slowing down despite what the meteorologists claimed was an earlier squall, they pulled out a few lanterns, threw a bunch of drop pillows on the carpet around the coffee table, and fell into a happy little rhythm of good, clean, and entirely unassuming fun.

Anna shifted the tiles around in her holder, trying to come up with a word that would play well with what Iron had left her to work with. The move wasn't strategic so much as distracting. Despite all the questions he'd graciously answered, there were a few she hadn't quite been able to bring herself to say out loud.

She picked up a tile and went for the only easy points available, in the game or otherwise.

Iron arched a brow. "*Wyverns*? Really? There are, like, four S tiles in the entire game and you blow one on pluralization? I'm going to need you to show your work on that one."

Anna shrugged. "Points are points, and my strategy is my own."

"Silly me. I thought you wanted to win."

"Who says I don't? It would be unwise to assume I don't have a plan just because you can't see the complexity of my moves just yet."

"Hmm." Iron tracked her fingers as she plucked out her replacement tile. "Didn't figure you for the ruthless type."

"You, my friend, have a *lot* to learn."

Iron took another pull on his beer. "Can't wait."

The tone of his declaration sent an unsettling chill coursing down Anna's spine. For anyone else, those two words, spoken in a lighthearted and casual manner, would have been dismissed as quickly as they'd been said. But for her, they dredged up memories of another man who, just a few short months ago, in this very living room, had echoed sentiments that had plunged her life into one of sorrow and solitude.

"Can't it wait, Anna? I've got a call in ten minutes."

"It'll be quick, I promise. I want to show you something."

That *something* had been a positive pregnancy test and the biggest irony bomb to ever hit her, for the destruction it wrought contained very little in the way of anything positive.

Turned out, Travis had had no interest in waiting nine months for the next chapter, but she would. So, yes, she could wait. She'd waited for Travis for six years, until his enthusiasm ran out. She was still waiting. She was the fucking queen when it came to waiting.

"Everything okay? Where'd you go?" Iron asked, assessing her with those bicolored eyes that spoke more of concern than condescension. To her surprise, she realized he wasn't hurrying her along but genuinely wanted to know if she was all right.

So she answered him.

"When you were dreaming about me, what was it like?" Mortified and totally clueless as to why she asked, Anna held up her hands and started shaking her question away. "No, scratch that. I didn't mean to—"

"Waiting, mostly."

Anna's mind roared to a stop as she swallowed past a gathering of emotions and was beyond grateful her abrupt halt in speech didn't do the same to his.

"I never knew when I was going to see you or how much of you I would see. I'd never heard you speak, not until recently, so I had no way of knowing if you ever would. I had no intel on what caused it all or what you were to me. All I knew was that every night I would fall asleep with an eagerness to just . . . wait. Waiting to see whether the dreams would still come or whether they would finally get pulled out from under me. And after many weeks when the dreams *didn't* stop, I knew that, eventually, if I waited long enough, I'd see . . . something."

Iron dangled the beer bottle from his forefingers and let his eyes haze over. "Usually, it all started off as a bunch of smoke and mirror bullshit. Just a lot of white mist and ether, with nothing to touch, nothing to orient myself toward. But then the mist would part, and I'd see a beacon of golden copper." He gestured with his drink at her braided hair, his gaze lingering over the bound strands. "You would float over to me sometimes, and it almost seemed like your hair wanted to greet me, the way it would drift toward me. But every time I tried to reach for it, reach for you, the mist of your form just . . . darted away."

"It was the same for me, mostly," she said. "I only ever saw the suggestion of you. I knew you were there but didn't know what was happening."

A pointed silence seemed to sustain the conversation. Then he asked, "Were you afraid?"

"No," she answered, and the truth of her words stunned her for a moment, until an unfamiliar courage found the rising nugget of her anxiety and, for some reason, sat on that shit like a high school linebacker squashing an eighth-grade bully. "I felt . . . safe. Alarmed and a bit uneasy, sure, but always safe. Like I knew you wouldn't harm me but also that I was being shown something others normally weren't. I remembered your"—she bit her lip—"form."

Iron halted the beer traveling toward his mouth but said nothing.

"I couldn't see anything, mind you. For months, you were just this suggestion. In the dream, the mist would kind of swirl around you, painting an abstract picture of a strong masculine frame. Muscled but also tense, like you were bracing for something. It always worried me."

"Why?"

Anna shrugged. "I didn't know whether you were expecting an enemy and whether that enemy was me." As she slid her mug back onto the coffee table, it shifted the coaster beneath it, sending two tiles tumbling to the floor.

She bent forward to scoop up the tiles, but Iron's hand was already there, covering the pieces. Their knuckles bumped each other, but when she went to pull her hand away, Iron lifted his thumb and lightly trapped the tip of her thumb against his index finger. Stuck, the rest of her fingers fell on top of his.

Iron was on one knee again, but this time, there wasn't a living room's worth of space between them or the foggy mist of a limitless dream world. There was just him and her and the pulsing waves of magnetism that beat off him like a drum's rhythmic seduction. He dipped his head lower, closer to hers, until his light breath tickled the exposed column of her throat, pulling up sensations she had no framework for.

"Anna," he whispered, letting the fingers that covered the tiles lift and cocoon hers in a soft embrace that was as overwhelming as it was subtle.

Subtle and terrifyingly exhilarating.

"Is this the soul bond thing? Is that why you're still here? Because you can leave now, technically, right? Can't you fly out of here or something?" she asked, filling the minute space between them with fractured words that had always ever been the only weapons she'd been expert in.

Iron didn't say anything, nor did he pull away, and Anna had exactly no idea what to make of any of it other than the fiery flutter of hope that kept blazing within her chest.

She missed this, even though she had no idea what *this* even was. It felt familiar on some level, like the ethereal warmth of her dreams whenever she'd drifted close to him through the fog. Had she really drifted, or had she been pulled closer by something?

"I'm not sure I believe any of this," she confessed, desperate to fill the silence and search out answers she wasn't sure he could give, but she'd try for them regardless. "I feel silly." Then she dipped her head down, tearing her gaze away from his. "Sorry, it's the hormones talking."

She slipped her hand out of Iron's grip, and he let her but only so he could grasp the side of her face, his fingers grazing over the underside of her jaw in comforting strokes.

"I got you, Anna. I got you."

He sealed his lips firmly against hers, crowding out any remaining questions.

CHAPTER 15

Whatever pain Iron thought he'd feel when he closed the distance between them was nothing compared to the wells of suffering packed into the pools of Anna's eyes. Even among the light from the meager camping lanterns and her handful of battery-operated flameless candles, he could see the trembling effects of what happened when a woman had been forced to rely on her own strength for far too long.

He wanted to comfort her, to hold her hand properly and impress upon her some of his strength—mages knew he had enough of it—but she had been far too close. When he first arrived at her cabin, he'd only ever meant to look after her. Make sure her generator was up and running and that she had something to eat other than Red 40 and high-fructose corn syrup. The rest, he'd told himself, would come later. It had too.

But that was before her lips parted against his mouth and a gentle mewl of delight vibrated through her chest and into his. Iron gripped the sides of her face with both hands, testing the feel of her beneath his palms. She fit so slightly against him, so much so that he feared he had no reference for the delicacy required to cradle such a creature. Her skin was soft, yet cold. Her jaw was slim but proud and stiff, urging closer with each drugging pull she sought to take against his lips.

The action tugged a pained growl from his lungs, and she swallowed it down as she explored him further, mapping out his mouth with plundering precision that set his blood to boiling.

"You taste . . ." she said, pulling away just long enough to speak the words but never opening her eyes. A gathering of wrinkles collected between her brows, giving her the effect of one understanding an emotion but not the enormity behind it. "You taste like . . . smoke. Something woodsy and fleeting."

She leaned forward and kissed him again, this time pressing her mouth to his in short searching pecks. There was care and consideration in the act, as if she were sampling a tasting menu. But every pull of her pillowy lips teased out of him more of an urge that he'd not experienced since his past had consumed his present and future.

Trapped beneath the silken brushes of Anna's boldness, he let himself forget—forget all about the war and a home that he wondered whether his honor clung to more than he did. He wanted *this*, more hours with this soft beauty who, in such a short time, had overwhelmed his mind more than any mage ever could. He wanted to learn more about her, to praise and pamper her, to ask about her interests and see the changing seasons through her eyes. These were desires he'd not allowed himself to entertain for so long, and he hadn't realized just how much of a prison his abstinence had become. How fucking lonely it was.

Iron pulled his mouth from hers and dragged his lips along the edge of her jaw. "You taste . . . better. So much better than any of it."

Just as he was about to plant a secret kiss behind her earlobe and nuzzle at the juncture of the downy hairs there, a surging heat clenched every muscle in his body. Flames, hot and damn angry, flooded his frame. His cock, thighs, biceps, everything seized up and held him prisoner to his own power.

Shit. It's happening.

Banking the roar that threatened to burst free behind his clenched teeth, Iron punched through his paralysis and tackled Anna to the floor, smothering her as much as he dared and tucking her head against his chest.

"Iron! What are you—"

"Close your eyes. Just keep them closed."

He felt the instant his angel fire was lost to him. The powerful celestial comfort that had always sat at the ready within his core leached from his body in banded ribbons of blue flame. Anna lay beneath him, her head cradled in the crook of his shoulder, her hands having no other recourse but to cling to his back.

And then he knew. When the sharp bite of her fingernails began scraping at his scapulas, he knew she saw it. The fire—*his* fire—engulfing them both.

"It won't harm you, Anna. Just breathe through it. Remember what I told you. The heat isn't real. The spark of your soul is calling to mine, pulling my fire from me, but the heat isn't real. Let go, sweet one. Relax your body and return my fire to me."

Anna's frame shook beneath him, and as he braced his thighs around her hips, securing her with his strength, a new fear took root. She was pregnant and mortal. What if his flames didn't play well with wild cards? What if he was causing her baby distress or far worse?

Her muffled screams beat against the wall of his chest as the flames rose higher and brighter around them. He'd managed to kick the pillows away, but there was no helping the rug beneath them. If he couldn't calm her down soon and regain control of his fire, they were in a very bad way. Iron lifted his head and glanced at the tinder box of their surroundings. The snowstorm outside was a blast of cold he desperately needed, but using his power to puncture the window with an iron rivet from one of the ceiling's wood planks would only feed the flames more oxygen.

Iron bit back a curse.

He'd asked too much of her. Far too much.

At a loss and out of options, Iron called on his wings using the only magic he still had available and draped them around him and Anna. The flames spread wide over his wings, keeping the worst of the din away from her. Then he dropped his head low, pressed his lips to her sweat-slicked forehead, and held them there. After a beat and beneath the arc of flames surrounding them, he pulled away from the kiss and said, "You take all the time you need. I'll be here for you when you come out of it."

There was nothing more he could do. He'd dragged her into a mess of his own making and had left her stranded, helpless and hopeless, fighting to control a power that she had never even known existed a few hours ago. Iron clutched his wings more tightly around them both, gripped the back of her neck, squeezing his support into her, and waited.

Slowly, the nails at his back lessened their assault. As Anna unlatched each finger, the flames around them sank lower and lower, until finally she let her hands fall to the floor and his full angel fire funneled back into his core. Once he was damn certain he had complete control of his power again, he sat up and looked at Anna.

"Are you all right?" he rasped out. By the mages, she looked terrified. Paler than he'd seen her and braced against him like a woman barricaded behind a door with the enemy surrounding her.

Fear bled from every feature.

Iron hauled himself off her and made damn sure there was a good ten feet between them, though he would have preferred ten miles if it took away her fear. Once her vital signs returned to normal and his celestial senses were satisfied she wasn't in any pain or harm, he risked speaking again. "I'm sorry. I'm so fucking sorry. I shouldn't have touched you. I knew the risks, and I took them anyway. I won't do it again. You have my word."

Anna sat up and rested on her elbows. "I-I'm okay." Then her eyes grew round as she tracked the arcs of his wings, and he cursed again, forgetting he'd yet to call them back.

"It's too much, I know." It was all too much. His past, his magic, the responsibility he'd heaped on her shoulders of helping him reunite with his full power so he could, what, give his brothers back their lives while robbing Anna of hers?

Fuck that.

Iron shook his head, disgusted and wishing like hell he had a charmer to dismember instead of taking on the hack job he was thinking of doing on himself. Standing taller than the three fucking inches he felt, he recalled his wings and went over to the door to shove his feet into his boots.

"Where are you going?"

"That was a lot, and I don't expect you to process it with me taking up all your air. I can't change what happened, but I can keep my promise going forward."

"What promise?"

Iron grabbed his jacket from the coat rack. "I don't know what my fire will do to your baby, and neither do you. You're fine now, but the more our bond is tested and strengthened, the more unknowns we'll have to contend with, and I'm not willing to put either of you at risk. Other supernaturals don't go through the flaming process with angel fire that mortals go through once the soul bond is realized. And the other mortals who my brothers have successfully bonded with"—he looked away—"none of them were pregnant."

Then Anna's face fell with a new awareness, one she clearly

hadn't considered as she sat up straight and rested her hand on her stomach. "Oh."

"Look, the worst of the snow should be moving out soon, and since you've seen my full power, there's no use hiding it anymore. I'm going to use it to see about moving those branches blocking my truck before I shut down the generator for the night."

He couldn't risk looking back at her. He didn't want to see the crumpled human he'd left on the floor, with her board game tiles and coffee table detritus scattered around her living room like he hadn't just brought a fucking inferno into her safe house.

Iron adjusted his coat sleeves over his leather bracers and shut the door behind him. The wind was a bitch, but now that he could don his metallic armor, it would be more manageable.

Snow he could live with. Fallen trees he could live with. What he could *not* live with was the destruction that came with mortal attachments.

He'd survived it once before, and he was still paying for it. He couldn't bring himself to live through that again.

CHAPTER 16

Anna's aging metal kettle whistled a shrill protest from the stove, though whether it was in defiance of the home shopping channel's host currently selling a far fancier glass electric kettle or in pleasure at finally being heard over the din of the storm, she had no clue. All Anna had to go on were two things: the storm, at last, was dying down, and even muted, her television was still her most reliable companion.

It had almost been a full day since the Flaming Debacle, as she was calling it, and Iron had made himself about as available as a groundhog who'd not only seen his shadow but had thought up every possible predator who could lurk inside of it.

On the one hand, if she hadn't had so many things to work through, she would have given him credit for the manner and skill with which he'd avoided her. On the other very discerning and hyperaware hand, she didn't really care how much food he'd left her or how he'd managed to use his magic to begin clearing her property out from the storm. Abandonment was abandonment. Mental, physical, it didn't matter. Which pissed her the hell off, because she barely had enough energy left in her emotional reserves to manage her own hurt, let alone the obvious pain that being in her presence was causing him.

Anna poured the hot water over the very caffeinated coffee grounds—because, desperate times and all that, time of day be damned—and let the steam seep into her pores while the water funneled through the coffee filter. The heat was a mellow kiss that chased away the cold just long enough to let other memories filter in, ones that contained a far different kind of heat.

Her entire body had been set on fire, and that was *before* literal flames had engulfed her and Iron. She'd felt the pull the instant he'd shifted his fingers from those game pieces so hers were in the cage of his own instead. A pulsating force had warmed within her belly, an acknowledgment of not only her desire but a confirmation of his as well. It was a punch designed to knock out everything she had previously thought was load bearing, and she'd fallen into it gladly, desperately. Wantonly.

She couldn't remember the last time she'd been kissed like that, with the same thoroughness and wonder that called explorers to mountaintops. There were promises in that kiss, the way his tongue slid over hers in satiny caresses, and she would have happily stayed there searching out every last one if it hadn't been for the power she'd called out of him.

Yes, she'd known what to expect. Iron had told her as much. During one of her many rounds of twenty questions, he'd explained all of it. How the soul bond connection grew in correlation to the physical intimacy of those who were bonded. The more he touched her, tasted her, knew her, the more power she'd pull and command from him until, eventually, she'd set his full angel fire free and his celestial power would no longer be a prisoner of the clock.

The flames erupting around her had been a shock but not nearly as much as the regret on Iron's face once the dust settled.

Anna took up residence in her armchair and eyed the couch over the lip of her coffee cup. He'd slept there again last night, even though he likely didn't need to, now that she knew the full extent of his powers. Just as before, her quilt was folded neatly on the arm of the couch, and there was barely even a depression to hint that Iron had trusted her furniture enough to support him through sleep.

Every step and movement Iron took in her house spoke of obligation, including the ones that led him outside, where he currently was, doing what he needed to do to clear a path for his truck down the hill. Angel fire, celestial strength, and metallic manipulation worked wonders on tree and snow removal, apparently.

She was far deeper in thought than was healthy when Iron walked through her front door, shaking the snow from his hood and boots. "Tree's all cleared, and I got enough of your driveway and the road to your house cleaned out so, come morning, you should be able to make it into town okay. The worst of the snowfall is behind us, and the all-wheel drive on your Subaru can handle the rest. Already heard a few plows taking to the main streets. And if the power's not back on by morning, I can" —he twisted his lips and seemed to debate over a word—"*play* with the transformer that supplies power to your private road."

Play. Ah. He means work his metal magic.

"That's good. Thank you." Anna looked out her picture window, and despite the evening's dark chill that had descended around them, the moon still put in a good effort to illuminate the snow, which had gone from a downpour to a dusting.

Strange how winter's purpose was called into question the moment it stopped snowing, as if its relevance was only measured in relation to what it could either provide or pummel into powerlessness.

Anna smiled back against the morose metaphor, having no

interest in picking at that barely healed scab just yet. "Are you getting ready to turn off the generator for the night?"

Iron rubbed the back of his neck. "I was going to ask whether you wanted me to do it now or come back later to take care of it."

She brought the coffee away from her lips. "What do you mean?"

"I mean that I'm going to head out." He shifted away from her, as if he already had half a mind to end the conversation before it began.

As if he'd made a monumental mistake in trusting a crazy single pregnant lady with his secret and would rather be anywhere else.

"Iron, wait. Can we talk about this? I feel like you've been avoiding me, and I don't know what I did wrong."

"I'm not avoiding you, and you didn't do a thing wrong. I'm just trying not to overwhelm you. Trying to keep my distance, you know? That's some scary shit that I put you through, and I don't want to be responsible if you decide to pretend the whole thing never happened."

"Hold up." Anna held her palm out in front of him. "First, you are a thousand percent responsible for the fact that I even had anything to eat beyond cupcake wrappers and cereal box cardboard. And second, why the hell would I want to pretend any of this never happened?"

"Because I almost set your house on fire," he hissed, his flare of aggression catching her off guard. "Because you have a baby growing inside you, one that relies on you to be as happy and healthy as possible. You don't need the stress that comes with living in my world, Anna."

"Don't tell me what I need," she gritted out. "Did you ever stop and think that maybe I needed to feel special, for once? That it felt goddamn wonderful to kiss you, to feel you kiss me back, to actually have someone *want* to kiss me back, even though I'm pregnant with another man's child?"

She lowered her shoulders away from her ears and tried not to let the wave of disappointment take her out again. "It was *nice*, Iron, being with you, having you here. I kind of forgot how lonely it can be sometimes, and how frickin' hard it is pretending that being single and pregnant is no big deal. So, yeah, I've been a little starved for company lately, and even though I don't understand your world *yet*," she emphasized, hoping like hell he got her meaning, "I'm willing to be over-whelmed by it for a little bit if it means I can keep seeing you from time to time." Then Anna plucked down the thought she'd been worrying over all day. "But if my pregnancy bothers you so much—"

Iron's hand stilled on the doorknob. "You have no idea what you're asking, Anna."

She tried not to cringe when he silently sidestepped around her fear in favor of spotlighting his own. "So, tell me. Keep talking. I like talking. Hell, I talk into a computer for a living. You'd be surprised to find that I'm actually really good at it."

A smile teased the corner of his lips, and she had the audacity to hope that it was enough to convince him to keep talking to her.

"If you leave," she added, "will I see you again, in person or otherwise?" The *otherwise* in question being a dreamworld that held even more unanswered secrets than the ones he clearly wasn't yet willing to share with her.

"I don't know."

White-hot slashes whipped across her memory, scraping new gouges of abandonment into her war-torn flesh. "Oh."

"But I'll call you. Look," he said, running his hand through his hair, "I don't know how to keep you and your baby from getting wrapped up in my world—a very *dangerous* world."

"You found me, though. That shard of the relic, it was seeking me out, wasn't it?"

"Yes," he agreed. "And that's why I need to go, at least for a little while. Now that I know what it was pointing me toward, I want to try and figure out what it all means."

"You mean, beyond just getting your full power back through the soul bond?"

"Yeah."

"I don't understand. Isn't that something you want regardless, after so long being without it?" It was as close to repeating her earlier plea as she could bring herself to mention without groveling and completely hating herself in the morning.

Iron's gaze struck her, and she gasped at the fiery topaz flames burning there. "More than anything."

"Then why can't we at least get to know each other better?"

"Because I have enemies, demons who would love nothing more than to slit your throat and watch the light of your soul bleed out just to fuck with me."

A dark coldness snaked along her skin, and Iron's even darker grin froze her body further.

"That's right, Anna. The beings I kill don't go down quietly, and they aren't above using the most brutal tactics to ensure they get what they want. Which is why I need to be sure I'm doing the right thing here."

"What is the right thing?"

"Keeping you safe from my sins."

"What sins?"

Iron shook his head. Exhaustion had carved lines into his features. "I don't want to do this."

"This? You mean deal with me?"

"No."

"Then what?"

"I just . . . I just need some time to figure things out."

"Do I get a say in any of this?"

"Anna . . ."

"No, I'm serious." She leaped to her feet and put her hands on her hips. "You can't perch yourself on my doormat and say that none of this is personal or spout some of that *it's not you, it's me* bullshit. You are literally standing where Travis was when he walked out on me. Because I became inconvenient. Because *our baby* became inconvenient. A problem to be dealt with or handled. So, forgive me if I'm not willing to put up with that same line of crap from another male who thinks they know what's good for me."

Anna pointed a finger at her chest. "*I* know what's good for me, and after dreaming about you for three months, it was a damn blessing to know that I wasn't crazy and that there was a reason for the dreams. The idea of a soul bond may send you running, but you know what? For me, it feels really damn nice. The concept that I could be on someone's team and I would make them more powerful, more meaningful in their mission, is an intoxicating feeling to wrap one's head around. Do I have a shit ton more to learn? Sure, you bet, but I'm willing to do the work and explore what it all means, regardless of the baby I'm bringing into the world. So, if you feel more comfortable walking out that door than having a conversation and learning right alongside me, then I can't help you."

Anna put her mug on the kitchen counter and stomped down the hall. When she got to the bathroom, she stopped, placed her hand on the wall, and spoke over her shoulder. "Feel free to turn the generator off. I'm done for the night. And when you're willing to talk, you know how to reach me. We shared a mind for months, Iron, and despite how alien this all is to me, I'm not willing to have the door slam in my face because you're too afraid to hold it open for me."

She kept going down the hall, and only when the wood of her bedroom door kissed her back, bolstering whatever strength she had left, did she finally let her body sink to the floor. A short time later, Iron's boots retreated from her living room, the cabin grew quiet, and the generator shuddered its final tremors into the rafters.

She was alone. Again. But this time, there was no unseeing her circumstances or shirking off the cold that no amount of blankets or hot tea could ever have the hope of fighting off.

CHAPTER 17

Iron stood among the ruins of an abandoned strip mall two towns over and wondered how mortals capable of creating the word *irony* couldn't fucking understand it when they saw it. He narrowed his eyes at the sign before him, reading it over for the third time and failing to connect it to the landscape before him.

Notice: This property is scheduled to be demolished. Trespassers will be prosecuted. Entry is strictly prohibited. Keep property free of litter and debris. If you see anyone violating this ordinance, contact the Mayerville Housing Division.

Iron craned his neck around the sign and shook his head at the landfill's worth of shit that had accumulated in every nook and cranny of the landscape. The area wasn't known to harbor too extensive of a homeless population, but it sure as shit served as the mecca for every college-resume-primping junior varsity and varsity athlete. Rivers of sports drinks and liquor bottles made up the formerly painted parking lot lines, while anything that could be once identified as a sidewalk or building wall was now home to a glitter bomb's worth of glass and what had to be the least inspired graffiti he'd ever seen. Someone had painted a winky face poop emoji right next to a stick figure peeing on a cluster of questionably drawn block letters declaring *Skool Sux, and So Does Your Mom!*

The rest of the site wasn't any better, with half-crumbling building facades doing jack shit to block the frigid wind. The entire thing was one CBD vape away from moonlighting as an Escher painting, with a mutilated chain-link fence decorating the perimeter for good, though ultimately useless, measure.

If the devil was in the details, this place had paid for the sins of every sex trafficker, war criminal, and crime lord with fucking pastel spray paint and atomized concrete. And that was *with* the decreased visibility nightfall afforded. He shuddered to think what sort of things slithered to the surface once the noonday sun baked the concrete landscape to an inhabitable temperature.

The metal structures the strip mall left behind, though, were still useful, and that was why he was there.

Iron toed something that looked like it had begun its life as a Powerade bottle out of his way and let the bright glow of his phone spotlight his presence so his brothers knew where to touch down when they arrived, which would be any minute.

He did *not* kill time—and his sanity—by hovering his thumb over the only name he hadn't been able to get out of his head since he'd left her cabin three days ago.

If he thought he'd known hell, he hadn't expected the dick punch that came with seeing Anna curl up into the smallest form of herself while he dressed her down like she was a child who hadn't thought of the repercussions that came with having ice cream for dinner every night. But the truth was, she'd been three steps ahead of him before he'd even gotten through the door. Not only did she want ice cream every night but she'd already mapped out healthy and feasible options for every other fucking meal, thus bringing balance to the force and making damn sure she wasn't only relevant but needed—that she wasn't *inconvenient.*

He hadn't expected to be called on his bullshit so eloquently, and the efficiency with which she wielded the knife terrified him, sending him into a tailspin that had him questioning every step previously laid out before him.

So, like any male well-versed in not seeing the forest for the trees, he decided that once power had been restored to her cabin and major transit lines had opened back up, he needed to focus on a new damn forest for a bit.

The steady *whump whump* of large angel wings beating back the night air recentered his purpose.

He quickly pocketed his phone and ducked through a patch of broken fence to join his brothers. "Thanks for coming."

Tungsten, their prime sentinel, was the first of the angels to land and step forward. "You've made some headway, I take it?"

"Not sure about headway. Let's call it a working theory."

Bronze jumped off a pile of concrete rubble and slapped Iron on the back. "Working theories don't abandon everyone for three days. They tend to come up for air once in a while. Have you even seen a set of four walls that wasn't the library or the armory recently?"

Iron shrugged him off but didn't put much effort into the rebuke. "I've seen enough to test a theory about the relic's shard, but I need all of us together to do it."

Bronze rubbed his hands together. "Are we going to blow shit up? Please tell me we're going to blow shit up."

Titan shared a look with Tung, then folded his arms across his chest. "I'm intrigued. What are you thinking?"

Oh boy. Here's where things get interesting.

Iron exhaled and pulled out the shard, which was still resting in its little test tube sanctuary. "What's something that everyone wants?"

"Power," Bronze offered.

"No. Everyone ultimately wants what they can't have." Iron raised the relic higher. "*This* is what Cyro can't access. The power of the Empyrean. He's hardwired to be repelled by the stuff. That's why he's been working overtime trying to find a way to circumvent its power. He's trying to mutate it with dark magic so its innate properties won't be so toxic to him that he'll risk his own destruction. But at its core, this puppy is pure Empyrean light and life. Blessed by the celestial mages and imbued with our Sealing powers that we impressed upon the gates when we were cast out. It's the literal antithesis to Cyro's being, but we've been looking at things all wrong."

Chrome pulled out a square of peppermint gum from his back pocket and popped the thing in his mouth. "How do you figure?"

"Because this thing is a toddler's dose, when we need fire hose quantities." Iron uncorked the test tube, grabbed the shard, and walked it over to a clear patch of concrete that was the only area concealed by the meager bits of building still standing. Then he retreated several steps back. "I want us to hit it with our angel fire."

Seven heads with identical question marks floating above them all whipped around at the same time.

"No, hear me out. It's been gnawing at me for days, why Cyro's been spending all this time trying to manipulate Empyrean magic. The asshole's risked exposure, capture, and finite resources trying to corrupt it and bend it to his will. Why? Because he's fucking terrified of it and of what would happen if we suped that little thing up to not only full strength but nuclear levels."

All through Iron's explanation, Chrome was nodding with what Iron hoped was understanding, though with Chrome, it was hard to tell. "So, we fire at that thing and then what?"

"Then we wait, see what happens, and go from there."

"What if we destroy it?" Brass replied.

It was Tung who fielded that one. "Impossible. It's of the Empyrean, as are we. Our power is symbiotic. It flows between all beings and things born of the prime mages. If it truly is a piece of the gates, it would recognize our fire and respond accordingly."

"The thing's already been following me around," Iron added, "firing up like a damn compass whenever it wanted to make the soul bond known to me."

Titan lifted a brow at that. "*The* soul bond? Not *your* soul bond? Does she not have a name?"

"I'm not talking about that right now," Iron gritted out.

"*That* or *Anna*?"

Bronze swept his hand out, palm up. "Dude, you brought her up. Titan has a point."

The needling wasn't just an act of love from well-intentioned brothers who wanted the best for him while teasing him about his worst. It was the kind of perpetual prodding that had followed Iron around with a weight that held as much significance for him as it did for his family.

"Just get in position. Spread out in a circle around the shard. I don't need this to take all night. I'd rather my theories fail earlier than later."

With his giant *hold your tongue or I'll cut it out* message being received loud and clear on every stony jaw within kicking distance, Iron went to take a stance on the far side opposite from where he'd been facing the shard.

He would *not* think about Anna or the betraying thoughts that would creep into his mind about what would happen if his plan didn't work.

If he *didn't* find a way to unleash the relic's power, make it back home, and stop Cyro.

If he *could* imagine a few more Scrabble games and soft kisses while he made sure she and her baby were fed and cared for.

Iron didn't wait for a three-count. Didn't give a shit about making sure everyone was in line or in sync. His fire punched out of his fists in a blaze of blue so pummeling, he didn't care if the damn shard atomized on contact.

He wanted an out, and he wanted answers. And as more streams of electric flames joined his, lighting up the sad demolition site like fiery wheel spokes, he finally got what he asked for.

CHAPTER 18

Brass's tense expression was what finally had Iron wrenching his power away from the shard, extinguishing his flames, and doubling over onto his knees. Around him, his brothers had all adopted the same stance, with a few rolling out their necks or cracking their jaws to soothe whatever the hell they had all just lived through. Once the thrum of his power had passed, Iron shook off the rest of his fatigue and forced his legs into the jog that carried him toward the relic's shard. The thing was glowing brighter, its curved stem pulsing with the ethereal light of their combined angel fire. But when Iron went to pick it up, the thing shivered out of his grip, dancing and spinning along the flat slab of concrete, until it finally puttered out and seemed to power down.

Titan joined him at his elbow, crouching down to examine the lifeless relic. "Huh. Not sure what I was expecting exactly, but I was hoping for something . . ."

"Exciting? Productive? Something along the lines of a fireworks show that could pump out enough magic to power up one or two galaxies, instead of the alarm clock's worth of wattage this thing gave off?" Chrome picked up the lone dingy arm of a mannequin that was getting far too handsy near his foot and drop-kicked it into a not-so-nearby junk pile.

More of the angels joined Iron as he lifted the shard and snuck it back into its test tube. He wasn't usually one for letting his emotions show, but certain levels of disappointment were impossible to hide, even for him. Iron's shoulders fell. "It was barely warm. I can't believe that didn't do anything. We're all almost back to full power. And the thing was clearly resonating with that! Shit, I was hoping—"

"It *did* do something."

Brass stepped forward, his stature having mostly recovered from whatever effects dispelling his fire had on him. His long black trench coat painted his form in its usual quiet lethality, except something in his posture belied the casualness of his composure. A lingering tension, the one Iron had noticed a moment ago, still held sway over his brother, and that shit had bad news written all over it.

Iron tucked the shard into his flannel pocket and bobbed his chin at Brass. "Talk to me."

"I need to know what everyone's feeling. Right now, tune into your celestial senses and tell me if you notice anything different."

The demolition site grew eerily quiet for several heartbeats as each of the angels closed their eyes and did exactly that. Steel, Rhode, and Bronze were the first to return their attention to the group, with a whole lot of headshaking happening. Chrome, Tungsten, and Titan, however, came away with a more solemn look, and Iron's insides twisted into a knot. All three of them wore an expression that had been . . . triggered. Whatever they'd finally picked up on wasn't enough to notice outright, nor was it enough to ignore entirely once it'd been made known to them.

Iron, on the other hand, sensed absolutely bupkis.

Chrome massaged the center of his chest. "What the hell is that?"

"Do you remember what it felt like to move through the realms?" Brass asked.

There were headshakes, thinned lips, and a boatload of disappointment as every one of them tried to recall a behavior that had once been as natural as breathing.

"My flames were the last to hit the relic," Brass added. "When they did, I got sort of a kickback of energy. It was like a returning ripple after you've floated your arm through the water. A sympathetic bump against my power. Almost like an acknowledgment."

Iron scratched at his beard along his jawline. "The magic was calling to you?"

Brass shook his head. "I'm not entirely certain what to make of it, but it damn sure reminded me of what it felt like when I used to move through the realms. When I'd pulse my celestial power out and hear the energetic reverberations from each of the different worlds. That was how the tracks were laid down, if you remember. It was a magical call-and-answer sort of system."

"Holy shit. Yeah, I remember. Man, I haven't thought about that in so long." Steel ran his fingers through his short blond hair and let a smile of bygone fondness break free.

"I felt it," Brass said, punching at his chest. "It was the echo of that magic, the magic we used to use to travel to the Empyrean and other realms. Don't get me wrong, that stuff was faint, but it was there. Like the hum of a car battery that needs just a bit more juice before it can fire up fully."

A torrent of shock had punched all the air from Iron's chest. He threw his hand out, grabbed the first thing he could find—a graffitied jersey barrier—and plopped his ass in front of it, more than happy to let the steel-reinforced hunk of concrete support him for the moment.

The ramifications spiraled out of control from there, with every one of his brothers running through the very likely scenario that they could, one day soon, actually make it back home.

A soft relief tickled the inside of his chest as every single sentinel and seraph around him let the weight of the discovery bring them to the ground in one form or another.

"We can finally go home," Titan breathed, leaning his athletic bulk against the side of a dumpster.

Damn. He'd gone and said it. The five words that had eaten away at them for eons. The main thing that ruled their actions in a world that could barely rule itself. Each one of his brothers had found sparks of the Empyrean's guiding light on Earth. Each one of them had not only regained their long-lost powers but found their soul's bond and purpose.

Each one of them had finally found a means to return to their home and deliver the might of the Empyrean down on Cyro's head once and for all.

All of them except him. He was the broken axle holding the caravan back, and the reason had just been illuminated for all to see.

"I need my full fire," he whispered, knowing everyone could still hear him. "Once my powers are free, we'll all be able to hit the relic with the full force of our celestial magic. There won't be anything to hold it back, no restrictions or breaks in the resonance between realms." He swallowed around the enormity of it all. "We'll be able to return to the Empyrean."

A sad awareness passed from one brother to another, until their combined realization settled heavily on Iron's thick shoulders once again.

If he wanted to make sure his brothers finally made it home, he needed Anna to help them get there.

And for the life of him, he couldn't see a way around it.

ANNA SMILED into the screen and settled for adjusting her glasses, instead of rubbing her palms into her eyes like she wanted. The morning was off to a banger of a start. It was only her first nutrition counseling session of the day and already she was fighting off the eye twitches.

She'd somehow misplaced her low-grade glasses, the ones she wasn't worried about accidentally dropping in the toilet or sending skittering under the bed, as she'd been known to do when pregnancy coordination hit her hard during her three a.m. bathroom visits. That pair had been her default when she wasn't working, and the frames were the most comfortable, unlike her work glasses, which still felt too stiff on her face, even after months of owning them. The result was her having to finally adapt to her proper prescription and muddle through the visual transition that came with it. Likewise, the coffee had been a mistake, but there was no going back from that. She'd broken the seal on the habit the second that bag of ground beans had found its way into her cabin on the heels of a snowstorm and a reluctant angel savior.

She'd have to cut it with decaf tomorrow.

"And that's why I had to buy a new food scale. As you know, I have no love for the imperial system, and the scale I have doesn't do grams. That's why I overindulged in those twenty-five-percent-less-sugar brownies, I think. You know, the ones with the added fiber? I even put black beans in them like my neighbor who's in that weekly walking group recommended. Not sure why she wanted to bite down on beans in her brownies, but once you get past the texture, they weren't bad." The sallow face of the man in front of her was only heightened by his balding pate and equally shiny mustache.

Martin Belknap, a sixty-year-old with an eye toward retirement and a sudden penchant to reverse decades of damage caused by the Sad American Diet, was always her first appointment on Wednesdays. Ever the punctual client, Marty usually sat in her virtual waiting room for a good fifteen minutes before she opened up the call each session. No matter how many times she reminded him he didn't need to be so early, he always responded the same way: "If someone's carving time out of their day to spend it with me, the least I can do is show up. I never want to have someone waiting on me. Besides, life's too short to owe anyone what you could easily give for free."

She used to think it was cute, that it was some sort of wisdom he was saving to pass down to his progeny when he finally became a grandpa.

Now, that adage rang like a record scratch on repeat.

"I hate owing people. That's how ghosts are made."

Her own words, the ones that had carried through a pre-storm maze of cellular towers to a pseudo-stranger's phone once upon a time, seemed like forever ago, and despite what had happened between her and Iron, she couldn't help but think she was still stuck around waiting.

Anna tapped a pen on her notebook, making sure to keep it out of the camera's view. "I think you're supposed to usually blend the beans up with some water first, then add them to the brownie batter," she responded as helpfully as she could. "Next time, when you have a sweet urge like that, it's perfectly fine to portion out a regular brownie. Not everything needs to be about fiber and sugar. A treat is a treat, and we all need those in our lives. Problems arise when we rely too heavily on them in our diets or, conversely, neglect them to the point where they occupy the majority of our focus. It's all about balance, and that's the hardest lesson to learn."

"Don't I know it," he said, patting the top half of a stomach that greedily took up more than its fair share of the camera frame.

From across the hall in her bedroom, her phone rang. Good thing that part of her virtual office policy mandated that she leave the thing in a different room. Fortunately, she had time to take the call, as she'd already gone fifteen minutes over with Marty and her next client wasn't for another forty-five minutes.

"I think we'll end there for today. A new scale sounds like it might be a good fit, if it'll create habits that promote consistency. I know data accuracy is important to you, so try it out for a week and we'll go from there."

Anna said her goodbyes and, after hanging up her headset, went to grab her phone. Her stomach lurched.

Two missed calls. From Iron.

Just seeing his name on her screen was enough to send her into a tailspin. The hurt that clogged her throat was still there, pressing reminders into her trachea of how they'd ended their last conversation, with her defending not only her judgment and decisions but her desire to know more about a man who was clearly running scared. And people said some fucked-up shit when they were scared. She should know. But after three days of trying to process that which couldn't be processed without more information, she was left with nothing to do except wait and hope he'd keep his word and call.

Now he was doing exactly that, apparently. Then why was she so uneasy about it?

The phone started chirping in her hand again, and she answered it.

He was in her ear before she even had a chance to dole out her greeting. "Anna."

"Hi."

She was wrong if she said his voice didn't still affect her. Oh, it did, and she hadn't realized how warm her small cabin felt when his baritone words were drifting around her, bouncing off the rafters with their soothing vibrations.

"You doing okay?"

Could there be a more loaded question?

Her mind drifted to the half-demolished box of Fruit Loops

on her kitchen counter and the fruit bowl she'd left untouched since he'd last arranged it days ago.

"Yeah. Just fine." *If you count thinking less and less of yourself because you, once again, make questionable decisions when it comes to men. And even though you're so good at it, you hate waiting. Like, a lot.*

The phone fell silent for a beat, then Iron's heavy exhale forced her to take a seat on the bed. "I'm sorry," he said. The phrase was quick but not clipped. "I need to address a shitload of misunderstandings."

"Well, it's always best to start at the top."

"The top." He scoffed. "How about we start at the core? I left something unsaid, and I need to correct that."

"Oh?"

"To me, you and your baby are a package deal, and yeah, at first, I didn't know what to make of it."

"You didn't know what to make of a pregnant woman?"

"No! I didn't know what to make of . . . Fuck, I didn't know why the prime mages, if they even existed at all, put you and your baby in my path to care for. I couldn't parse out that sort of responsibility or how to nurture what I desperately wanted to without putting you both at risk. And I realized recently that I can't."

Outside her window, there was no wind. No angry snarling weather. No torrential rain or drifting snow. There was nothing to portend the Doom 2.0 that was coming for her when Iron finally let the other shoe drop. Already, her nose began to twitch with the increased blood funneling to her cheeks and tear ducts.

"I realized," he continued, "that I can't be willing to play high stakes without high risk as well."

Her eyes had just begun to mist over when her brain stalled out. "I'm sorry. What are you saying?"

"I'm saying, if you're up for it, I'm willing to try. I'm happy to bring you and your baby into my world, meet my family, their mates, hear all the stupid theories that come out of Chrome's mouth whenever he gets a few microbrews in him. All of it. I'm willing to hold your hand, guide you through the very messy and, to be clear, really fucking dangerous shit show that can be my life, if you're willing to spend some more time with me. Time where we're not waiting out a storm or battling over word scores."

Anna sniffed. Shit! She didn't mean to let him hear that. "It wasn't really a battle, I don't think. The game just ended early. I would have won eventually."

He chuckled softly. "There's no doubt in my mind about that."

A dark flutter kicked at her insides, and she grinned behind the back of her hand. "But also, you need to know something."

"Shoot."

"From here on out, when it comes to what I want, I will absolutely one hundred percent not wait around for anything or anyone a single minute more." Her mind spun around a thought, and she fired it out before she could summon the courage to corral it back. "And I want to kiss you again. I want *you* to want to kiss me again."

Iron's breaths grew heavy in the receiver, and for a second, Anna worried she'd said too much. But then his voice was in her ear once more, laced with an edge that was far more foreboding than she'd ever heard. "You can't say that stuff to me."

"Why not?"

"Because there hasn't been a single minute of the last three days where I have not stroked myself to the memory of your taste."

Holy fucking shit balls!

The heat in Anna's cheeks rocketed up to volcanic levels. Then her unhelpful sex-starved pregnancy brain took over the controls. "I'd like to see that sometime."

She clamped a hand over her mouth. Whoever this woman

was who'd hijacked Anna and replaced her with a creature who cheerfully spoke her mind without regard for consequences either deserved an all-expenses-paid vacation to the Tropics or a prison sentence. Jury was still out on that one.

"Deal."

"I, uh, haven't accepted your apology yet, you know."

"I've noticed. Tell me what to do to change that. I can be very accommodating and open to persuasion under the right circumstances."

Do not think of him stroking himself. Do not think of him stroking himself. "You need to do something for me, something that'll make you as uncomfortable and anxious as I've been."

Regret heightened his tone. "I can't apologize enough for what I've done. My actions were beyond shameful. But if it's my discomfort you're after, I may have the perfect thing."

"Oh? That's what?"

"Fuck. I can't believe I'm going to even bring this up."

"The horse has left the barn now. No use trying to call it back."

"Fine. Tomorrow night, I'm picking you up at six."

"Where are we going?"

"A bar."

Any excitement that had previously flushed her body red-hot quickly began evaporating. Bars and pregnant women didn't usually mix. "Oh."

"It's not what you think."

"I don't exactly know what to think, because you haven't told me."

"Do you really have a response for everything?"

"No. Sometimes I sleep."

The boisterous laugh that bellowed through the phone was like air rushing into the lungs of a drowning woman. The happiness chasing it at hearing his joy was enough to erase every gloomy thought from the past three days.

"There's a bar me and my brothers go to every now and then on Thursday nights."

"Your . . . brothers?"

"Yup. All seven of them, plus their mates. It's about as socially grueling for someone like me as you can expect, and not because I don't love my family."

Anna gripped the phone tighter. "What am I missing? What happens on Thursday nights?"

Iron groaned into the phone, and for the first time, she began to question the bargain she'd just struck with him.

"Trivia."

The Thursday night crowd at the Cider Citadel and Brewing Bastion was well thinned given the time of year, but that didn't stop the diehards from attending trivia night. The bar was what Anna expected: lots of dim lighting broken up by random fluorescent beams advertising one brand of beer or another, a few high-top tables, an only-mildly-sticky floor, and pint after pint of some house ale or another.

The whiteboard was a surprise, as was the microphone setup. However, that made sense for emcee and scoring purposes if trivia was indeed the main item on the menu that evening.

However, an entirely different set of questions raced through her head, none of which would fall under the *pop culture* or *sports and stats* categories.

No, her qualms fell more in line with "What will everyone think of me?" and "Can I keep the bathroom trips to a reasonable number?"

"Can I take your coat?" Iron asked as he ushered her toward a cluster of tables at the back of the barroom. His hand never left her lower back the entire time, guiding them both through the meager crowd with bladed purpose. Every time he pressed against her just a little more firmly, piloting her away from any of the well-lubricated men who'd gotten a head start on their evening's enjoyment, she recalled the rough thrill of his fingers when they'd caged her own during a far different type of game.

Not for the first time since she hastily swept on some mascara and broke out her one tube of questionably salvageable lip gloss earlier that evening, she wondered whether she was in over her head.

"I might just keep my coat on for a bit." He didn't need to know how grateful she was for the crappy lighting because it would hide her threadbare maternity leggings, which were the only pants she wore these days, and her very much *nonmaternity* cardigan, which was dipping and pulling in places a pregnant woman need not call more attention to.

Iron eyed her carefully, then nodded. "Whatever makes you comfortable."

"Are you? Comfortable, that is? I'm getting the sense that I may have asked for too much from you."

The corner of his mouth kicked up. "Let's just say you're about to witness a very crude display of family bonding." Iron caught the eye of whoever he was walking toward and nodded. "And that's just when Drea and Rose get teamed up. Molly tries to keep the peace when she can, but those women come up with some answers during the wild card rounds that would put Chrome's penchant for cursing to shame."

Anna laughed softly. "They sound wonderful."

"They *sound* like a designated driver's worst nightmare. And here they are, Trouble One and Trouble Two."

Anna took a deep breath to center . . . whatever the hell it was that usually got centered when people took a deep breath and smiled at the assembled crowd.

Or she tried to, at any rate, because the second Iron escorted her to their table, she was swept up in a warm hug of Amazonian proportions.

"Oh my gosh, you're Anna, right? Iron's told us absolutely nothing useful about you. I really don't know why Chrome and the others keep him around. I'm Drea, by the way."

When the hug was finally relinquished, Anna was staring into the violet exuberant eyes of a six-foot-tall blonde woman whose breath and braid already carried the scent of a good time.

Mental note: discuss definition of the word trouble *with Iron.*

"Hi. Yes, I'm Anna. It's nice to meet you."

"To clarify, we keep him around because he knows the Wi-Fi password. Chrome. Pleasure." A behemoth of a man with a military crew cut and two beers in hand winked at her, then passed one of the longnecks to Iron.

"Drea is Chrome's soul bond, and Chrome is about to spend some quality time with the blunt end of my mace."

Anna stifled a giggle and spoke out of the side of her mouth to Iron. "Well, he did just confirm your Wi-Fi password theory, so maybe he's not all bad."

"Oh, I like her! I like her so much! Can we keep her? I'd like to keep her." Drea was bouncing on the balls of her feet like a kid who'd just cashed in their Skee-Ball tickets for a prize that was actually worth something.

Iron rolled his eyes and put an arm around Anna's shoulders before gesturing to the group in front of them. "I'm probably going to need something a lot stronger than beer pretty soon, but before I get to that, let me introduce you to everyone. If you need name tags, let me know. I have absolutely zero problem slapping some *Hello, My Name Is* stickers on their shirts. That adhesive is hell on cotton fibers, and some of these clowns could use some humbling."

They had four tables reserved for their group, which was the only reason Anna was able to keep anyone straight, especially when it came to the set of twins: Rose—Trouble Two, Anna presumed—and Tammy. Rose was soul bound to Titan, second-in-command to Tungsten, the sentinels' leader, who Tammy was mated to. Thankfully, the twins were on different teams. Also, the two women not only had different hairstyles but wildly different personalities, which helped separate them in Anna's mental catalog. Rose was sarcastic and endearing while her sister was a bit more reserved and studious but sweet as all get out. Validating Iron's apparent fears from earlier, Chrome and Drea were paired with Titan and Rose.

At Tungsten and Tammy's table sat another couple, Bronze and Clara. Iron explained that Bronze's soul bond didn't normally attend human functions because, her being a lycan, metal didn't agree with her molecular makeup, but she could usually manage short periods without any major hiccups.

Brass and his mate, Molly, a woman who Anna recognized as an owner of one of the restaurants in town, sat at another table, their heads bowed over in strategy with another couple. Neela, who was the first female charmer and former kin of Cyro, and Rhode, the only angel among them created of the seraph class. Now, *that* was a relationship story she'd like to hear someday.

Then that left Steel and Bridget, who both had lighthearted gamer smiles plastered on their faces.

Before Anna could say hi again, her words were cut off when Iron spoke in her ear. "We'll be on their team. They're the least stressful to play with. Of all the characters I've introduced thus far, these two are the only ones who know this is still just a game. No pressure. Just fun."

"It's wonderful to meet all of you."

Bridget smiled at her. "Likewise. Would you like something to drink? They have really good mocktails here."

Anna shot Iron a questioning look, which he addressed with a single nod. "They're aware."

She dipped her head low so only he could hear. "Were you gossiping about me?"

His beard brushed against the shell of her ear as he replied, "You're the first female I've ever introduced them to, and secrets don't fly among our soul-bound family. Not anymore, at least. We've had to learn and grow on that front and have no interest in repeating mistakes. That means everyone you see here is protected, including your baby."

Steel piped up. "Tell me about it. Talk to Bridget if you need more horror stories on secrets." He shuddered in mock affront, and Anna raised a brow at Iron.

"Celestial senses," Iron added matter-of-factly. "Sound travels fast for us."

"Ah, got it. In that case, sure, I'll have a drink." *I can't inadvertently say something stupid if there's a straw in my mouth.*

Bridget slid her a menu, and Anna selected something with blood orange, sparkling coconut water—that was new—and yuzu.

The emcee took the stage, which was just a section of floor that had hardwood as opposed to laminate, and grabbed the microphone. "All right, my friends, it's time to get the party started! Great to see so many of you here tonight. Let's begin by going through the evening's categor—" The sound cut out, a scratchy *tsewmp* popped through the two amps stationed at the front, and the overhead lights above the whiteboard began to flicker.

A few tables over, the white shock of Clara's hair fell forward as she bent toward Bronze. "Oops. Sorry."

The auburn-haired angel smiled wide and lifted her knuckles to his lips. "You're always stealing the show."

"Okay, that was weird," the emcee said. "No matter, I'll just— what do they call it in theater classes?—not yell . . . ah, project! Can everybody hear me all right?" After several nods from the room gave him his greenlight, he announced the categories, and they were off to the races. "The first category is *superheroes*. Who is the leader of the Avengers?"

Bridget and Steel had an answer down before any of the tables around them had finished deliberating, which was fine with Anna, while Drea, Rose, and Chrome were locked in some sort of heated debate over source material. When time was called, teams threw up their cards. Anna's team guessed Iron Man, which was correct.

Chrome, however, waved his card proclaiming Captain America as their answer at the emcee. "Hey, are we basing the answer off screen adaptations here or the comic books? Because if we're talking about the Marvel Cinematic Universe, there were entire movies and subsequent plot lines devoted to the ambiguity of the Avengers' leadership."

Then Rose stood up. "Yeah, and how long are the terms of leadership we're talking about? I can literally think of a time when every single character in the original comics took on the Avengers mantle of leadership. So, are we talking over the course of a battle, a mission, a day, years? It really is unclear."

"Oh, for fuck's sake. Here we go." Iron knocked back his beer, gestured to the waiter for another, and returned his attention to Anna, as if he were gauging her tolerance for ass-hattery.

He needn't have worried, and she smiled to let him know as much.

This was freaking *wonderful*.

Over the course of ten rounds, one wild card battle, and a bracketed system that included several complicated knock-out sequences, Anna's cheeks had found their new happy place supporting the wings of her smile. The drinks were yummy and the verbal battles more than entertaining, but that wasn't what had her skin tingling and dopamine flowing.

Somewhere near the fifth round, Iron's hand had taken a particular liking to hers. It started with gentle bumps and brushes whenever he'd slide her a napkin. Then those gestures turned into something more than simple courtesies. When she'd spent too long gripping her drink and she'd pull her hand away to wipe the condensation off her fingers and warm them up, he was already there holding out his palm to her. She'd give him her hand, and slowly, gingerly, he'd rub and dry away any traces of chilled wetness.

The contact was in everything he did, even when it wasn't as apparent as touching. The way his arm was already bracketed behind her seat when she'd return from the bathroom. The new drink he always made sure took the place of her empty one, with special attention paid to ensuring the straw was facing her and that the drink wasn't too close to the edge of the table lest she accidentally bump it. His unspoken removal and acceptance of her coat after she'd unbuttoned it, even though she'd been afraid to remove it for fear of exposing her clumsiness to her new friends and knocking into the table, sending her drink spilling across the response cards.

If Travis had been consumed with convenience, Iron was consumed with acts of service. With each small, warm kindness the angel showed her, the layers of ice that had dammed up around her heart slowly began to thaw, until she found herself reaching for his touch, craving it and all the promise it offered.

"Fuck," Chrome bellowed as the winning team—Anna's table—was announced.

Drea's palm collided with the back of Chrome's head before the *k* in his curse had the chance to run free. "Don't swear in front of the baby," she hissed, then slanted an apologetic look Anna's way.

"It's fine," she replied, patting her belly for reassurance. "I'm fairly certain its ears aren't fully formed yet. Though, I'll find out tomorrow."

The look of relief erasing Drea's admittedly inebriated concern was heartwarming on so many levels. Iron had explained how Drea's former life was lived as a messenger mage in the Empyrean. Between her time there and her largely controlled interactions in the mortal world before she'd mated Chrome, she had relatively little knowledge about babies and fetal development.

"See," Chrome said, gesturing to Anna. "It's fine!"

Iron leaned close. "What's tomorrow?"

"My sixteen-week checkup. Not my favorite thing to do, but kind of necessary." Around her, tables were beginning to clear as guests shrugged into coats and paid their bills.

"Are you nervous that something might be wrong?" he asked, standing and holding out her coat for her to slide into.

"No, not at all. It's just a very couple-y experience. In the beginning, it wasn't so terrible because I could just pretend I was there for a regular pap smear or something, but now that I'm starting to show a bit more, it's clear I'm pregnant and flying solo. Again, not a problem, but it just feels a bit . . ."

"Inconvenient."

Anna hadn't expected Iron to finish her thought or remember Travis's adjectival weapon of choice that the bastard would fling at her heart. "Sometimes, yeah."

Anna shrugged on her coat and worked at the buttons. When she finally got them all to line up correctly—a frequent problem most days—she lifted her chin and was nearly struck dumb by the expression staring back at her.

It was Iron, but . . . not. He was silent and enigmatic like always, but a look of consternation warred across his strong features in a way she hadn't seen before. Then he held out his palm to her, and knowing there was some significance to his offering, she placed her hand in his.

"How would you feel if I joined you?"

Her world stalled on his axis. "What?"

"At your appointment tomorrow. How would you feel if I went with you?"

"I-I'd feel . . . like you'd be needlessly subjecting yourself to an abnormally large number of hormonal pregnant women."

He chuckled softly, massaging the fleshy pad between her thumb and forefinger. "It's not needless if you don't want to be alone."

"Are you sure?"

"Sure as anything."

She didn't know what to say, but thankfully, she didn't need to. Her body took it from there. Anna threw her arms around his neck and kissed him. Right there, in front of his brothers, their mates, and whoever else decided to take their sweet-ass time leaving the bar to gawk at strangers. Let them. If this was a show to be put on, she'd do it a thousand times over if she got to feel the strength and warmth of his arms banding around her, lifting her off the floor like a treasure to be secured.

Iron brought her impossibly closer, and her breath hitched as, even through their coats, her body remembered how the hard planes of his muscles felt against a softness she was so afraid to show anyone. She angled her head, and an appreciative greedy moan vibrated from his lips into hers. Anna had no problems with greedy. She could be greedy. She could be—

"Ow!" Neela's startled shout broke Anna and Iron from their embrace. Someone, a man, must have bumped into Rhode's soul bond and knocked her into the server behind her, sending a tray of drinking glasses and beer bottles clamoring to the floor.

"Easy, lady. Just had to reach for my keys. You're fine." A muscled man with long hair tied back in a low ponytail had righted himself after leaning around Neela to grab a rusted key ring complete with two keys and a bottle opener from a nearby table. A large stain bloomed across his white T-shirt, accompanied by the stinging bite of hard alcohol that, in high doses up close, always made Anna's nose tingle.

Rhode was moving before Neela had a chance to regain her balance. The fool hadn't even pieced together just what was happening to him when the seraph had his hands on the drunk man's shirt collar and dragged him on his toes out the door.

While Anna watched the impressive display of waste removal, a few other men stood from a table near the door and walked out right after Rhode. Iron's grip shifted to her hips and tightened. Then his eyes flashed that brilliant fiery topaz, and he quickly pulled her behind his back.

"Iron, what is it? What's going on?"

Around them, the other angels had stood as well, flames dancing high in each of their eyes, painting their features in hard brutal shadows that hadn't been there a moment ago.

"Charmers."

CHAPTER 20

Tung stepped forward while Titan quickly gathered the women behind them.

The prime sentinel then jerked his chin at Chrome and Steel. "We split up. You two stay with Titan and me. Get everyone to safety back in the den." That pewter gaze high with fire and barely leashed rage slashed to Iron, who'd already begun to make his way out the door with Brass and Bronze. "Find Rhode. Ensure the charmers are dealt with quickly and quietly."

"Understood."

Like any sort of confirmation was needed on that, though? Just the sight of a demon this close to Anna had already made Iron's fire dance at the tips of his fingers.

He snuffed his flames into his fists, then pushed through the sparse dining room, with his brothers trailing as silent harbingers of their lethality. His boot was barely over the threshold when a jarring sensation halted his stride. Tucked into the corner of the dining room was a round wooden table adjacent to the door. A foul hum of dark magic coated the tight area, slinking over his skin like an oily caress. It was concentrated. The bastards had been there awhile, sitting, observing. Learning.

"Shit," Iron ground out.

Brass leaned down and swiped his fingers along the wood in spots. "Scratches."

Bronze narrowed his eyes. "New or old?"

"Very fucking new." Iron curled his fingers into a claw shape and ran them over the grids of pale lines Brass had noticed carved into the wood. There were sets of them, each evenly spaced with five lines. "And they're sending us a message."

Iron bit back a curse he didn't want his brothers hearing. He'd become so goddamn distracted over the past several months that he'd let the very basics of battle float to the floor of his mind. Charmers didn't move through the mortal realm without leaving signs. Yes, they shifted shape. Yes, they ate, fucked, and fought just like any other human, but certain parts of themselves were always visible, always at the ready.

Their nails. For the mystic conjurers, the magic users, they always kept them long, almost clawlike. It made it easier for them to swipe against an abrasive surface, create a spark, and feed their dark magic into it quickly to ignite their spells. Only the mystics behaved this way. Elite kept their nails trimmed for ease of combat, and apex kept their thumbnails long so they were more adept at fighting and casting.

These were essential details about the enemy ingrained into every sentinel and seraph, and he'd been so fucking focused on Anna that his celestial senses hadn't even picked out when the assholes were in the goddamn room with her. Sharing her air. Hearing her heartbeat—and the heartbeat of her unborn baby.

Iron burst through the door, his chest heaving to accommodate the flood of fire raging through his frame.

"Around back. Near the lake." Brass was off and sprinting,

with Bronze and Iron fast on his heels. The bar backed up against a pond-turned-manmade-lake that had been carved out a good century ago, serving as a bucolic focal point for Aurora and its wildlife. It also offered great shoreline forested coverage, and Iron had never been more grateful for the camouflage. He was going to light those fuckers up and use their ashes to polish his weapons.

Up ahead, a flash of silver swiped through a catacomb of trees. Iron pushed his legs faster and pointed. "There! Rhode's engaged!"

Bronze shouted, "I see him!"

The three of them finally penetrated the tree line. Rhode had already shifted into his metallic armor, wings out, twisting and slicing at the mystics like a blender blade. Whatever human forms they'd taken to conceal themselves in the bar had long been shed. Now, their characteristic bald heads and swirling teal and gold tattoos decorated their skin in a fashion that set Iron's heart pumping, triggering the most brutal facets of his need-to-kill reflex.

"Are they all mystics? I count six!" Brass hollered as he palmed his firearms and started shooting off angel-fire-laced bullets left and right, landing against shields of green electrified magic that the mystics threw up.

Fuck. When the hell had they managed that trick? Angel fire was the one thing charmers had always been susceptible to, and if they'd finally found a way to spell against it . . .

Rhode paused his assault to adjust his grip on his knives. Blue flames arced up the blades to the hilts. "These two are elite. They're mine."

They all sank into the familiar ebb and flow of battle. Iron crouched low, summoned his wings wide, and leaped into the air. Two of the mystics paused their readying assault to track him. Good. Iron didn't waste time with handheld weapons.

True, he was more of a blunt-force trauma kind of guy, but his mace and ax weren't the kinds of things he could conceal easily at a mortal bar. Instead, he punched his power free, sending streaks of fire arcing directly at the targets of bald heads below. One shield went up, snuffing his flames, then the other.

But when the charmers didn't see any expression of frustration greeting their defense, Iron smiled slowly, letting every ounce of grim glee shine in the shadows of his visage instead.

Bingo.

"You're cooked, motherfuckers!" Bronze leaped from a nearby tree branch and heaved two fireballs at the first charmer, who still held its shield high, its attention on Iron and expecting more aerial attacks. Fire slammed into the creature's knees from the side, burning through its kneecaps, cartilage, and bone. Screams shot high into the air as two severed stumps toppled to the ground, crisping to ash in moments while the rest of the body followed suit.

The other mystic lowered its magic shield and sent it hurtling toward Bronze like a glowing electric green discus. The angel threw his wings out and managed to wrap himself within them as the magic hit, throwing him into the air until his back met a tree. He grunted hard and slid to the ground.

Below, Rhode had incinerated one of the elite but was still battling the other. Blood and acid wounds from before he'd shifted streaked down the side of the seraph's face as he dodged the arc of the charmer's bone blade. Brass was squaring off with a mystic who had two acid bombs levitating above its upturned palms while muttering some dark incantations. Those projectiles would fly free soon, and none of their metals could withstand magically altered acid attacks for long.

"Burn them all! Now!" Iron punched his fists out in front of him, angling his body like a flaming beacon. He tucked his wings and dove toward the charmer who'd flung its shield at Bronze. Magic struck fire in a sizzling explosion. They both tumbled to the ground in a ball of battling fury. The mystic raked its claws down the size of Iron's neck, snagging a strained tendon. Iron roared, and his fire sputtered out. He tried to breathe through the pain and call his fire back, but only slight sparks responded. The well of celestial power deep within his core was failing, in desperate need of regeneration this late in the evening.

Fuck!

"I do believe something is wrong with you," the mystic taunted, smiling through teeth coated in its black blood. Then the thing pitched itself up and over onto Iron's back, pinning him to the ground while it pressed its contorted magic against the weight of Iron's wings, crushing him into the snow.

Iron bucked and writhed, but the unnatural heaviness weighing him down only increased with each movement.

"It'll be over soon. We already got what we came for." The mystic fired more pulses of dark magic against Iron's wings, singeing his flight feathers and forcing his mouth and nose farther into the snow.

Around him, the sounds of fighting had begun to die down, replaced by muffled grunts and far too much hissing. Dammit! He couldn't tell whether they were from acid burns or angel fire incineration.

Iron pulled at his power again, begging, pleading with everything he was and had ever done for it to punch forward.

All he got were the silent reverberations of sorrowful echoes.

He tried to strain his face away from the snow, to see who or what was around. A branch, a rock, a fucking leg that hadn't incinerated fully yet. Something!

Then he felt it, the pull on his metal. It took Iron half a thought to recognize what it was and where it was coming from, and the other half of his thought to act.

He freed a hand and reached out toward the small body of

water near him. The lake's frozen crust crackled, then erupted into a shower of icy shards that rained down crystalline sprinkles along the remaining unbroken surface. A long curved piece of black metal pierced through the air from the water below and hurled toward the charmer on Iron's back.

A sharp grunt ripped from its lungs as the previously submerged car fender slammed into its middle.

Iron wasted no time. Now freed, he shot to his feet, not liking how slow his equilibrium was returning, and powered that fender right into the nearest tree. The sound of creaking metal had never been so sweet as when it was called into service after a long slumber. The pulls and pinches were just *so* satisfying, especially as Iron wrapped that fender around the mystic's middle like he was trussing a turkey.

"Steel's one of my favorite iron alloys to play with, you know." He spat blood into the snow and held his hand to the wounded side of his neck. Then he called out to no one in particular. "A little help here!"

Eager as ever for the final fireworks, Brass and Rhode hobbled to their feet and simultaneously called forth their full angel fire.

"You're too late!" The mystic snarled, a disembodied glee stretching its features as the combined beams of flames shot toward it from behind Iron.

And that was when he saw the error he'd made. It wasn't just blue that reflected back at him from the charmer's wide golden eyes but green as well.

Iron spun but didn't see the sixth charmer until it had already cast open a portal. A dull *whoomp* resonated through the trees, then green electricity crackled and flared around the edges of the magic door. The forgotten mystic smiled at him, gave a two-fingered salute from its temple, and stepped through. The portal dissolved around the charmer's heels.

In the quiet that settled over the decimated forest landscape, punctuated only by the labored breaths of his brothers, Iron dropped to his knees, sank below the weight of his injured wings, and screamed into the night sky.

Cyro soon would know about Anna.

CHAPTER 21

An hour had passed since Anna had seen Iron. The slow tinkling of water dripping through a coffee maker was the nails-on-a-chalkboard equivalent that rubbed against her already abraded nerves. The sixty minutes of worried time spent in his brothers' care was the longest freaking year of her life.

When he and the others finally pushed through the solid metal door to their home, there was no such thing as a spared glance his way while she maintained some semblance of decorum on her part. Nope. She gave up on discreet courtesy the second she and the other women had been dragged into the angels' home—a feat of construction best described as an underground palace with Wi-Fi, espresso on tap, and enough weapons to arm a small country—with only mild murmurings of "Charmers" and "It's not safe."

So, yeah, when Iron walked in with all limbs intact and an expression that could sour vinegar, she wasted no time. Anna abandoned her chamomile and fired herself at him like a heat-seeking missile. He caught her with an *oof!* but still banded her to him with an arm around her back. One arm, not two.

Then she saw why.

"Holy shit, you're hurt!" Anna let him lower her to the ground and flew into full mother-hen mode, peeling his fingers away from the bandages at his neck. Up until that point, she'd never successfully nurtured anything beyond the mold colonies that grew in the back of her fridge, yet this somehow felt vital and instinctual. "Let me see it."

"It'll heal," he said in tones far gentler than she was used to, but he didn't resist when she lifted the—nope, not a bandage—wad of cocktail napkins from the bar away from his neck. She gasped. Angry slashes shredded the skin there. Each shorn edge of flesh was mottled with pockets of charred burns.

"How will this heal? This is in no way a heal-on-its-own thing. This is way more than a cat scratch. We need to get you to a hospital!"

Iron gathered her trembling hands and laid them against his warm chest. "I've got everything I need right here." Then he dipped his forehead against hers, and the tense torso muscles beneath her fingers relaxed slightly. "The mountain will heal me."

"What does that even mean?"

Tungsten, who'd stayed with her in the great room until everyone returned, stepped away from his conversation with Brass and the others and joined them. He rested a reassuring hand on her shoulder. "This mountain contains minerals and elements that call to our metals. When we are wounded, those earthly components commune with our magic, regenerating our strength and healing what our bodies naturally cannot. It is why we built our home beneath it."

"Right," she acknowledged, feeling slightly foolish. "I should have remembered that."

Iron stood straight but didn't let Anna's hands go free. "You don't have to remember anything."

"But I'd like to," she urged, impressing the importance of her conviction into her words, though hating how she still struggled to keep anything about his world straight. "It's just that some thoughts are harder to keep in my head these days. Can you at least tell me what happened?"

Around them, several of the other angels began peeling off shirts and gear. Rhode came back from the kitchen with a fishing tackle box stuffed with first aid supplies.

Tungsten threw a chastising finger out at Bronze, who was already on the sandstone-colored couch, picking off flecks of charred skin from his bare chest and toned bicep like one would peel a sunburn. "Hey, keep it off the furniture. Tammy likes to read there in the mornings." Then he returned his attention to Iron. "Anything we need to know?"

"There were six of them. Five dead. One lucky fucker escaped through a portal." A penetrated silence settled through the room before Iron spoke again. "They saw Anna at the bar with us, with me. It's safe to assume they'd be more than happy to use that intel against us. Oh, and they have angel fire-blocking shields now, which was fun."

Muffled curses from every angel bounced through the great room, then Rhode said grimly, "I wouldn't be surprised if they cooked something up with what they still have of my DNA." Haunted shadows cast over the seraph's eyes. "Regrettable but nothing to be done for it now."

Anna knew the gist of the reference but only through surface-level context. Iron had explained how, before Rhode had come to live with the angels, he'd been a prisoner of war in Cyro's camp for untold years. The experiments done on him were the stuff of nightmares and things he still had difficulty talking about.

But before Anna could ask any more questions, Iron's hand was at the small of her back, urging her out of the room. "All that shit is a problem for another day. For now, let's get some rest." Then he growled over his shoulder, "And keep your goddamn shirts on when you're in the den's public spaces. We have bathrooms and an infirmary for a reason."

Bronze craned his head up, a chunk of charred skin dangling from his fingertips. "Isn't our home private, though?"

Tungsten wadded up a sweatshirt and tossed it at Bronze's face.

Anna managed to smother a snort, which was saying something about her brain finally responding to the right social cues given the unfunny circumstances. Then Iron was leading her down a dark stone corridor. Though she'd been given a tour of the place when the others had first brought her in, she was still amazed at the craftsmanship and smoothness of it all. It was the difference between knowing a masterpiece existed and actually feeling the materials used to create it. Evenly spaced electrical lanterns, pristinely arched ceilings, and giant metal doors that, before the angels had welcomed their soul bonds into their home, had only operated by the magic of their metal alone. It was all the stuff of fairy tales. A belowground modern-day enchanted castle of sorts.

And here Anna was, desperately trying to hold a wad of cocktail napkins near Iron's wound so she could prove her usefulness and keep some of the blood off the granite floor.

"This one's mine." Iron halted her in front of yet another massive door, this one located at the end of the hall where the other living quarters were. When the slab of metal creaked open, it was the final welcome ushering her into a world she'd only wondered about.

Iron's suite. The place where he laid his head each night.

But when she took a turn around the room, she had to stop herself lest she trip over her jaw.

Every single wall of his space was made up of floor-to-ceiling white marble. It chased away any lingering darkness that had followed them in from the evening's horrors and set up shop like a field of blooming wildflowers hell-bent on taking a stand against insufferable sadness. Already, Anna's cheeks pinched against the rims of her glasses as she smiled wider than she could remember. It was impossible not to. There was just so much . . .

"Light," she breathed. Anna walked over to the closest wall and ran her fingers along the ridges of the stone. It was sensually smooth, with dappled striations etched in rivers of gold and silver. "How did you get this here? We don't have this kind of white marble in New Hampshire. Did you clean out Vermont's marble mines or something?"

She followed the track of one of the marble veins, which led her to mounted wall displays of massive weapons, instruments she recognized but couldn't immediately place, and various clay masks and other ceramic artifacts. Did the man know he slept in a museum? Crap, should she have taken her shoes off?

"The marble came from the Carrara quarries in Italy. It's just an overlay, though, and is only about an inch thick. I bonded it to the granite some time ago."

Iron shut the door and walked over to a dark oak dresser situated beneath a massive mirror. He reached into his flannel pocket and removed the test tube he always carried around with him, then placed it in what looked like a ceramic teapot. He then balled up his flannel shirt and chucked it into a nearby hamper.

He was rummaging through his drawers when Anna asked, "How the hell did you bond marble to granite?"

He shrugged, his back muscles doing interesting things to accommodate the gesture. "I played around with the iron oxide in the marble. There isn't usually much of it in marble since the stone's mostly made up of calcium carbonate, but what's there was enough for me to use my metal to make it adhere to the granite."

"It's truly breathtaking. It sure as hell beats the pastel paint chips I have in my desk drawer back home. Somehow, the idea of repainting my office with some variant of not-white-marble suddenly feels like a disservice." Anna sank down on the bed, suddenly getting hit with every ounce of exhaustion her adrenaline had been keeping from her. "You know, I think I need more light where I live, something that brings out a smile, like this," she said, gesturing at the walls. "I imagine the baby would like that. Poor thing's been in the dark for so long, after all. Can they even detect light yet? I have no idea."

All at once, images of her dream cabin pelted against the fortress she found herself in, and the beautiful wooden space she'd carved out for her and soon her small family seemed like a dreary default to a life she should have upgraded long ago. But like anyone who refused to install the latest software for fear of losing what they loved about the old stuff, it was futile. The world was a master at planned obsolescence, always changing and evolving, and if she didn't change with it, what would that mean for her baby?

There were a few sharp rips, then papers crinkling. More rummaging in a drawer, then the sound of it snicking shut before Iron joined her on the bed. He'd taped up his neck with fresh gauze and medical tape and had a bundle of folded clothes in his hands. She studied his face and tried to find the fear she was harboring reflected back at her, something large and heavy enough to overwhelm her to the point where she'd run screaming right back up her mountain and into the cozy socks and shielded comfort she was used to.

Instead, what she found was Iron's russet hair unbound and tumbling in waves around his shoulders, which were bare except for what his tank top covered. He wasn't smiling, but his eyes were cast down at the corners, as if in resolute acknowledgment that something had shifted between them, but the scales hadn't yet settled on whether it was good or bad.

"Those glasses suit you," Iron said, skimming his gaze over the rims of her pale pink cat eye frames that, up until a few days ago, only her virtual clients ever saw her wear. "They play well with the green in your eyes. It's a stunning effect."

"Thanks," she replied, tucking her hair behind her ear. "Kind of lost my old pair, so I'm having to get used to the higher prescription."

"The *proper* prescription, you mean?" he asked, and she thrilled at the teasing lilt to his tone. Man, she liked this Iron. The one who battled her in Scrabble and chastised her about her empty-calorie addiction without ever needling the whole *aren't you a nutritionist?* point to death. He knew, just as she did, how much of a walking contradiction she was, but living that role was fun and easy with him and made everything about their time together in her little cabin feel warm in a way the space never had felt before.

"Quiet, you," she said, narrowing her eyes, before finally working up the courage to ask the question that had been worrying a hole through her chest ever since he'd returned. "You got that injury because you exhausted your fire, didn't you?"

All the air got sucked out of the room on the wisps of her query, including bits of whatever essential stuff always starched his shoulders. "Yes. But I still got the job done. I always do."

She shook her head. "You shouldn't have to find a work-around, though. Your fire is a part of you. It's heartbreaking how you can't access it when you need to."

It had been a nagging worry that had dug its claws into the back of her mind and then army crawled its way into every thought that had surrounded her time with him.

"I'm pretty sure I'm not the only one in this room who has trouble accessing deeper parts of themselves."

"What's that supposed to mean?"

Iron dropped the pile of clothes into her lap. Another one of his flannels sat folded on top, but she didn't realize there were more clothes beneath it. A pair of mesh athletic shorts and a T-shirt. "I think you know or you wouldn't be hiding."

Anna ran her fingers along the flannel, not daring to meet his eyes. "You're casting aspersions." She winced, even as she spoke the words. That was a phrase her mother had always tossed around the house like throw pillows meant to cover up their family's otherwise gross lack of morals. It was a proper phrase meant to chastise in a proper way while concealing exactly nothing. She fucking hated it, yet the defense came flaring to life on demand regardless.

She *was* hiding, but was it worth it to come aboveground if the sun she was seeking kept avoiding her behind the clouds?

Iron exhaled a sadness far deeper than she thought him capable of, and it worried her. "Look, I'd like you to stay here tonight, with me. I mean, not *with* me. I'll sleep elsewhere, but here, in my suite of rooms. Those clothes are for you, to get comfortable."

That had her head shooting up. "Why?"

"Because I can't take you back home tonight. I'm gassed, I need to heal up and recharge a bit, and you'll be safe if—"

"No, I mean, why won't you stay with me?"

Entire chasms could have opened between them, and still, there wouldn't have been enough space to keep her question from pelting him against the forehead and for her to expect an answer in return.

An unsettled heat ignited the air between them, filling it with heartfelt promises they'd yet to find a way to voice, but dammit all to hell, she wasn't about to let him off the hook without trying.

"I could have stopped him if I had my full fire." A pleading note sat behind his words, unnerving her further. "My fire failed me, and it was only by the stroke of dumb luck that some poor soul had likely ditched their car into the lake and my metal latched on to it before it was too late. But it came with a cost."

Fire returned to his eyes, a heated fury searching for an outlet that could either soothe or stoke what burned within. "They know about you. They know you're important to me. Because I got cocky and, for a few unbelievable hours, got to play pretend and live a life where happiness and laughter were the orders of the day." He placed his hand over hers on top of the clothes, his knuckles brushing against her abdomen. "Where I got to envision taking you to the doctor tomorrow and asking far too late whether you'd let me come in the exam room because I knew it'd frazzle the fuck out of you." He swallowed hard. "That you might secretly want me there but couldn't bring yourself to ask. I got to create a moment in my mind where I saw your face light up at hearing the sound of your baby's heartbeat and handing you extra tissues to wipe the excess ultrasound goop off your belly."

Then a dark cloud stormed over those would-be memories, robbing her of the promise of those happy thoughts. "And I erased it all by putting a goddamn target on your back. By the mages, how can you even look at me, let alone want to share with me where you lay your head at night?"

"Because I want all of that, too!" she screamed, tossing the clothes to the floor. "I want you to take whatever you need from me that would bring you closer to your fullest self. I want you to go with me to the doctor and stare down every nose-in-the-air guy in that waiting room who assumes the worst of me because I'm a single thirty-four-year-old pregnant woman, as if that's such a goddamn crime. I want to get closer to you, and I think you want that, too, but I am absolute shit when it comes to mind games, so what the hell am I missing, Iron? What aren't you telling me?"

"I can't return to the Empyrean unless I have my full fire back!" he rushed out. "And neither can my brothers." His chest heaved through the exertion of his emotions, and it was enough to stun her back into silence. "Whatever we have, it would be a transaction. A *temporary* transaction."

"But you said the soul bond was forever."

He looked away from her. "Yes."

"Can two people be bonded and live apart like that, with you in the Empyrean and me here?"

More silence and then, "I don't know."

"So, you're not certain about any of it, yet you've already made your decision that I shouldn't have one."

He didn't respond at first, then replied, "I don't want you to get hurt, but I don't know how to stop the course you and I are both on."

She sat straighter on the bed, running through words spoken and scenarios described, but above them all was the pounding need in her chest. The need to be needed, to explore and provide in a way she'd never been afforded before. It was a transactional relationship of a different sort, one with a potential time limit, but one she couldn't help but reach for with both hands.

"What if I don't want to stop?" she asked, then set aside every fear hen-pecking at her logic center and did what her body had been urging her to do since she'd first dreamed of this man.

Anna rose to her feet and slid onto Iron's lap, straddling his hips and wrapping her arms around his neck.

"What are you doing?" he asked, and then she brought his hands to her waist, settling them there like the anchors she needed them to be.

"Living for the moments we have while exploring whatever joy you and I are capable of. Am I scared? A bit, but not when I'm with you. And I'd rather do it scared than hide back in my cabin with only dreams to keep me company. I want the real thing, warts and all."

Iron's fingers fanned along the expanse of her ribs, pressing possessive divots into the negative spaces. Before he could voice any asinine words of so-called reason, she silenced his lips with her finger.

A burgeoning heat ignited between them, tightening her abdominals and prickling her skin.

She wanted this. Oh god, she wanted him, and if he spurned her one more time, well, she wasn't sure she had it in her to bounce back from that type of rejection. The very idea of it felt dire.

But then his lips parted, and the heat of his tongue licked a wicked current along the pad of her finger.

Any breaths and lingering concerns she had were soon lost to the mesmerizing cove of his mouth.

CHAPTER 22

Iron was so goddamn right. Anna tasted better than any delicacy dreamed up by mortals past or present. In that same vein, as he savored the flavor of her skin, he knew, with absolute certainty, another cell-altering truth: he was equally goddamn screwed.

The difference this time was his ability to care.

Iron slipped Anna's finger free from his mouth and dropped a kiss on her palm, right where some mortal cultures believed a lifeline resided. He had to smile at that, given the way his own life had changed so drastically since she'd been in it. She flinched slightly, then curled her fingers around the side of his face and ducked her forehead against his shoulder.

Was she . . .?

"I didn't know you were ticklish."

Anna rocked her head back and forth against him, refusing to break the contact. "I didn't know how soft your beard would feel against my skin there."

"I knew how soft you'd feel. Been dreaming about it."

"Oh my *god*. I can't believe you're talking like that."

"Believe it and don't ever doubt it."

The assurances fell easily from his lips, surprising him at just how few convictions he'd hung on to once he'd gotten Anna in his arms. All it took was one breathy little laugh against his collarbone and everyone one of his duty-bound burdens vacated the space between his ears until all that was left was what his soul needed to keep the woman in his arms right where she was.

Anna leaned back, removed her glasses, and placed them on the nightstand. He caught her hand before the frames hit the wood. "No, leave them on."

"Why? They'll just get in the way."

Iron brushed his hands around the sides of her neck, then used the backs of them to fan out her glorious hair so it fell about her shoulders. He sifted his fingers through the soft strands, smiling at how he was finally able to touch them without some evil mind mist yanking her away from him again. Then he held her stare and made damn sure she saw the seriousness of his belief, and much more, reflected back at her. "I want you to see what I see. And what I see is a stunning creature who knows what she wants and has had to blind herself in a blurry world to be accepted. You don't need to do that with me, because when you can see clearly—*really* see clearly—you'd be able to tell how just how fucking gorgeous you are."

He didn't wait for an answer, didn't want to hear any more self-doubt creep in or witness her warring with a life she'd known versus a life he was trying to show her. Instead, he slipped her glasses back on her face, cupped her jaw, and sealed his lips to hers.

As he angled his head and took more and more of her into him, every worrisome thought knocking around his noggin vacated in favor of a far more basic and primal incentive: need. It was lust on the winds of logic. Pleasure chasing the most delicious sort of pain. And when Anna squirmed against his cock, rubbing that luscious bottom in time to the drugging pulls of his mouth, he damn near lost it.

Iron palmed her ass and stood, sucking down her sharp moans of approval. There was no fear, no tension in her body or uncertain jerks of meager touches. In this, they were in sync, as they seemed to have always been.

Anna fell onto the bed, but before she tried to scoot herself back to allow him to join her, he halted her movements, hooking his hands beneath her knees.

He knew all too well the ramifications of what came next, of what he *really* wanted to do, and if Anna had been any other woman, that cardigan would have been nothing more than evergreen-colored shreds on his floor hoping for a second life as a bathmat. He knew what he looked like and damn well knew how big he was. And there were times when he used that to his advantage in the bedroom, when only certain types of females could scratch only certain types of itches. One woman, in particular, had made it seem like that was his crowning achievement and offering. A glory only he could provide.

But Iron pushed those thoughts away in favor of the feast before him. Anna flushed and panting, color spreading high in her cheeks that he had put there, looking at him with a fiery desire.

A fiery desire reflecting the topaz flames of his celestial power.

Shit. It was happening.

"Are you in pain?" he asked, a sprout of uncertainty bumping up against the bedrock of his need.

Anna shook her head. "Pain's the furthest thing from my mind. Like, the literal furthest thing."

He squeezed her knees gently. "Are you warm?" By the mages, he had to do this right, had to know if she really wanted this. Already, his fire was punching through his gut, raging to course through his body with unmatched speed.

"Hot."

"But not in pain."

She smiled and then parted her legs, widening the cradle of her hips before him. "Not a bit."

Those three little words of confirmation were all his lust needed to stomp down his worry and pounce.

Iron grabbed her sweater's hem and slid it off her. Fabric? Gone. Bra? Tossed to mages knew where. The leggings went next, then any barrier that prevented him from getting his hands on her bare flesh. Once she was laid out before him, perfect and preening, he moved to kiss her in the one place that had been tugging all his allegiance.

Her lower belly welcomed him with its plushness, the spot that housed a life Anna had trusted him with keeping safe, as well as her own. Iron whispered words against her flesh he knew she couldn't understand or even hear, and that was fine with him. Those words weren't for her. They were for another soul who he one day hoped to meet.

When he lifted his head, Anna's neck was craned as well, and a curious sheen wetted the fiery eyes behind her glasses. He couldn't let himself dwell on the moment too long. No good came from such introspection.

Instead, he grinned, ripped his shirt over his head, and crawled up her body. "If you're tearing up, I have more work to do."

He kissed her again, a quick searing claiming, one just forceful enough to break up the roadblocks behind her eyes and redirect her focus to where he was dragging his mouth next.

Dusty pink nipples stood erect and ready, twin peaks offered at the altar of her full breasts. He palmed her lush flesh carefully, mounding each globe with only as much force as Anna's gasps dictated, and brought his mouth to the taut peeks that seemed to beg for his touch.

"Oh my god," she breathed, hitching her hips higher each time he passed his tongue over a stiffened tip. "They're so fucking sensitive all the goddamn time. You have no idea how distracting it is, but whatever you're doing feels *sooo* good."

Iron smiled against her rib cage and hid his humor beneath a kiss to her sternum. "So, nipple play brings the cursing out of you. Good to know." It was equally distracting on his part because every filthy warning that fell from her lips found its corresponding anchor in a jolt of his pleasure.

"Iron," she whimpered as she dragged her eager fingers toward the fly of his jeans, letting her legs fall open even wider.

It hit him, then. The scent of her arousal was a lightning bolt that forced his fire into overdrive. It was a cataclysmic power that stripped him bare of any higher reasoning and had him pulling away from her eager hands so he could get on his knees with an eagerness of his own. His mouth hovered at the juncture of her thighs before she could let out her next breath.

Then he devoured her with a conqueror's single-mindedness. Even the silken flesh of her hips filling his hands wasn't enough to distract him from the pleasure he sought to wring from her. Iron gave one slow, strong lick, then he did it again in time to the tremors of her thighs bracketing his ears. He chased her moans with blade-like focus, closing his lips around her clit and sucking so there was no quarter. Iron wanted all of her, to capture every passionate cry and shuddering pleasure that had been wasted on a world too limited to appreciate the limitless wonder he cradled in his care.

Iron's angel fire grew hotter in his core as he slid a finger into her, pumping in time to his heartbeat. He risked a peek at her face, just one, just so he could see the spark of confirmation blazing in her eyes—eyes that still reflected the topaz fire of his power.

Anna's passion blew apart when he added a second finger and her entire body trembled through an orgasm as she clamped down on him, tearing free a scream.

Iron's full fire erupted within his core, blazing to life in a heat without flames. He saw it the moment Anna registered the sensation as well. Her eyes widened—eyes that had returned to their natural jade depths—and she reached for him. Powerless to deny her anything, Iron moved up but paused his ascent into her arms when his mouth lingered over her womb. There, he impressed upon it another devout kiss before joining her, enveloping her against him as his fire's nature receded, leaving behind the tingling ripples of its footprint.

He brushed his lips against her slick forehead, relishing the feeling of the woman and wonder beneath him.

"Oh!" A surprised gasp bubbled out of Anna, and he quickly lifted off her, ready to fling himself across the room if need be, when her gentle laugh pulled him back down. It was her smile that did him in for good. Pure brightness and heat infused a mouth that had spent far too much time frowning, and he was done, captured as much as he was captivated.

She must have read the question in his face, because she grabbed one of his hands and brought it down low over her abdomen. A very slight tremor, almost imperceptible if not for his celestial senses, *whooshed* against his palm.

"It's not really a full kick yet. More like how I imagine a goldfish flutter would feel, but it's there." Anna grinned and waggled her eyebrows like a cartoon supervillain. "Someone liked your moves. And speaking of moves . . ."

She was off her back and undoing his belt buckle all while his batty brain was still hung up on the previous thought.

The baby. I felt it.

Anna nearly had his cock free before he gently stilled her hands, remembering her doctor's appointment tomorrow morning and how late it was already. Though he'd love nothing more than to continue, it wouldn't be right. He wouldn't be that guy, the one who took so selfishly at the expense of another. She was tired, though she'd done a hell of a job convincing him otherwise. It was in the speed at which her heart rate slowed and how insistent her heavy eyelids had become.

The fire in her wanted to continue, but her body was putting its foot down.

Iron quickly kissed the resentment away that had been brewing behind her eyes when she perhaps realized why he was pausing their activities. Right on cue, a yawn stretched her jaw wide.

"Let's get some sleep. It's after midnight already, and I want to make sure you have enough energy tomorrow morning to give me the rundown on just how many soon-to-be dads I have to leer at in the waiting room before they fuck off back into their phones."

"Stop being so smart," she said, still accepting the comforter he wrapped her up in. Then he shucked his pants and climbed into bed with her, grabbing her back to his front. She fit in his arms like a cherished memory.

"Don't tell Chrome you said that."

"Why?"

"Because I told him how I beat you in Scrabble, and he's been dying for a reason to test my skills."

"You didn't beat me." Even her insistence had begun tucking itself into bed.

"*Yet*. I didn't beat you *yet*. It was inevitable. Just ran out of time."

"Yeah, because you *kissed* me."

Iron squeezed her midsection, loving the feel of her warm breasts cushioning his forearms. "See? I'm smart. Now go to sleep."

Anna laughed, but there was no malice in it. "You're really going to take me to my OB appointment tomorrow, aren't you?"

"You want me there, then that's where I'll be."

She draped her arms over his and snuggled closer to him. "I want you there," she said softly.

He smiled, turning the lights off with his power. "Wouldn't miss it for the world."

It was the only promise he'd made to her that he knew he could keep.

CHAPTER 23

Anna walked back into the doctor's office waiting room from the bathroom and rejoined Iron in the seat next to him. "Mandatory urine sample before the appointment. Think of it like the coming attractions to a movie. They'll call me in soon."

"Call *us* in."

Iron snatched her hand up and settled it on top of his thigh. It was a possessive gesture that thrilled Anna to no end, especially when the three other men in the waiting room sitting with their partners had all developed unexplained ants in their pants.

And Iron wasn't even wearing the bloody bandage on his neck anymore.

While Anna had been checking in, Iron had stood behind her, so they were back to back, with him facing the rest of the room. She didn't know what happened and could only offer up half an ear lest she pull out the wrong credit card to cover her copay, but when she accepted the urine sample cup from the receptionist and looked back, it was quite a different scene than she was used to.

The three female patients waiting for their appointments all had annoyed looks on their faces, which Anna enjoyed immensely since none of those glares were directed at her for a change. No, they were all aimed at significant others showing the damn near dingiest true colors Anna had ever seen. One man kept trying to desperately hush his partner while she was going on about why Anna was told she'd be seen first, despite the woman arriving before her. Another guy, who was probably only a few inches taller than Anna but was decked out in all sorts of designer finery that made him act two feet taller, immediately vacated his chair and abandoned his wife to examine something suddenly fascinating inside the hallway elevator. And the last man had picked up a magazine off an end table and buried his nose between the pages instead of sweeping another judgmental pass over Anna's lounge attire.

She didn't have the heart to tell the guy he was reading a *Highlights* magazine. Wouldn't want to insult the little kids who came there with their mothers and have them think their favorite doctor's office time-killing material was favored by manboys as well.

A medical assistant opened the door to the waiting room. "Anna Malone?"

"That's me."

"Oh, is this your partner?"

"He's my . . . uh . . ."

"Yes." Iron's declaration slammed down like an asteroid in the small waiting room, casting out ripples strong enough to bring every woman in the vicinity to their knees.

Except the medical assistant, who seemed pleased as punch at the opportunity to escort Iron behind the curtain, so to speak. "Wonderful! Follow me."

As Anna followed behind the woman, with Iron bringing up the rear, she overheard a sharp slap echo from the waiting room along with the words "Why don't you ever pipe up like that for me?"

"Here we are. The doctor will be in shortly. Anna, you know the drill."

"Sure do."

Once the door closed, Iron asked, "What's the drill?"

Anna kicked off her shoes and hopped back onto the examination table. "Weight and blood pressure, to start. Lots of poking and prodding around my belly. Some abdominal measurements, and I believe they'll do an ultrasound this time around. It won't take long, but hopefully, I'll get sent home with some pictures."

She said that last part with a smile, but Iron's far-off look had her second-guessing the whole outing. His cheeks had taken on a slightly redder complexion, and his gaze bounced around the modest exam room as he took in the cherubic artwork of mothers and their newborns right alongside an anatomy chart that made her embarrassed on his behalf.

Was it too much? Had it been a mistake to drag him to this? There was decidedly very little that was sexy about pregnancy, especially considering what was brought up during these appointments. The topics du jour tended toward fluids. Lots and lots of fluids. Fluids they took out of her body, fluids that left her body (some without her say so), fluids above the belt, and fluids below the belt . . . just a whole lot of talk about liquid matter in general. It was as unsexy as a wet diaper, which, yeah, oddly enough, had also been brought up at one point.

For the first time since Anna had been coming there, she finally understood why all the guys in the waiting room always seemed more interested in the post-appointment lunch reservation than the appointment itself.

Why in all that was holy had she thought Iron, who had already acknowledged the temporary nature of whatever the hell their attraction was garnering, would want to come with her to her OB-frickin'-GYN appointment? Would he see her differently if he knew what was in store for her over the next several months?

"You know, it's not too late to bail if this is making you uncomfortable. You can wait outside, if you prefer. It's honestly not that interesting. The doctor just—"

The door to her exam room was halfway open before Dr. Li started knocking on it to announce her arrival. Anna bristled and bit back a curse. Why the hell did they always do that?

"Hi, Anna."

"Hi, Dr. Li."

"I heard you brought a guest today. So exciting. Quite a few of my patients bring loved ones to their sixteen-week appointments. Well, any time between sixteen and twenty weeks, really. What can I say? Family photos tend to bring out the crowd." Dr. Li walked over to a dispenser on the wall and shot a dollop of hand sanitizer into her palm before rubbing it in, then gestured toward the scale. "All right. Let's get you measured, chat a bit about how you're feeling, what to expect over the next few weeks, and then we'll take a look at our little lemon."

"I thought it was an avocado."

Anna had just put her second socked foot on the scale when the sound of Iron's gruff voice debating the fruit-shaped merits of her baby nearly sent the scale into full tilt. She smiled and, after Dr. Li jotted down her weight, returned to the table, laid back, and lifted her sweater over her belly. "Maybe it's the size of a navel orange or something."

Iron scooted his chair closer to her. "Not sure what kind of navel oranges you're eating. Some of those things are the size of small rodents."

"A persimmon, then?"

"Nah," he said, taking her hand and twining his fingers with hers. "A few varieties of persimmon can be weirdly flat, like if an animal sat on it or something. I don't like the idea of your baby being so misshapen."

"True," she said, nodding seriously while Dr. Li measured her. "Although, I can't think of a fruit more misshapen than an avocado, to be frank. Maybe a strawberry, but we've already passed that stage of fruit development."

"Damn. And here I thought I was being original." Iron winked at her, sending an entire meadow's worth of butterflies alight in her abdomen. The baby even seemed to get a kick—ha! —out of Iron's teasing. Now that Anna knew what to look for, she smiled every time a school of fish swam through her lower belly, as it did just then.

"You two are a riot," Dr. Li said. "I hope he can make it to your appointments more often."

"Me, too," Anna said, stunned by just how much she meant it.

Anna and Dr. Li chatted more about how the past few weeks had been going for her. Yes, she was mostly out of the morning sickness loop. No, she didn't have any sciatica pain flare-ups. Yes, she was eating well and paying attention to the nutrients her body needed. (Yes, Anna occasionally considered the sugar in her cereal a nutrient. No, she did not tell Dr. Li that, and thankfully, neither did Iron, who just arched a brow when that particular topic entered the conversation.)

Then Dr. Li pulled out the tube of ultrasound gel. "Are we ready to see your baby?"

"Definitely."

After what had to be a punch-bowl-sized amount of goop was applied to her belly, Anna squeezed Iron's hand as they waited for Dr. Li to lift the curtain on the star of the show. There was a fair amount of hunting and pecking on the doctor's part, owing to the little one's size, and then it was front and center in all its black-and-white grainy glory.

"Now," Dr. Li cut in. "Before I go any further, you've previously indicated that you don't want to know the gender, Anna. Is that still the case?"

"Yes, that's correct."

Iron rubbed his thumb over hers, drawing her attention back to him. "Why not?" he whispered.

She shrugged. "No reason."

He eyed her warily and gave her a look that told her they'd be circling back to that conversation, but he thankfully dropped it for the time being and returned his attention to the monitor.

"Heart rate is going strong, and I'm happy to report that all arms, legs, fingers, and toes seem to be accounted for. Bones are a nice bright white, which tells me they're forming nicely. Ears aren't quite in the final position yet, so you still have some time to continue debating what fruit you think the baby's most likely to resemble before it could hear you and possibly take offense." Dr. Li winked and actually managed to get a chuckle out of Iron.

But when Anna looked back at the angel, all she got was the strong profile of his jaw. So engrossed was he in what was filling the screen that he'd even let his grip on her hand loosen a bit, to the point where she'd begun tickling the underside of his palm to see whether he'd notice.

He hadn't.

Oh, no. This was dangerous. Anna knew better than to drink in the sight of Iron this way. She'd grown used to his attention, however uncomfortable it'd made her at first. But now that another beautiful little life seemed intent on stealing it away from her, she wasn't sure what to make of it.

Hers was a path of just-enoughs and right-under-the-wires. She had a house and could support herself, but the word *barely* tended to rear its ugly head most months where that was concerned. She wasn't old by society's standards, nor was she considered young enough to be a young mother. She was good at what she did and had built a satisfying career she could do from anywhere. But unfortunately, because she *could* do it from anywhere, she more often than not chose to do it from her hole-in-the-wall office, where sunlight and vitamin D were optional because the only doctor she saw regularly wasn't checking her vitamin D (provided all was well with the baby, which it seemed to be).

And here was Iron, holding her hand, meeting her baby, and welcoming her into a family that didn't usually take well to outsiders. He may otherwise leave her once the soul bond was fully enacted and he could finally return to wherever he came from. He was a man of responsibility, regardless of emotions. She knew that now. If she asked for it, she suspected he'd likely go anywhere with her, whether or not he wanted to.

The realization was enough to dim the cheery glow that had cocooned them ever since they'd been shut into the exam room together.

Dr. Li continued her docent's tour of Anna's uterus, touching on relevant phrases like *stretch mark prevention* and *staying hydrated*. But it all turned into dull background noise, like the constant roar of plane engines—necessary to fill the silence so Anna's other senses could focus on what rose to the surface.

Duty was etched on Iron's features, in the proud slope of his brow and the taut lines of his jaw. But conflict lived there, too. It was in the dusty shadows beneath his eyes, the ones that were often overpowered by his distracting gaze and rich beard.

His presence in the dinky chair next to her broke her heart as much as it held it together, painting whatever future visions that occasionally flashed through her mind with a skim coat of sludge.

She feared she could either be right or happy, but not both.

"Here's your souvenir. Enjoy, you two, and I'll see you in four weeks."

A square slip of photo paper danced in Anna's periphery,

held out between Dr. Li's fingertips, but before Anna cleared her thoughts enough to realize what it was and take it, Iron had already accepted the offering.

"We'll be back," he said, never lifting his eyes from the image of her baby.

That image, the one she mentally snapped and stored of Iron holding what he could of their unlikely future together, would have to be enough to last her for however long until his conviction finally caught up with his character.

Until then, she was happy living in a fantasy, the one that all started with whimsical dreams and wings.

CHAPTER 24

Iron wanted to punch something, which wasn't the usual reaction one should have when staring at an ultrasound printout that his soul bond had propped up against his dashboard while he drove her home. Never, in all his years, had he thought that something so grainy and nondescript could hold such a significant place behind his breastbone. When the doctor first pulled the image up on the monitor and he saw this white blob starting to look less like an amorphous mass and more like a tiny human bobbing to the groove of its mother's heartbeat, it twisted a perspective he'd never had the luxury of examining too closely.

What if I stayed?

And even more concerning . . .

What would that future look like if I did?

Iron gripped the steering wheel more tightly as he turned onto the road that led to Anna's house. Beside him, she was cheerfully playing with his sound system, making damn sure he knew how much of a crime it was that he still listened to *terrestrial* radio, whatever the hell that meant. She could have chastised him for anything, the color of his leather seats, the angle at which he kept his heating vents, his complete lack of fast food containers littering his back seat—which, yeah, he could totally see her complaining about. He would have happily listened to all of it if it kept her smiling and stroking that picture while she sat next to him, dreaming in safety of the wonders that would soon come her way.

Fuck if he didn't want to experience every single one of those wonders with her, even if they were never really possibilities for long. At best, he could promise a few months, and at worst, well, he and his brothers had lived lifetimes with mortals never knowing about their existence. It wouldn't be that hard to get gone for good, especially when a golden ribbon had been decked across the finish line at the end of the exit ramp they'd all been falling over themselves to reach for years.

Too bad for him he'd seen that exit ramp before, and there had already been a time long ago when he'd been tempted to turn off it prematurely. Abandon his brothers, his mission, all of it, and just opt out of a duty he'd lost faith in ever being able to fulfill.

That ended about as well as a nuclear bomb detonation, one he still hadn't recovered from.

Then why the fuck was his mind drifting toward those promises again?

Iron pulled his truck up to Anna's house and killed the engine. She'd already plucked the ultrasound picture off his dash and had begun hopping down out of his truck, which must have felt like falling from a pole vault jump given how small she was in comparison to his vehicle's lift. Jesus Christ, couldn't she wait for him to at least come around to her side and help her down? Did the woman *want* a twisted ankle?

"You know, I normally would have just tacked it up in my office next to my window, but that just doesn't feel welcoming enough. Work is work, and for the most part, I don't like to go into my office when I'm not on the clock, so maybe I could hang it in the kitchen? I would like to see the thing regularly. Though I worry steam and aerosolized food grease would wreak havoc on the picture. That is, if I ever decide to actually use the cast-iron pans above my stove for anything other than decoration at this point."

Anna bounced up her front steps with all the exuberance and, to Iron's great frustration, lack of care similar to a puppy who didn't know its bones weren't connected yet because its growth plates were still too soft. Oh, he'd cleared a good path for her after the snowstorm, but that didn't mean things didn't ice over in the mornings, especially at those higher altitudes. He'd even put a bucket of salt out for her next to her front door —a bucket whose lid still sat askew at the exact fucking angle he'd left it five days ago.

He shoved his fists into his pockets, muttered some choice curses, and followed her into the house. He had to kick a sizable chunk of ice out of the way before he walked through the front door, hating how his gaze kept landing on a million and one things he could improve for her if his options weren't tied up in his duty to his family. There was a small water spot on the living room ceiling that had grown slightly since he'd been there last, the pilot light ports on her stoves needed a good cleaning, and don't get him started on that fucking shed out back.

Iron shook his head and tried to unclench his fingers before the indentations they left in his palms became permanent. This wasn't his place, even if the mages had thrown the two of them together for some reason. His place was, and always had been, by his brothers' sides, defending the actions and intelligence of celestial mages who'd, lately, occupied his mind far more than he suspected he ever did for them. If he had, he wouldn't have had to lose pieces of his soul when—

"You seem awfully far away for someone who's only ten feet from me."

He looked up to see Anna standing in front of the hallway,

her jubilant features from a moment ago now sagging with a frown that looked all kinds of wrong on her face, not the least of which because he was likely the asshole who'd put it there. She'd already changed into her standard uniform of comfy lounge pants, thick cozy socks, and an oversized T-shirt that practically swallowed her whole. On any other day, he would have thought how she dressed around him was a testament to how comfortable he made her feel. Now, all he saw was someone that much more in need of a protective outer shell.

"You have any clients this afternoon?"

"No. I took off today because of my doctor's appointment. Figured I wouldn't be in the mood to remind people about good nutritional choices when I've just been measured and weighed like a 4-H heifer and am thinking of diving spoon-first into some ice cream."

"Ice cream? It's, like, two degrees outside."

A single razor-sharp brow lifted toward her hairline with a resolute speed that gave him just enough time to rethink the next words out of his mouth. "And?"

"And . . . if you tell me the flavor you want, I'd be happy to excavate it from your freezer for you before I head out. That icebox you've got is one Tetris brick away from collapsing. You sure there aren't any body parts in there I should be worried about finding?" He meant it as a joke, a small quip set to diffuse and deflect any of that prying gaze Anna was so good at throwing his way.

But, like goddamn always, his efforts fell short when it came to her.

"Why would you head out?" The question speared him through his core hard enough to send his fire scuttling to safety inside him.

"Figured you'd want some space after your appointment."

Anna put her hands on her hips. "And if any of those words held even a modicum of truth, I'd have told you that a woman does not invite a man who is not the biological father of her baby to her frickin' OB appointment without planning to spend the rest of the afternoon *with that man.*" Then she folded her arms over her chest. "What's going on?"

"Why don't you want to know the gender?" It was the question that had been bouncing around his mind all through the ride home and one he hadn't been able to figure out an answer for.

"What?"

He struggled to keep the regret out of his voice, but in doing so, he somehow managed to let sparks of his indignation punch through. "Why don't you want to know? There's got to be a reason, because this is America. It's default information overload all the goddamn time. So, what makes you so different here? You're not the type to love surprises, so why don't you want to know the gender of the life you're carrying? Seems like it might make things easier with the planning and all."

Anna hugged herself tighter, and he waited, *waited* for the blast of censure she was sure to fire at him for running off his dumb-ass mouth to a pregnant woman *about* her pregnancy, as if he had any skin in the game on that front. And if he'd honestly thought it'd help her get a clean, deserving shot at him, he'd open his coat and flannel wide enough so she couldn't miss.

But then her eyes tipped toward the floor, and he didn't overlook the sheen that coated them before she stole all that sad sparkle away from him.

"What if I'm not enough?" She whispered her confession to the floorboards.

Iron could have been in the track of an entire solar system's worth of space garbage and, after hearing her heartbreaking words, still wouldn't have had the wherewithal to move out the damn way. "Anna, you can't be serious."

"Of course I'm serious." She swiped at a tear while all he could do was stand there, horrified that he'd made her cry in the first place but far too dumbstruck to work out which problem to tackle first—all of which he feared he had a hand in starting. "Since the day Travis left me, I told myself I was better off, because I wouldn't let that asshole within sniffing distance of my new family, and him leaving was the best of both worlds. I promised myself that I would be such a magnificent goddamn mother that there would be no room for my child to ever wonder about who helped create them. I'd be the best. The best entrepreneur, have the most successful online nutrition counseling service in the state, always be there for my baby whenever they needed me. I would smother that child with enough love to squeeze out Travis from the picture entirely, until he was never even a thought in our lives to begin with."

The conviction in her voice felt forced but well used, like a coat of armor that never fit quite right but had been called into countless battles regardless. Her strength was astounding and totally fucking heartbreaking.

"But when my doctor first asked me whether I wanted to know the gender, there was something inside me that kept scratching at whether I might be wrong. How will I react if I see Travis in my child? Will I see his judgmental attitude shaming me behind my son's eyes or his coloring monopolizing every prominent feature of my daughter to the point that people don't even recognize her as mine? I thought that, if it was a surprise, at least I'd have to find a way to deal with the hand I'd be dealt and that maybe some of my anxieties would be stripped away. But what if all my intentions and self-talk fly out the window as soon as I find out what kind of baby I'm giving birth to? What if I'm not really strong enough to do this on my own and all my motivational mumblings wind up feeling as hollow as they sound?"

His heart finally finished splintering. Just full-on shattered into a thousand shards that scampered further away from him on the peals of her pain. There was no hope of collecting them again, for he feared that whatever he'd manage to save would be so battered and bruised that there wouldn't be any love left in them to care for the child that desperately needed the love it previously housed.

In the absence of anything useful to wield against a foe he had no experience fighting, he offered up the only thing he could think of.

Iron closed the space between them, gliding across her living room in two giant strides. His hands flew to the sides of her face, offering his strength even as he thumbed away her tears. Just the sight of her heartache was enough to send his heart, whatever was left of it, into a painful spasm. She didn't deserve this, and he was the piece of shit who had pressured her into unraveling a hurt he'd not known she'd carried, all to satisfy his curiosity.

"Listen to me, Anna," he said, softly shaking his insistence into his embrace. "You are so much more than enough."

He couldn't help himself, couldn't hold back anymore. There were a thousand scenarios that saw him turning on his bootheels and leaving her to a life he logically knew her to be better off in. But only one of them had her in his arms, pulling her closer, while he stroked the smooth skin down the sides of her neck, doing his bumbling best to massage away the tension he'd brought into her home.

Only one scenario saw him slanting his lips across hers, absorbing the anguish of her tears into himself.

Only one scenario had her responding, her arms curling around his neck, returning his possessive embrace with a claim of her own, or him lifting her high against his chest and carrying her to her bedroom.

If she didn't think she was enough, he was going to spend whatever time he had left in the mortal realm showing her how very wrong she was.

CHAPTER 25

It was on the tip of Anna's tongue to ask Iron to kiss her—or beg, to be frank. It would have been a million times easier to get lost in the heady flavor of him than to slice open more of the wound she'd been trying to cover up ever since she found out she was pregnant. She never expected him to silence that noise by stealing bits of her broken soul into him. Hadn't even known that was possible, just like so many things when it came to this man.

With the mental clamor gone, or at least silenced for the time being, she dove headfirst into what *she* finally wanted.

Anna let Iron carry her far away from whatever anxiety had spilled out of her mouth and onto her living room floor. Whether it evaporated into the ether or chose to fester into a larger problem for her to deal with later, she didn't care. All that mattered was Iron's mouth on hers and the feel of his solid strength supporting her.

Iron kicked her bedroom door closed behind them. The slam of the wood was a definitive statement, shutting out her problems while barring entrance to anything that wasn't supporting her body with his strength. But when Iron didn't immediately carry her over to the bed like she expected, she forced herself to pull away from him. The look etched on his face nearly stopped her heart.

Whatever master had previously taken their chisel and hammer to Iron's features had replaced their tools with lust-fueled flames. A tempered need flashed high in his eyes, which had yet to land on any part of her and *not* ignite her skin with reciprocal force. Anna blinked, then focused her gaze on where her forearms rested over his shoulders, double-checking for heat that was surely rippling off her skin.

Nothing. Nothing except a frenzied desire to rip off the far too many layers of clothing he still wore, including his coat, and run her scorched palms over every mound of muscle she'd only ever dreamed of touching.

Which had been fever dreams, clearly, because holy shit, it was hot in her bedroom. Even the air felt arid, and that was quite the problem, because if he kissed her like that again, she was going to need entire atmospheres of the stuff just to keep up with him.

With a groan she felt in every single one of her vertebrae, he attacked the side of her neck with a renewed enthusiasm that had her tumbling over whatever cliff he'd brought her to. "You have no idea how much I've wanted you." He palmed her ass, spreading and massaging her through her pants, maneuvering her right where he desired. When he squeezed the flesh there, gripping her with just the right amount of force, her pulse kicked higher against his lips. "Mmm, perfect. I want your wild heartbeats, Anna. I want everything about you, all the frantic, messy bits no one sees. Let my arms be that safe place for you, where you can come apart without consequences."

"Yes," she breathed, shocked at the emotion in her voice. She wanted all of that. *God*, she wanted all of that, to hold Iron in her messy world and be held in return, free of any rebukes or reprimands. She wanted—

"I need the sun on your skin."

Iron whirled them both around so fast, her thoughts and words had no time to catch up. The temperature shifted on her next breath, and then her back was against her bedroom window, her ass on top of the dresser. A sharp gasp was robbed from her throat. Then he was kissing her again, deeper than before. She was lost in the pleasure of it, of the frosted glass chilling her from behind while the heat from Iron scorched her front. It was impossible to keep it all straight, even as her body tried its former-gifted-student best to make sense of what was being asked of it.

Together, they slid their hands over each other, attacking and peeling off whatever got in their way. Iron's heavy coat hit the floor first, followed by whatever remained of his flannel shirt and tank beneath it. She was about to lift off her T-shirt when his large hands covered hers. "No. Let me take care of you."

She didn't have a chance to object—though, c'mon, like she would have? For the first time since she'd been pregnant, all her body parts had finally gotten on the same page. Every nerve ending snapped into sync, standing up to take notice when Iron slid his hands gently beneath her shirt, then lifted it over her head, along with her lounge bra.

Bare before each other from the waist up, Anna breathed through the still moment between them while basking in the heated glory of Iron's strength. If his face had been chiseled from the granite of the mountains around him, his chest had been carved from the boulders beneath. She sat forward, eager to slide her fingers down his wide chest just to memorize the paths each valley and divot charted. Thickly capped shoulders, sloping biceps, exquisite contours. She wanted to discover them all and experience what it felt like to be protectively wrapped in the armor of such a man. His physique was a curious wonder for the ages that her questing fingers couldn't get enough of. And the heat. *God!* The stuff radiated off him like a furnace.

She was just about to say as much when he leaned forward and pressed a kiss to her breastbone, then swept his lips over the sensitive skin of her breasts to toy with her nipples.

Damn. The bastard remembered.

"Oh god!" she cried, bucking against his head, pushing more of her into his mouth. When he pulled away, he blew cool air across one heated peak, before repeating the delicious torture to the other.

Anna's smile was teased wider with the fade of the sting, and she sat up higher, eager to see what he'd do next with that wicked tongue.

Then a prism of colors landed on her belly, a byproduct of the sunlight beating through the window behind her. Iron noticed it too, then traced his fingers over the small rainbow, which was no bigger than her pinky. A knowing smile teased his lips. "The sun's in on the secret, too."

"What secret's that?"

"Knowing how much the light suits you. It craves you, Anna. It would share with you all its beauty if you let it."

"You can't say stuff like that to a pregnant woman," she replied, cupping her palm around his stony chin, fighting to speak through the tension in her throat.

He leaned into her caress. "Why not?"

"Because it messes with our brain chemistry. It'll make me want to think of spending time in the light with you, and this is supposed to be transactional. Temporary. And that kind of talk feels more—"

"Permanent."

The word hovered around them, suspended above the flames that crackled unseen between their panting bodies. It charged the air and bolstered every breath feeding into Anna's lungs. And like a volley of atoms reaching critical mass, the release was inevitable and one she knew she'd never come back from.

Iron spun her over, pushing her onto her knees on top of the dresser. Then he caressed her bare arms and positioned them out in front of her so her palms were flat on the frosty window glass. There was nowhere to hide from the sun. It draped over every part of her, from her exposed breasts to her quivering belly, bathing her in an existence that she'd not let herself dream of revisiting for fear of what it would reveal. A broken, discarded woman whose judgment think tank was always running on E.

"Keep your hands here," Iron said, his words pushing back the fog of doubt creeping in, anchoring her to the present she craved. "The light needs all of you, Anna. *I* need all of you."

The heart in her chest pumped wildly against her rib cage as he curled his fingers into the waistband of her pants and slowly slid them and her underwear down over her hips. Carefully, tenderly, he helped her out of them, including her socks, until she was completely stripped save for the goose bumps prickling her flesh.

Behind her, his belt buckle tinkled, clothing rustled, and the stiff denim that had abraded the backs of her thighs a moment ago was gone, replaced by a stolen kiss deposited at the base of her spine.

"Iron." His name became a plea on her lips, a supplication to both begin and end the lives he'd uncovered inside her. She wanted her old one to die so she could be reborn with the knowledge of what it meant to be sustained by this man.

His fingers traced a path along her inner thighs, then stilled when they reached the slickness that waited for him. She could feel the virile heat spiraling from his body, urging every magnificent sensation that had yet to be fully realized between them higher. His knees hit the floor, and his mouth took her to heights she'd never dreamed of. He ravaged her wet heat with a devotion that could only be perceived by the absence of all else. With his mouth on her and his appreciative moans sending shivers everywhere throughout her body, she was lost and limp, tossed about a choppy sea of pleasure with only Iron's strong hands on her hips as an anchor.

She came apart on his tongue in wave after wave of satiated bliss. But just when she thought to let her delicious exhaustion claim her and allow her to crumple to her bedroom floor in an orgasm-replete puddle, Iron stood and placed his hands on the backs of hers, holding her to the window. The dark leather wrist bracers he always wore were little more than smudges pressed against the bright canvas he'd created.

"I'm not done with you yet."

It was ten kinds of exhilarating to be such a singular focus of his attention, to pant with need in time to the shivers he sent down her spine, knowing he'd make good on every promise he bestowed on her body.

"Please, Iron. I need you. It's all too much."

"Anything you want, it's yours. Always."

"I want you. All of you."

"You have me."

The tip of his cock pressed against her entrance, robbing the breath from both of them. He sank in farther, stretching and filling her with its exquisite invasion. The moan that left her lips fogged over the glass in front of her, creating a slick surface for Iron to interlock their fingers against.

He was at her ear, commanding her attention and forcing her to look at him with that blazing gaze of his. It was no longer a mix of brown and hazel, but that of the burning topaz that came out when his fire needed to play. Then he pounded into her with purpose, pulling heat from within her soul higher to the surface with each thrust of her breasts against the glass. Anna couldn't look away from him, even as he played her body like a finely tuned concert instrument. Her skin slicked over with sweat, and a fresh bloom of warmth coiled tighter in her belly every time he sank into her.

Still, he pierced her with his stare. Always watching. Always devouring. Always demanding she do the same.

Each time he seated himself fully, her body trembled with the fulfillment of all his promises. Every kiss, caress, and claiming brought something out in her, foreign feelings that lit her soul from within, until it felt like her very skin was pulsing with a fire that instinctively would never harm her, nor would it stop from erupting around her.

Anna leaned toward Iron, straining to kiss him as he sent her diving over an edge she'd not known prior to this man. Before his mouth captured hers, however, swallowing down a searing orgasm pulled from a place she'd never ventured, power rippled over his body. Flesh turned to armored iron beneath her fingertips. He pulled away, growling his release as he slammed his hips against her with unmatched ferocity.

Her body trembled around his cock, her core clutching him even tighter through pulses that somehow blinded her. Brilliant light flooded her small bedroom, its energy seeming to spark from her core connected to his. At her back, his fire erupted. Blue electric flames rippled over his metallic body as he let out a roar into her neck that could have toppled mountain ranges.

Anna collapsed back against his chest as the final pulses left both their bodies. The flames subsided, his armor gone as quickly as it appeared, leaving behind a slew of answers to questions she'd never gotten the courage to ask.

Iron held her back to him, curling around her curved form like a protective shell. Then he lifted her and rolled them both into the bed next to them. They lay there, flat on their backs, caring not for the mechanics of covers or how they were going to chase what they'd just done with some big spoon, little spoon consolations.

Anna turned to face him, but he was already looking at her, a stern expression taking over the wonder she'd hoped to see there.

Then she realized he wasn't looking at her, so much as her wrist, which lay next to her ear facing up.

Anna reached for his hand, knowing full well what was likely now tattooed on hers based on what Iron had told her about the soul bond ritual, and kissed each of his knuckles. And when she was finished with one hand, she moved to the other. She didn't stop there. She kissed everything she could. His pecs, biceps, the caps of his shoulders, that delicious divot in his chin, the perpetual furrow between his brows. All of it. She wanted to taste and own all of it.

Then he finally wrapped his arms around her and held her to his chest. The heart hammering back against her ear was the sweetest rhythm she'd ever heard next to the heartbeat of her unborn child, and one she'd happily guard for as long as he'd let her, even if it meant wading through the waters of mortal overwhelm in a supernatural world.

"I've got you," she whispered against his neck. He tightened his hold on her, still shaking with the aftershocks of all they'd just shared and all that he'd gained. She kissed his jaw again. "Whatever happens, I've got you, too."

CHAPTER 26

Iron stood before Anna's bathroom mirror, tracking the rivulets of water dripping off his beard onto his bare chest. The droplets peppered their points home every time he splashed his face with another frigid dose of the stuff.

He finally had his fire back and had swept up Anna as his full soul bond in the process. Strange. He thought it would feel far different somehow, to share not only his strength with another person but his innate celestial makeup as well. He didn't know what to expect, really, but nothing short of a full-on Macy's Thanksgiving Day Parade seemed appropriate, complete with nationwide marching bands and Broadway performances. After all, when one had been on the hunt for solutions to literal world-ending problems for longer than mortals had a metric to measure it, you kind of expected to feel . . . *something*. At the very least, a sense of relief or achievement.

Instead, all he felt was . . . complete but not the satisfying sort. Not the kind of completion one enjoyed after ticking off tasks on a list or finding the right food storage container lid to go with its mate. No, this completion was more finite, more absolute.

It was the end to a soul's endless search and the eternal rest of a restless power long starved.

Anna.

Iron shut off the faucet, wiped any lingering chill from his skin lest it travel to hers, and hurried back to his mate.

Fuck, his *mate*. His soul bond. There was a ring to it that, for so long, he'd only associated with others, but now that phrase held a weight that made him rethink his allegiances or, at the very least, reprioritize the hell out of them. She'd set him free, released his full fire. How, by the eternal wisdom of the prime mages, was he supposed to still go to work and do his fucking job like his world didn't now hang on whatever the woman in that bed needed?

It was a unique kind of cruelness, to finally know such a connection and freedom, only to have it placed on hold while you went off to fight the good fight no mortal would even know whether you won or lost.

Glory had never been the endgame, but Iron was beginning to wonder whether the duty he'd pledged his life to had been misplaced.

Iron turned the corner and was about to enter the bedroom when Anna's serene form slowed his momentum, yanking him to a halt. He leaned his shoulder against the doorframe and smiled, marveling at the voracious creature who'd trapped him in her bed and kept him there for the better part of the afternoon.

Half-draped in the comforter, with a lone foot peeking out at the base of the bed, Anna looked like she'd wrestled with an alligator and had not only won the match but convinced the creature to gleefully turn its hide into a pair of boots for the privilege of worshipping at her feet. Half of her long copper hair coiled around her outstretched forearm, while the other half sprawled across the pillow he'd just been using. Her bare shoulders and flushed complexion still bore the markings of their recent exertions. And though he was man enough to acknowledge that her mesmerizing glow could have been attributed to her pregnancy as much as his rather thorough attentions, he couldn't be mad at it. She was a vision of the dreams he never wanted to stop having and the desires he'd been too afraid to voice.

But what he *could* be mad at was the disturbed furrow between her brow and the faraway look in her eyes that had her ten seconds away from mindlessly twisting the ends of her hair into snarls.

She looked lost, like a wandering listless thing, and his heart seized at the sight, worried about how far her mind might wander away from him.

"You can't do that," he said, hoping to penetrate her deep thoughts.

Focus sharpened her eyes, dragging them away from wherever she'd gone. "Do what?"

"Go places I can't follow you."

That serene smile returned to her lips, the one he'd coaxed out of her earlier when he kissed the space between every single one of her vertebrae before entering her again. It was one of many memories that would color the remainder of his days when the darkness became impenetrable.

She lifted the covers aside, treating him to all that luscious bare skin, and welcomed him to join her again.

That intoxicating woman could teach courses on how to convince mountains to move and make a killing by upselling her methods for getting stubborn horses to drink as well. Before she took her next breath, Iron was beneath the covers and had her against him, with his forearms bracketing her ribs and snuggled beneath her breasts.

It had quickly become his favorite position.

Anna sighed and ran the pad of her finger over the swirl of glowing gold on the inside of her wrist that was only visible when she held it out to the sunlight streaming in from the window. His heart still kicked up at the sight of it.

"What was it again? Your celestial name?"

"Daegan."

"Daegan," she repeated. "I like it. It suits you."

"It suits a ghost. I haven't been called that in quite some time. Not sure I could even respond to it anymore."

Anna's touch slowed, then her palm covered the tattoo entirely. "You don't like it?"

"No, it's not that." He grabbed her hand, turned it over, and kissed his apology along the pad of her palm. "Just reminds me of things I'd rather not think about at times. But not you. Never you. I haven't been able to get you out of my mind since you stole my sleep that first night." Then he nipped at the flesh there, forcing her fingers to curl around his jaw just the way he liked. "Little thief that you are."

It was true, all of it, and that shocked him as much as it soothed him.

Anna indulged him with a loving caress down his beard, and damn if he didn't have a new appreciation for that tail-wagging shit dogs always did to get their humans to pet them. "Does it have something to do with why you always wear these?" She took her hand back and tapped out an entreaty along the leather of his bracers.

Perhaps it was the soft sadness in her voice or the way he despised how he'd made her feel like she needed to walk on eggshells around him. Whatever it was, he didn't want it to linger in these few moments of bliss, tainting the happiness they'd both finally found.

Iron shifted Anna slightly so he could have full use of his arms. Then, crosshatch by crosshatch, he unstrung the leather cords that fastened his cuffs and covered skin no mortal had ever seen.

When he peeled them off, he was beyond grateful Anna

didn't gasp or make some exclamation over the state of his wrists. He'd never been one for pity and wouldn't know what to do with it if someone were to fling it at him.

Anna's care and compassion, however, was an entirely different brand of emotional weapon, one he had no way to prepare against. She didn't move, didn't squirm, didn't try to lift his arms closer for her inspection. She didn't try to run her gentle fingers over the mangled skin or, mages help him, kiss away whatever hurt she perceived to be there.

Instead, she stayed quiet, waiting for him to explain a set of circumstances no one outside of his brothers knew about.

And he'd give her what she wanted. He knew now he always would.

"Centuries ago, I loved a mortal woman." He tested the weight of the words on the air, half convinced they'd turn into spears that Anna would want to heave right back at him. When that didn't happen and his soul bond just lay in his arms, patiently listening, if not slightly more tense, he tossed the rest of his reservations aside and continued removing the stones that he'd piled up around his past.

"Her name was Abigail, and she lived in a village not too far from here. She was a horsewoman and worked with her father and brothers to breed the beasts and sell them to the highest bidder. Her family was well known for being the best of what they offered but also for being equally aloof. Abigail never ventured into town much or had many friends. But she always had her horses. Looking back on it, that should have told me all I needed to know about her. She had a thing for beasts, and at the time, I had a thing for raven-haired beauties."

"Well, who would blame you?" Anna offered in her achingly helpful way.

"Shhh," he said against her forehead, brushing a kiss along her hairline. "There's no need for that. Save your sweetness. It was a long time ago." Before she could argue, he grabbed her hand and began stroking his celestial symbol on the inside of her wrist, offering up the only distraction he could think of that would help him get through what he'd promised himself he'd share with her.

"Abigail saw me as the mountain of brawn I was and had no problem getting her fill from a dangerous man. The charmers had only recently begun to settle into the colony that would eventually become New Hampshire, and there was an air of disquiet among the people. No one ever really knew who was friend or foe, and as Abigail and her family did business with everyone, she wasn't quite so discerning when it came to her lovers. She was greedy and liked her sex flavored with all the roughness she expected to come with bedding a brute of my size. She'd never had an interest in slow passion or furtive caresses. Her only interest was in my strength and my cock and how I could use both to thrill and excite her."

"That doesn't sound like you at all."

"Again, it was a different time, and I was a different person. More bloodthirsty, more desperate to slay charmers so I might move on to hunting for what I really craved: my fire and my home. I am . . . not that man anymore. But back then, I thought I'd come to love Abigail, that she would ultimately be my soul bond, the one who would set my fire free and deliver to me my full powers. You have to understand, my brothers and I didn't know then all that we know now about the bond. I was unaware of how the progression of intimate connections worked and how our twin sparks spoke to each other, only that they must surely exist and make themselves known at some point. Despite our many physical encounters with no signals revealing themselves, I was still convinced Abigail was my mate and that it would just take time for things to be realized."

Iron swallowed hard and gripped Anna tighter. "The area where her village was located is where the old Chlor-Chem Labs site is now."

Anna turned her head toward him. "Isn't that place a Super-fund redevelopment project? I always got the impression it was all contaminated land at this point."

"It is, and because of its lack of mortal interference over the last several decades, it's one of the locations Cyro used as a base of operations. It was where Rhode was being held captive before we got him out of there."

Anna burrowed farther against him. "That's awful."

"It was just one of the many atrocities Cyro had a hand in at that location." He forced himself to look at the puckered skin snaking over his wristbone. "One winter night, the charmers had grown particularly bold. They raided Abigail's village, slashing the throats of every mortal they could find just to watch each soul's light bleed slowly from their necks. Every soul snuffed out by a charmer is robbed of its opportunity to return its spark to the Eternal Flame, weakening the power of the Empyrean. It's our great plight and what my brothers and I have fought to prevent for so long. I thought I was in love with Abigail, that our souls' sparks would eventually find each other, giving me my full power along with my soul bond. When the raid started, I was screaming her name, searching frantically for her. And then I found her, clutched against the chest of an apex who had its bone knife to her throat."

Anna inhaled softly. "You don't have to say anything more. I can imagine what—"

"No, you can't," he growled, hissing at the memory as much as his former self. "I couldn't reach her in time. My fire had already been drained in the earlier fighting. The bastard knew this. I flew toward him anyway, my flaming ax held high, but he was quicker. The knife he slid across her throat just finished its arc as my weapon came down on his shoulder, cleaving his arm from his body."

"Oh, god."

"All three of us hit the ground at the same time. I scrambled for Abigail, screaming as her soul's light left her body and was slowly released into the smoky air above. I waited for it to come and find me, certain that my soul's own light would finally be revealed and join with hers so I might save her. But her light never reached for mine, never even attempted to make a connection. It was then I realized that she'd never been my soul bond, despite the trust and love I'd shown her." Iron expected the anguish to pinch his vocal cords the way it always did whenever he thought of Abigail, but this time, the tension didn't come. Without that roadblock, he no longer had an excuse to bow out of shining a light on the ball and chain of his consequences.

"I was careless to assume the apex had promptly perished after my ax had struck him. Oh, don't get me wrong, he was well on his way to dying. My fire was doing its thing but nowhere near fast enough, and amid my grief, I didn't check on the bastard's progress. That was when the apex lifted its other hand and held out a glowing orb I hadn't seen before. Later, I learned it contained all sorts of nasty dark magic laced with acid and mages knew what. It exploded in my face. I threw my hands up and punched out my fire, but I wasn't fast enough to block all of the spray. My gloved hands were spared, but my wrists and lower forearms weren't. That shit coated my skin and would have eaten through my flesh entirely if Chrome hadn't been nearby, healing me as best he could with his power. Likewise, when the blast hit, my fire mingled with the dark magic, temporarily blinding me in one eye. I eventually regained my full vision, but the jumble of colors in that eye remained."

Anna's warm arms wrapped around his ribs. "I'm sorry you had to go through that. I know it's a stupid thing to do to apologize for something you had no part in, but it's all I can think to say. I'm so sorry, Iron."

He hugged her back, letting the feel of her soft skin drag him away from terrors that had dug their claws into him for far too long. "After Abigail, a lot of things I had always believed as truth started looking a little grimier. I didn't care how I killed, so long as I took down every single fucking charmer within sniffing distance. I realigned myself with my purpose, turning far more ruthless than any of my brothers thought healthy. I craved the routine and became a devoted student of it. A killer without a conscience. I focused on my duty to the celestial mages, rather than any trust I might have still had in them. I let *that* be my guide."

Iron breathed deeply, holding hard to Anna's sweet scent. "It took me a long time to realize I had no true love for Abigail, nor she for me, but she still didn't deserve to die the way she had. For centuries, I thought the fault lay in her and her sex. That there was something innately untrustworthy about women and their judgment, that perhaps they were just like the celestial mages. Creatures I should have a duty toward, but nothing further."

"Not all women are bad, just like not all men are. And believe me, it took a hell of a lot of bottomless bowls of M&Ms for me to get to a point where I could admit that and believe it."

He chuckled and kissed the top of her head. "I know that now. You've helped me realize that my concerns with trust stem from issues with my own judgment, not the judgment of others."

"But you trust your family, your brothers, right?"

"With my life."

"Let me ask you a question," Anna said, shifting slightly so she could look at him. "If you could do anything in the world that would bring you joy, what would it be? And *no*, don't give me that look. For the purposes of this conversation, I'm taking myself off the table. I mean for *you*, Iron. What would make you happy if Cyro wasn't a factor and you weren't beholden to anyone? What would Iron want for Iron's sake?"

"No one's ever asked me that before."

"Well, I'm not no one, and I'm asking. What would you want?"

He thought for a minute, then moved his hand lower, cupping the rounded softness of her lower belly. "This," he breathed. "I want this."

His answer flew across the small bedroom, lighting up every corner until there was no place for his deepest desires to hide. "I want a home. A *true* home. With space for all of us, my brothers, their mates, you and your baby. Everyone. I want to see your child born and cared for. I want to give you a family and have that baby passed around from uncle to uncle while I take care of you properly. I want to have so many damn buildings, we'd need our own zip code. As we are, half of us are scattered. Our den is underground, but we're all over the place. Bridget and Steel are in Boston once a month, Rose and Tammy have their apartment with all their shit still there, and Clara and Bronze spend most of their time in lycan territory. We're about as far-flung as possible, to the point that I doubt we could even call ourselves a real family anymore." Iron sat up and gripped the side of Anna's face. "I want a home, and I want you and your baby in it."

Anna's eyes turned liquid as she gripped his wrist, the one part of him he never let another soul touch. "I want that, too."

Iron kissed her, fiercely, furiously. He kissed her with a punishing precision that had erupted inside him from the single spark of her curiosity. *Home.* He'd never allowed himself to dream of it before.

And as Anna parted her legs and welcomed him into the warmth of her body, a new unshakable truth emboldened his frame, filling his muscles with a conviction there was no going back from.

He would give Anna and his family a proper home, even if it meant he'd never get to see it.

CHAPTER 27

The beginning of spring was always a doozy of a deception in New England. It either served up the ultimate omen of good things to come or plopped down the cruelest twist of climate trickery. Some years, several of the shops and restaurants in Aurora would offer special treats for tourists brave enough to bet their vacation dollars that the quaint little town would have been thawed out by then. Between the piles of unmelted snow and the curious crocuses, it wasn't uncommon to find offerings of free ice cream cones or iced coffees during those early days of the season. Whether the springtime celebrations actually held any sway over Mother Nature was anyone's guess, but it didn't stop Anna from bundling up in her puffer coat and nabbing a free waffle cone with soft serve mint and chocolate sprinkles every time.

The only difference on this occasion was the angel holding her hand while he escorted her to a park bench where they could enjoy their ice cream.

The past several days had been a whirlwind of emotions Iron had forced Anna to dredge up from her sentiment basement, dust off, and wrap around her with all the luster of a new pair of patent-leather shoes and ultra-glossy lipstick. Under his *very* persuasive encouragement, he'd gotten her out of the house almost every single day for a lunch date. And on the days when the weather decided to show its ass, as it often did in the weeks leading up to spring, he was at her door, takeout in hand, and his metallic power humming its *you power down or I'll do it for you* warning around the finer workings of her laptop. She'd learned the hard way early on that if she didn't start enforcing her time limit boundaries with her clients and let those calls bleed into her lunch hour, she'd have an apology e-mail to send later that afternoon explaining how her laptop mysteriously shut down mid-call.

Yeah . . . it'd taken only two of those e-mails before she, and her clients, got the literal memo going forward.

One by one, Iron had begun breaking down walls Anna had never even realized she'd put up. Things like mostly nutritionally balanced freezer meals and granola bars had been replaced with home-cooked spreads and *really damn good* granola bars. Like, the soft and chewy kind made by one of the bakeries in town that loaded each bar up with just the right amount of maple syrup, nuts, and chocolate morsels.

The kind of food with an expiration date that wasn't measured in months or years but days.

And her body freaking loved it.

At some point, Anna forgot to apologize for her pregnancy cravings, regardless of whether they were food or sex related. For a woman who had lived her entire life expressing regret for her natural inclinations, whether they be nonreciprocal kindness, her sweet tooth, or occasionally wanting sex anywhere other than the bedroom, it was a whole new world.

Iron, too, had been just as voracious and accommodating, to the point where she no longer had to ask, then justify what she wanted. The habit, which had been ingrained into her since she was young, had been scrubbed away with the sturdy strokes of

Iron's presence in her life. He was always there, feeding her, pleasuring her, supporting her in ways she didn't know how to accept, and like being repeatedly exposed to any foreign custom, she was learning. And loving it.

She just wished the weight pressing down on her core wasn't solely related to the baby.

"Your next OB appointment is on April fourteenth, right?" Iron settled them both on the bench and handed Anna her ice cream cone with an obscene number of napkins wrapped around the base to prevent leakage.

Oh, that man.

"Yup," she said around a mouthful of soft mint. "It's at nine thirty in the morning."

"You taking the afternoon off again?"

"Not this time. My afternoon's booked a bit too tightly, and two of my clients are going on spring break the following week, so it was the only time they could fit sessions in before they're away for a bit. And trust me, when clients have impending vacations, they usually don't skip sessions. Oftentimes, they'll book extras."

"Makes sense." He sat back against the bench and wrapped his arm around her shoulders, staring out at the small pond that had finally thawed enough for the local mallards to sit up and take notice from time to time.

Anna waited for him to say something else, something beyond remarks about the weather, what she'd like for dinner, or whether there were any more packages of maternity clothes waiting at her P.O. box that he could pick up for her.

As dreamlike as his attention had been, it was all a distraction from the real storm circling off on the horizon. Sure, it had been wonderful to skirt around it and pretend that the honeymoon didn't have to end, but he knew as well as she did that bullets weren't meant to be dodged forever. Not to mention that the longer he put off testing out his full angel fire with his brothers and the relic, the more worried she got that her selfishness in wanting to keep what they had intact would soon spread resentment among his family. Would they see her as stealing him away from them, when he had a duty far more significant than making sure she and the baby were getting in their recommended dietary fiber intake each day? (They were, by the way. Annoyingly so.)

There was only so much guilt Anna could carry around before she toppled over, especially when she was already leaden with the weight of another life.

"Iron," she said, shifting into his open embrace and leaning against his chest. Was it cowardly to avoid looking him in the eye while bringing up the topic of conversation they were both actively avoiding?

Some would say so, but she preferred to think of it as strategic. With her snuggled across his torso and holding a precariously balanced ice cream cone over his crotch, he was far less likely to bolt into the pond. Or so she hoped.

With a deep breath, using his powerful strength beneath her as a support, she tried again. "Titan called me this morning."

His fingers tensed around her shoulder, but only slightly. Not angry, then, just . . . anticipatory. Good. She could work with that.

"He said he tried to talk to you before you left the den, but you ignored him."

"Had somewhere to be."

"Where?"

He gripped her more tightly. "Wherever you were."

Anna handed him her ice cream cone—the good parts were already licked off anyway—so she could wrap both arms around his massive chest. To no one's surprise, he took it and let her consume as much of him as she could given her growing belly and their shortening time together. "You can't do that, Iron. They're your family."

"So are you," he whispered into the crown of her head. "Which is why I'm okay telling you the truth of things." Then he cast his pensive gaze out over the pond. "I'm a bit scared about the next steps. And worried."

She had to smile at that, because any other reaction would have enlisted a wellspring of her tears into service, and neither of them had enough napkins to stem that tide.

"It's okay to be scared, you know. There isn't a height or weight requirement, or gender requirement for that matter, in order to feel the emotion."

"If we test my full fire with that of my brothers' against the relic's shard, I'm worried about what it will reveal and the decisions we'll all have to make depending on the results. I've been hammering that damn nail since the moment Titan first bonded with Rose several years ago, but it wasn't anything my brothers were willing to face back then. They were all too happy and relieved, hopeful, and like hell I was going to be the asshole to highlight the fact that love didn't remove the expiration date on our situations. All it did was push it back a bit."

"Then do it afraid. Do it anyway, despite your fear. And you're not allowed to *not* believe me here. I've got far too much experience in this department to be talking out of my ass. My entire adult life has been me learning to plow through the scary things despite the fear. I wish I could say it gets easier, but it doesn't, only more necessary."

"There is no going back from whatever is revealed, Anna. I need you to know that. If we can return to the Empyrean, we must. And if we can't, then . . ."

He didn't need to say the rest. She knew. They all did. If they couldn't return to the Empyrean, there was no way to stop Cyro for good. If he'd finally managed to find a way to go after the Empyrean and break through its gates, there was nothing the sentinels could do about it while they were trapped in the mortal realm. It didn't matter who they were trapped with.

"You need to know," she said, doing her best to keep her voice from quivering. "Either way, you need to know."

"Will you be there with me? When we do the test again?"

That warming power within her chest that connected the two of them fluttered a form of hope. "Of course. We should all be there. I think we need to be."

"You're all I need."

She swallowed hard and burrowed her face farther into the protection of his body. "My heart's breaking, you know." It was a quiet confession, one she hoped wouldn't influence the turn of events, but also one she couldn't keep in any longer.

Her revelation was gobbled up by the wind and carried off to who knew where. Then Iron stood, tossed the remaining bit of ice cream cone and napkins into the garbage can near their bench, and settled her onto his lap with her head tucked beneath his chin.

"I don't think I can stop that," he breathed out, a dark anguish tarnishing his words. She gripped him tighter at the sound of his desperation. "But I sure as hell can protect every single one of the shards that do fall. I'll collect them, cherish them, and combine them with the broken pieces of my own so your soul will always be cared for. No matter what happens."

There wasn't any more either of them could say. Anna's throat had tightened to the point of pain, and after the declaration that Iron had just sent on the wind, she didn't think he had it in him to argue the point any further.

So, they sat there in silence, both realizing what Iron's full power would likely mean for the angels' ability to return home and defeat Cyro, and weighing that against the possibility of a world devoid of such power but which none of them would be around to see.

Iron clutched Anna's hand tighter in his as he escorted her over a particularly precarious mound of rubble. The structural disintegrity of the dilapidated strip mall had, to no one's surprise, degraded to levels even disease-riddled rodents and starving dogs wouldn't entertain for shelter, and yet there he was, setting up shop with his family as though it was a fucking Fourth of July picnic.

Bronze and Clara crested the patch of broken concrete behind them, paving enough of a way through the corrugated mess that, though not exactly red-carpet coiffed for the mates to traverse, was at least moderately more likely to get everyone to the center of the site sans broken ankles.

Beneath the paltry moonlight, Anna wrapped herself more fully around his arm. Then she pulled him up short, drew a happy face with her finger on the cap of his shoulder, and waited. While everyone else had started strategizing about where they were going to position, not only themselves but their mates during the celestial fireworks show, his Anna was tapping out a secret message on his body she knew he couldn't ignore.

Mages, he loved her little quirks. This one meant she wanted a kiss and that he had to stop what he was doing to bend down and deliver the goods.

As if there was something that would ever claim so much of his attention when her lips were on the line.

There were so many of Anna's small expressions of humanity that he adored, all crafted in a language she'd created and one he'd become a studious expert in over the past several weeks. They were nothing like Abigail's blatant seductive pulls. No, any time Anna wanted anything from him, she always couched it under the guise of her particular brand of cozy cheerfulness.

Kisses in exchange for an extra splash of French vanilla creamer in her occasional contraband coffee. Writing her name with her finger across his bare chest, right over where his heart was, when she wanted to wear his flannel, and little else, after sex. The way she tried to keep her tone and demeanor *so freaking serious* during client calls when she knew he was listening to her from the kitchen as he prepared one of her favorite lunches: a grilled cheese sandwich cut into the shape of Mickey Mouse with a bowl of broccoli cheese soup served in a coffee mug.

It was all heart-achingly beautiful and had gone a long way to peel the ice chips off that leathered and near-calcified muscle that had passed for his heart for so long.

Iron leaned down and gladly kissed Anna, letting his lips linger on hers for however many moments the two of them had before the shard in his pocket called him toward a more pressing duty.

Given both the known and unknown nature of what they were all about to face, it had been decided that every angel, mates included, should be present for the next attempt at calling forth the Empyrean's magic from the shard. Iron hadn't kept his full bonding with Anna a secret, but he hadn't felt ready to share its significance with his brothers just yet.

For the rest of the sentinels, they had all had time with their mates over the recent months and years, time to love and learn and cry and grieve with the women who'd sparked the fire within their chests.

Iron had barely enjoyed a handful of weeks. It was pitifully and unfairly short compared to the eternity he'd be staring down if the gift Anna had finally unleashed within him couldn't live up to the hope his brothers had been harboring for so long.

Anna nipped at his lower lip, then pulled away and placed her forehead against his. "Don't do that," she whispered against his lips.

"Do what?" He smiled at the two words that had become their signature question to each other.

"Go places I can't follow you."

His world stopped short and his heart flung itself against the wall of his chest at hearing his decree fired back at him. Goddamn, this woman. There was a reason every single one of his recent days had been consumed with incessant thoughts of her. From what she was or wasn't eating to whether any of the products from the home shopping channel chattering in the background of her living room would make her smile to how long her cabin went in between oil heat refuels. If a thousand thoughts ran through his mind at any given second, nine hundred and ninety-five of them were about Anna.

Iron hugged her fiercely and cupped the back of her head. "I'm not going anywhere."

And he meant it, with his whole fucking chest. He'd find a way to fulfill that promise to her, even if the fulfillment of that promise couldn't look like what they'd both hoped.

It was Tungsten who took the center of the circle this time, with Tammy on his right side holding his hand, while Titan and Rose stood at his left. The male's presence, with his staunch expression and unflinching frame, was a reminder to every single one of them why he wore the mantle of prime sentinel. Whereas skepticism-fueled duty had been the lifeblood of Iron's will for so long, unabashed loyalty had been Tungsten's charge. Despite his title being bestowed upon him by the prime mages, he'd earned his place fighting among the Empyrean's legions regardless, not only as a leader but as a brother as well.

Bronze sidled up to Iron and whispered out of the corner of his mouth, "This has got to be the lamest family reunion we've ever had."

"I didn't pick this place for the ambiance, asshole."

"Are you sure? Because I think, with such little cloud cover, our combined fire would look killer against that open sky." Bronze nudged Iron in the ribs. "Admit it. You wanted to show off for your girl a bit."

"You're going a little hard with the humor there. Can't say I'm entirely in the mood at the moment." For the love of all the mages, couldn't his brother read the fucking room?

Bronze scoffed. "Oh, please. You're never in the mood."

"I've had a lot on my mind."

"Tell me about it. Otherwise, you'd have catered the shit out of this affair."

Whatever annoyance Iron had tried desperately to hold onto flooded from him, deflating his chest and carving out the exact right amount of room for the hard chuckle he couldn't keep from shaking his shoulders. "You're something else."

"I'm a goddamn delight, is what I am." Bronze clapped him on the back of the neck and squeezed deeply before stepping away to rejoin Clara.

It was another punch to the gut Iron didn't see coming. Bronze's ability to light up the scene—in their case, an abandoned strip mall—find someone's pressure release valve, and flick it just enough so that the worst of the tension oozed out and went elsewhere.

Every angel there had an essential part to play in each other's lives, in how they fought not only for their survival but for the survival of a race of beings that had no idea they even existed.

And whatever Anna had released within him was about to affect all of that.

"We've all come here today because the significance of what may or may not be revealed by the relic's shard impacts all of us," Tung said, his booming voice carrying the weight of his words far beyond the rubble. "Whatever decisions need to be made after this shall be formed by the findings." Then he squeezed Tammy's hand and kissed the back of her palm. "I cannot dictate how this will go, nor tell you what path you must walk down when it's over. All I require is that we take the next step together, in whatever way that manifests." His tone cemented a finality into their circumstances, illuminating a fact none of them had ever really thought they'd achieve. It was in the shifting of boots and the broken eye contact.

Somewhere along the journey, hope and happiness had become integral players in their eternal game of homeward bound, with none of them feeling ten kinds of confidence about the path to take anymore.

A path that had been so straightforward for so long was now clear as mud.

There wasn't anything left to say, which was just fine with Iron. He needed things to move a hell of a lot quicker than they were. The sooner he had information, the sooner he could act.

Iron placed the small shard of the Empyrean's relic on the same flat slab of concrete as before. One by one, the angels took their familiar places in a circle surrounding the shard. The mates wisely stood way the fuck back, covered largely behind a broken bit of stone wall.

That was good. He needed Anna to be out of sight, because if he caught one more look of worry-laced encouragement in those jade-green eyes, he was liable to walk out on the whole thing and kiss the concern right out of her.

Putting her from his mind, he focused on the shard in front of him and called his power forth. "Let's light this candle."

Iron roared his fire's full release, pummeling the tiny shard with a power capable of demolishing cities. His brothers' cries joined in, their beams of fire coupling with his and infusing whatever fate had planned for them all into a fragment no bigger than Iron's pinky finger. He went on like that for as long as he could, until his muscles quivered and his abdominals strained with the force emanating from his core.

Like before, he capped off his fire and let his depleted body land on whatever it needed to. This time, it was Anna's softness that supported him. She ran up behind him and caught his arm just as he fell to his knees. "I've got you."

He smiled and appeased her caregiving spirit by leaning some of his weight on her and giving the rest to the stones beneath him. He was about as willing to risk crushing her as he was willing to let her know that her five-foot-nothing frame was no match for his bulk, regardless of her desire to think so.

Rhode was the first to his feet and, with Neela at his side, walked toward the relic. "That looks . . . different."

This time, the small shard glowed with the vibrant light and health they'd all hoped for. It pulsed with a radiating energy that struck Iron hard in his chest.

"Holy shit," he said, laying his palm flat on his pecs. "The realm resonance. I can feel it."

But as soon as he said the words, he knew they weren't right. The pulsing power that had once been so familiar to his body when he used to pass through the realms with ease now hummed a very muted cord, like a newborn baby plucking a harp string.

Chrome massaged his chest as well and frowned. "Something's off."

Iron eyed the shard, which still glowed as brightly as a proud daisy finally pushing out its petals in spring. The thing was powerful, there was no doubt, and far more so than last time.

What the hell was going on?

Around him, murmurings of confusion and speculation passed from brother to brother. Errant theories or posited outcomes made the rounds for good measure, but none of them landed with any sort of sense.

"You all feel it, too, right?" Bronze asked.

Steel nodded. "Yeah. It's the hum of what used to pull me through the realms, but it's so weak. I can barely sense it."

"Should we try again?" Brass offered. "Give ourselves a few minutes, then hit it with more fire?"

Tungsten shook his head. "I don't think that will do anything. It's already glowing and maintaining what we fed it. I don't see how it could hold more."

Titan stepped forward, his fist curled beneath his bearded chin. "What if—"

"It's too small," Iron replied, dropping the curtain on the hopes of everyone around him. "The shard is just too small to hold the power needed to transport us all back to the Empyrean." He walked toward the shard and lifted the luminous thing between his thumb and forefinger as though he were examining a specimen. An awareness filled his soul, sparking its insistence straight into his core while effectively burying the rest of his hope beneath the rubble.

He knew at once what the magic was trying to tell him and wished like hell it had a different message to convey.

Fuck.

"There's only enough power to transport one of us through the realms, and that's being generous. Likely, it'll be a one-way trip for whoever takes it."

Chrome shook his head. "Are you serious?"

"Yes." Iron dropped his head and shoved the shard back in

his pocket as if it were no more significant than a scratch-off lottery ticket.

Rose stepped forward, her hands out in a pleading gesture. "Is there really no guarantee that someone could return? If that thing is supposed to take you to the Empyrean, doesn't that mean there's a whole freaking host of Heavenly whoop ass waiting for you guys up there?" Tears brimmed her eyes, and Titan held out his hands to her, but she skirted around them. "No, I need to know this. You've been working your entire lives to get back home. Are you telling me, with all the wonders you've told us the Empyrean holds, that there's no magic that could bring someone back here?"

"We sealed the gates for a reason," Iron said. "Cyro's armies were about to bust through. Who knows what kind of headway they've made since our time in the mortal realm. If we go back, there's no telling what we'll be walking into, what we'll be able to access, if anything. We could be plopped into a battlefield with no backup, no support, and no way to punch through the gates without a flood of charmers entering."

"But you've got your powers back!" She was screaming now, tears streaking down her face as she finally let Titan grab her and draw her against his chest.

"There are no guarantees, except that one of us has to make a choice. Otherwise, the rest of this realm might look a lot like what we're standing on now."

"Can't we wait?" Bridget asked, her hands fisted in front of her. "Do we have to send someone now? Or at all, for that matter?"

"Cyro has the rest of the relic," Steel reminded her softly. "There's no telling how long before he uses his dark magic to crack the code on how to get that relic's Empyrean magic to open the gates for him. We can't let that happen, love."

"But can't we wait?" she yelled, echoing Rose's hysteria. "A day? A week? This is all happening so fast. Can't we just take some time to think about this, even if the outcome remains what it is?"

Iron knew what she was doing. Asking for more time with her soul bond. Buying precious selfish minutes where life could go back to the way it was, where ignorance won out over reality for just a little while longer.

He couldn't blame her in the slightest, especially as Anna hugged him tighter, nearly squeezing his sanity right out of him.

Tungsten heaved a sigh, then said, "Bridget's right. This is . . . not what any of us expected. Let's take three days to consider how we wish to proceed. I do believe the mages owe us that much of a fucking kindness."

Silence overtook their tired trip home. No one said a word or offered a look of encouragement for the shit sandwich they'd found themselves unable to stomach.

Which was just fine with him. Iron didn't need to witness any more looks of pity or consolation passing between them. Not from his brothers or his precious soul bond.

Because he'd already mapped out his course of action the moment he'd pocketed that damn shard.

He'd give Anna and her baby the life he'd promised them. A life of care and comfort among his family who would watch after them for the rest of their days.

Which, if Iron had anything to say about it, would be a very long fucking time.

Because he was going home.

CHAPTER 29

The coldness seeping into Anna's limbs had nothing to do with the lingering chill that the promise of spring had yet to chase away. It was a bleak reminder that everything had a duty to fulfill, even down to the changing seasons. Eventually, the snow would thaw, and the flora would get its act together by popping up where it needed to. The ice would recede and all those migrating birds would make their way back to their warmer-climate homes in the 'burbs.

But as she walked on wooden legs into her cold cabin that had yet to be graced with the seasonal tepid goodness she'd been assured would arrive any minute, one thing had become overly apparent.

Time was ticking, and not in her favor. Whether it was in the sad abandonment of unfulfilled bonds or hopeful future encounters that had been robbed of their luster, none of it would look like the happy life she'd finally known in Iron's arms.

She wanted to call bullshit on all of it.

Anna toed off her shoes, threw her coat on whatever surface felt so inclined to catch it, and went to her bedroom. Vaguely, she heard the front door close and registered the familiar details of Iron locking them in safely at the top of her little mountain. Coats hung up properly, shoes moved to the boot tray Iron had bought her, curtains brushing softly against their rods as he shut them, blocking out all presence from the outside world. All pleasant domestic actions that had been stamped as past due and would soon be called home by their rightful owner.

Each sound was heavy and final in a way they hadn't been before. Movements that were once comforting and sturdy now felt like heavily punctuated goodbyes. How many more times would she get to hear Iron *thunking* through her living room, refolding her throw blankets so the corners lined up evenly? Or hand-washing her favorite mug that she'd put off enjoying her hot drinks in for so long because life had tumbled her a bit too hard for her to manage anything that wasn't dishwasher safe?

Anna peeled off her clothes and hucked them into her hamper, wishing they'd hit the bottom with the same force she'd put into her throw. They didn't. Then she grabbed her bathrobe, the one overly plush number that did a shit job of keeping both her breasts fully covered but made up for it with its length and softness, and cinched the belt high above her belly.

It was the only armor she had to protect herself against the events of that evening. Seeing every one of the angels unleash the full force of their celestial fire, and then being communally cowed by something no bigger than a long sewing needle, was as humbling as it was heartbreaking.

They couldn't go home. Not all of them. Not fully. None of them even knew what going home would look like when they did, but yet one of them still had to.

And the truly awful person inside of her had been frickin' glad for the raw confusion in the moment, the pinched brows and soft curses that bounced from each one of Iron's brothers as they all realized time had betrayed them.

Because it meant she got a few more hours to savor Iron

before the weight of his family's decision sent them all down a course they couldn't turn back from.

Iron didn't come to her. He didn't seek her out or check on where her mind was at while he was likely trying to keep his own from falling apart. Instead, her only awareness of his presence came in the form of the bathroom door creaking open and the shower rushing to life.

Anna padded to the bathroom and joined Iron in the small space. He'd already shucked his flannel, shoes, and socks, leaving him in his jeans and black tank top. The bracers lay on top of his shirt, an acquiescence he only ever made when they were alone like this, and his hair had been unbound, with its ends already curling from the shower's steam. But it was his eyes that took her breath away, just stole it right out of her lungs as he walked over to her and, without saying anything, parted the collar of her robe and delicately pushed the fabric over her shoulders, baring all of her to him.

The fire that burned in those eyes was desperate, the same kind of stuff she imagined could both destroy and rekindle entire star systems. It was a phoenix's hope that simmered there, carving its determination and service into every muscle that flexed before her as he placed her glasses on the edge of the sink, then grabbed her hand and led her into the shower.

The rest of his clothes hit the floor before the tile's chill had an opportunity to seep into her feet. Because then he was there, surrounding her with his unabashed strength and sex. Their bodies clashed with the unspoken warning of a thunderclap. She claimed his mouth with a fury of her own, gripping and pulling her frustration and agony into his scalp. Iron growled back against her tugs. Good. She wanted more, needed his outward display of savage heartache that could never be matched with words. Anything requiring communication was done through the slick movements of their bodies.

Iron grunted his crushing need into his kiss, then palmed

her ass and lifted her above him, dragging feverish caresses of his lips across her collarbone and breasts. Their frantic movements became a conversation of their own.

I fucking hate this, but it doesn't change the fact that you're mine.

Anna pushed the pad of her foot off the back of the shower wall, spinning them so he was caught in the spray and she had more leverage when he positioned himself just right so she could sink down on his cock.

I don't want to think about anything other than you.

Iron entered her with a primal growl, shifting his support of her to one arm while he braced his other against the tile next to her ear. He pumped higher, harder, his balls slapping crudely against her flesh, feeding parts of himself into her that she never knew she could hold.

I can't take you with me.

Anna cried against his onslaught, gripping him fiercely, tears leaking from the corners of her eyes and mingling with the shower spray that pelted his massive shoulders.

You'll be inside me forever. Nothing will change that.

Her orgasm shattered not only her body but her heart. Iron, too, bucked through the pleasure-pain of what he'd wrought upon her. The laments that erupted from them both were cast into the steam around them like the desperate howls of dying animals. It was breaking her. Every touch, kiss, and shift of muscles against her skin tore new holes into a soul that had already been patched together a thousand times, leaving her with nothing but the threadbare integrity of tenuous promises she knew he couldn't keep. Ripples of urgent and deeply seated awareness flashed through his eyes as she kissed him through the tremors of their connection, and she wanted to cry all over again at the sight.

His promises stared back at her, sorrowful yet determined regardless of themselves. They were the clingings of an anguished and hopeless warrior who had finally found his soul but was fated to lose it.

And all she could do was bury her wet head against his strong shoulder and hold him through the agony.

Among the strands of limp and soaking hair and the fog of steam surrounding them, Anna was struck with the one word she and Iron had refused to give voice to, despite the fusion of their bodies all but yanking it from them.

It was an ending to a beginning that had never left the starting gate.

Goodbye.

ANNA HAD no clue what time it was, only that the sun had recently gotten its act together without her. She stretched her body, smiling at the familiar soreness that her inner thighs hadn't entirely gotten used to but now knew there was no point in protesting anymore. Her whole body had been a revolving commuter train of activity over the past few months, having gone from off-peak operations lulls to rush-hour acrobatics. Even the large kiwi inside of her—or plum, depending on which pregnancy app she looked at—had taken to exercising, with movements decidedly more forceful than goldfish flutters.

Groaning, she rolled over and sighed at the cooling depression that met her palm. At some point in the night, she and Iron had finally collapsed into bed, only agreeing to give up the ghost of consciousness because it had been through unconsciousness that they'd originally found each other. He'd whispered his promise to her again, that he'd always find a way to care for her, and she'd shushed him mightily by placing her palm over his mouth and telling him to continue this conversation in the dreamscape.

It didn't matter that they hadn't seen each other there since they'd connected in real life. It was a thread she needed to cling to, one he had no choice but to oblige her with.

Too bad she'd dreamed of nothing.

The rustic scents of oatmeal and earthy maple finally pulled her out of bed, though let the record show she did so under extreme duress.

"Figures he'd already be making breakfast."

Rubbing the sleep from her eyes, she felt around her night-stand for her glasses. When she couldn't find them, she remembered how Iron had left them on the edge of the bathroom sink. Normally, he'd be attentive enough to make sure she had them near before bed, but like she could blame him? They couldn't even get their own speech to show up for work last night, let alone demand employment from any of the other parts of their brains.

Despair had that effect on people.

Anna got to her feet and threw on whatever clothes she happened to grab first—a pair of maternity jeans and a long-sleeve tunic—and made her way out into the kitchen. Before she got there, though, her hip brushed against Iron's coat, which he'd tossed over the edge of the couch in the living room. A sturdy case of some sort hit the floor, and she leaned down to pick it up.

"Going back out again?" She said this more to herself since Iron rarely left his coat anywhere other than the coat rack unless he didn't plan on being inside very long.

"Yeah. I was about to touch base with Titan but remembered you have a client call at nine and wanted breakfast ready for you."

As if either of them could possibly go back to normal after what they'd learned the night before.

It was on the tip of her tongue to say as much, and how she'd already planned to reschedule all her calls today and spend it with him, when her brain stalled out over what she'd picked up off the floor.

It was a rigid pyramidal gray glasses case with the designery-est of designer brand names stamped across the magnetic flap.

"What's this?" Anna held up the case.

The wooden spoon hit the spoon rest next to the stove, and Iron filled the doorway between the kitchen and living room. A chagrined look of unease twisted his features. Then a huge sigh collapsed his shoulders. "Open it."

Curious, she skimmed her thumb along the magnetic seam. Air rushed out of her lungs. Nestled within its plum-colored bassinet of a microfiber lens cloth was a shiny new pair of prescription glasses. She knew without even lifting them to her eyes that they were meant for her. The pale purple brushed metallic frames arched over lenses that were the perfect shapely mix of oval and cat eye. Wide but not distractingly so. The carved temple arms featured cut-aways of small, very subtle flames arching around the sides before bleeding out into the most comfortable-looking temple tips she'd ever seen.

"They're titanium," Iron added as if he hadn't just added another several hundred dollars to the wonder sitting in her palms.

"What? Wait, you can't mean what I think you're meaning."

Iron lifted a brawny shoulder as if the half a grand worth of eyewear she cradled to her chest like a baby bird was just no big deal. "I know a guy. Helps that he's my brother and knows a thing or two about titanium metal manipulation. Rose had fun playing with the color wheel on that pair, too, after I told her what I was thinking. And before you ask, yes, it's the *right* prescription."

Gently, he lifted the glasses from their case and settled them on her face. All at once, her world came into focus again, starting with Iron, all glorious and charming, smiling sweetly before her, and ending with the last time she'd seen her old pair of glasses before she'd lost them. Iron had been with her then, too, as he'd usually been.

"You had something to do with my old pair going missing, didn't you?"

"Guilty." But there was a calm, comforting edge to the admission, as though he didn't mind getting caught because he was looking forward to the punishment. Then he cupped the sides of her face. "I hated seeing you settle for whatever you thought you deserved to see of the world. And I also learned real fast that I was a pretty miserable bastard to be around when I was away from you."

Anna snorted. "How could you tell?"

He lifted her chin higher and silenced her with a searing kiss that stole her breath as well as her brazen teases. "It wasn't hard to see the writing on the wall. Brass poured his beer in my lap when he asked whether everyone liked the cranberry scones Molly sent him home with, and I neglected to respond."

"Her food's amazing, though."

"Oh, I know. I just had other things on my mind, and by the time I realized how loud my silence was, I had a crotch full of IPA and the insistence from several dubiously well-intentioned family members that I needed to fix my shit or they'd fix it for me."

He didn't have to say what had been on his mind. The heat in his stare confirmed everything she was already thinking. She tried to look away, but her heart was utterly captivated. The beautiful warmth pumping out of him was just so damn bright even for her soul.

"The next time I saw you and saw the pitiful condition of your favorite glasses, I swiped them, determined to give them an overhaul for you. It was a small kindness I could offer. I kept telling myself that if I could make sure you had groceries, that your oil heat tank was accessible, that your damn car had enough in her to get you down the mountain and back, that you'd be okay without me."

Anna let her tears slip, not caring a whit whether or not she smudged her new glasses. And like freaking clockwork, Iron was there to catch every single tear that slid down her cheeks.

He was always there, and she was fairly certain she'd no longer know how to exist in a world where he didn't.

Iron smoothed his rough thumbs over her cheeks. "At one point, I wasn't even sure I was capable of returning your glasses to you. I debated with that selfish part of myself and thought if I could at least carry a piece of you with me, even if that piece was a pair of seen-better-days glasses with a scratch on the left lens, then that was better than not seeing you at all. I couldn't bear not having some of you to protect and hold in any way. After all, you had already been taken from my dreams, and though we'd yet to figure out how to use the relic's magic, I'd always known I wasn't meant to keep you forever. Just like I couldn't keep your glasses either."

The dam burst free on every emotion that had been lodged deep inside Anna. She cried rivers onto Iron's shirt. Anger, love, betrayal, fear, acceptance, compassion, it all poured out in great ugly gasps. Iron held her to him as he guided them to the nearby couch. There, he let her unleash everything she'd been feeling, and never once did he shush her or tell her it was going to be okay.

Because it wasn't. None of it was okay. Not the fact that he and his family had an impossible choice to make, or that she'd just begun to truly know the man she imagined her child meeting for the first time.

Not the fact that she loved him.

That thought had slapped her soberly across the face but made itself known as nothing but fact when she hadn't retreated from the sting it left behind. Instead, she relished it, searching out more of what it would mean to love a man such as him.

And all of that newly unearthed wonder had been stamped with an expiration date.

Anna kicked and sobbed and screamed, and Iron just held her through it all, until, finally, she lifted her head away from his chest just long enough to confirm what she dreaded. "We have two days, right? We still have that, don't we?"

He squeezed her tighter and nodded. "Two days."

They had two days until he and his brothers would meet to decide how they would proceed. Two days to cram a timeless future into. Two days to pretend they could be happy while simultaneously watching the clock call bullshit on the endeavor.

Two days to live a life she'd only begun to realize had been finally worth living.

CHAPTER 30

Iron stared down at the text string between him and his brothers confirming the time they'd agreed to meet the day after tomorrow. Molly had insisted on hosting the event at her restaurant, as if the fate of the realm and the rest of their lives was a formal affair that needed proper catering and tablescapes.

He loved Molly, he really did. In the short time he'd come to know her and the other women welcomed into his brothers' lives, he'd begun to realize what a band of cantankerous assholes the sentinels had devolved into before the soul bond had saved them all. It was an amazing thing to see the toll that such a brutal grind of an eternal routine had taken reflected back through the eyes of someone with no experience of the suffering but adoration for the hard work regardless. The familial ties that had sprouted between all of them had grown so thick, interweaving in and around each other like an unbreakable mesh, that Iron couldn't help but smile at the little network they'd created.

And that was why he wouldn't be attending the meeting to discuss the angels' next steps.

He'd already decided what needed to be done.

Iron tapped back a quick thumbs-up to the meeting time and closed a group chat that had served as a lifeline with his brothers for mages knew how many years. He'd never deleted the thing, and thanks to Chrome's tech storage wizardry, he never had to. Which meant he was never far from pulling up any of Bronze's rude jokes, all of which had been crafted pre-Clara, one of Steel's coffee experiments, or Brass's ridiculous high Wordle scores. His participation had been limited to a handful of monosyllabic responses comprised mostly of *K* or *Cool* or *Asshole*, sometimes with a variation of all three.

Even though he never said much, he savored the connection all the same. So it was just another trouble stone to add to his stack when he finally shut his phone off and placed it in the mahogany-colored ceramic teapot on his dresser. It was one of his favorite artifacts he'd picked up in the Jiangsu province during his time in China some years ago. He guessed mortals referred to that time period as the Qing Dynasty, but he just called it a great vacation with kick-ass food and excellent kung fu training excursions.

Iron placed the lid on the pot and smiled as he remembered the way Anna appreciated the bit of stoneware also. If all went according to plan, soon it'd be hers, along with everything else he owned, as he'd outlined in the instructions he left for his brothers to carry out.

He hadn't been able to look at Anna too closely before he left her sleeping an hour ago. It took everything he fucking had to pry himself away from her body, which she'd managed to wrap around his trunk like a greedy barnacle intent on capsizing the ship and happily going down with it if it meant more alone time together. And while he'd never actually confirmed anything to her, that brilliant mind of hers had worked out a likelihood that didn't end with them holding hands and shopping for strollers or installing a car seat in her Subaru. (He'd made a special note in his instructions for Titan to handle that last one and for Rose to handle the former.) And just the fact that he had to put pen to paper on that subject was the only motivation fueling his actions.

If he dwelled on what he was leaving behind, he'd never move forward, and that would be as unforgivable as his selfish heart that screamed at him to take to the skies and get back in bed with Anna so he might finish out the moonlight with her draped around him and the two of them beneath it.

But he couldn't, because the moment he turned around and flew right up that mountain of hers, it would take an act of the prime mages themselves to pry him from her arms.

Throwing back his shoulders, he tightened the cords on his leather bracers, rolled down his sleeves, and plucked the relic's shard from his breast pocket. Not only had the thing never stopped glowing since they'd infused their combined fire into it but it now had the nerve to wink at him as though it approved of his conspiracy to abandon his family so that they might have the chance to remain as one.

He took it out of its test tube prison, placed it on the granite floor of his living quarters, then retreated a few healthy steps. He supposed there should have been more fanfare when a sentinel returned to the Empyrean after being away from it for so long. A finely pressed uniform and shoe polish seemed like they belonged in that scenario. But he'd never been one for dramatics. Instead, he kept to his usual combination of boots, jeans, and flannel shirt that he'd freshen up and buy in bulk at the outdoor apparel store once a quarter century or so.

Weapons were a different story. That shit he loaded up on.

Thigh and ankle holsters held a variety of blades while guns lined every usable inch of his waist, chest, and underarms, starting behind his back and snaking around to the front. Then he picked up his mace in one hand and his battle ax in the other and sank into the weight of the metal surrounding him. Combinations of iron, steel, titanium, chrome, all of it melded, calibrated, and perfect for his grips and preferences.

All of it was infused with boatloads of his full angel fire.

Without another thought, he pointed his mace and ax at the shard and released his flames through the metal. The shard danced and flared brighter under his power's onslaught. He gritted his teeth, pushing more of himself into the tiny thing, willing it to show him that which he had not seen in eons.

Then he felt it, that hum of a forgotten resonance thickening through the air. It coated his skin and wrapped him in a hug that vibrated celestial energy through every cell.

"Holy shit," he breathed. His eyes winged open, and his body shook against its soothing assault.

The room around him faded into nothingness as his form at long last dissolved from the mortal plane.

A GREAT CRY wrenched through him as Iron materialized in a barren landscape of scorched earth that was nothing like the Empyrean he remembered. Parched terrain beaten down by a dark and dusty orange mist stretched out before him and was accented by craggy rock structures that looked as pained as he felt.

His hand flew to his chest, checking that all vital organs were present and accounted for, when something strange abraded his palm. A carpet of charcoal-gray scales, which, individually, were no larger than his fingernails, enmeshed around his frame to form an armor he'd been so long without. Thickly ridged plates snapped over his shoulders, elbows, and other joints, all knitted together by the innate power of his celestial makeup.

My battle skin.

Iron tested the fit and strength of his old armor, twisting and flexing with a familiar grace that rushed into him with every breath he took.

"I don't believe it."

Then he patted his suit, searching for his weapons before remembering they were part of him now, melded into his battle skin and ready to be called upon whenever he desired.

But that wasn't enough. He needed to test the theory.

As if no time had passed at all, Iron stretched out his hands to call forth his mace and ax. Both shimmered into being and settled at once into his battle grip. Then his wings responded. Pearlescent energy blazed between his shoulder blades, stretching out far and wide. The feathers were no longer iron, as they'd been in the mortal realm. Instead, they pulsed with the primal celestial light and power of the Empyrean.

"It worked. It fucking worked." Iron tested his power and found it to fit and function as well as if it had never left him. It was beautiful, stunning. He was about to drop to his knees in praise of it all when a subtle warmth kissed the back of his neck.

Behind him, the Empyrean's gates shone with a brightness to rival the sun. Tall, gleaming beams of celestial fire encased each rung of the gates as they shot northward into the mist above. The flames glowed a crackling fierce electric blue and snapped and hissed as they arced between the supports in both vertical and horizontal fashions, locking all of the Empyrean behind a mesh of celestial magic.

The *sentinels'* magic. The same fury that, with the help of the celestial mages long ago, Iron and his brothers had unleashed from outside the gates to enact the Sealing.

The wonder of it all was a thick thing in Iron's throat. "It held. All this time, it held. Thank the mages." It had all been worth it. The battles, the bleeding, the terrible losses, and the innumerable number of souls saved.

It had fucking worked.

But his joy was short-lived. A heavy presence thickened the

air around him. The flames licking at the gates pulled away slightly from their posts, aiming their ardor at something emerging from the fog.

Iron turned and froze. A dark figure cut a path through the mists, followed by waves and waves of bald soldiers. There were so many, stretching on toward an end Iron wasn't sure existed. The closer they got, the easier they were to identify. Innumerable numbers of gold bands stretched tightly across throats winked menacingly in the light of the fire at Iron's back. Single bands, double, triple. There were so many of them, all signifying the different classes of charmers who served Cyro. The beings looked nothing like the versions he'd fought over the long years, with their black tactical gear and reinforced artillery common among their mortal presence. Instead, they lined up, bare-chested and bold, muscles, magic, and gold and teal tattoos on full display for whatever they had in store—not for him, he realized with horror.

For the Empyrean.

"I'm so glad you've come to join me, and by the looks of it, you've finally managed to connect the dots of what we've come to do here today." Cyro stood before his minions in all his arrogant glory, though the formalwear he normally favored had been replaced with a type of shadowy battle skin, one that draped him in plates of ashen bone with wisps of white smoke clinging to his frame. A lone fang-like object hung from his neck. The full relic of the Empyrean's gates that Iron's shard had been severed from.

Iron had zero interest in whatever dark magic the bastard had coated himself in, only how to cut the head off the snake. "You look like the goddamn anemic Michelin Man, bringing all that third-rate garbage behind you up here to me."

"I had a feeling it would be you. The one to crack the code, I mean. Chrome is too hotheaded, Rhode is too damaged—sorry about that—and Tungsten fancies himself too much of a leader to realize when he's being led around. Of all the sentinels, though, you were the one I was never quite able to figure out. Until recently, that is. Tell me, do you think it's a coincidence that, of all your brothers, you were the one I expected to finally meet this day?"

"I expect you to eat my shit." Iron's body erupted into flames. He crouched low, preparing to lunge.

The bastard smiled at him, flashing far more fang than Iron was used to seeing from the showboating asshole. A warning singed the hairs at the back of Iron's neck. "How was Anna before you left her? Was she well?"

Cyro stepped fully out of the landscape's mist. Iron squinted at the weapon the demon ruler held in his hand. Something long and pale, no bigger than Iron's ax. Then Cyro tossed it to the ground between them.

Iron's fury blazed a rage in his core.

It was no weapon. There was a wet stump of flesh and bone on one end. Five delicate fingers on the other. A shining symbol painted on the underside of a wrist that spoke to him and him alone. *Daegan.*

Breath punched from his lungs, but he forced himself to look closer. *Really* look. He could not be wrong in this.

And then his world collapsed. Pale purple nail polish, the exact color of the glasses he'd given Anna, dotted each fingernail. He'd painted them himself after she'd rummaged through her polish collection, proudly plucking the perfect color from the bin. She'd asked him to paint every finger and toe so that they'd match her new glasses, and he'd done so gladly, perfectly content to deny her nothing.

A beastly cry erupted out of him, scattering the encompassing mist outward in undulating waves. Green shields were thrown up in response, barricading the charmers from the blast of his fiery anguish and what else might carry on its heels.

The dark magic beating off those things pricked his nose

and thickened the tears pooling in the corners of his eyes. It was the same vile magic that had snuffed out his angel fire the last time he'd encountered them.

But now there were many. Too many.

His heart ached, bled, was fucking ripped open across the mist and depleted of all usefulness and meaning.

Anna. *His* Anna. Her copper-spun hair and sunlit smile, her laugh, her kind heart, and her terrible taste in junk food. Her fucking *child*. They were all gone.

Because he'd wanted to chase a dream he had no business believing could be real.

Iron wailed harder, louder, until his fire pushed out farther beyond the reach of his weapons, just past the edge of his rage.

Cyro's cruel smile widened, and he kicked at Anna's arm, sending it flying into the mist. "That's it, brute. Show me your belly. Let me see those wounds bleed." The relic at Cyro's throat taunted him further. Bone weapons coated in black magic leaped into the bastard's hands.

Iron sprinted toward the demon ruler, ax and mace swinging, power pumping, fire seething.

He'd take down Cyro and every one of those fuckers in a blaze of the Empyrean's might.

And then he'd turn it on himself, because any love he'd had for living had died along with Anna.

CHAPTER 31

Anna walked out of her OB appointment alone save for the little slip of photo paper depicting the sum total of her family. Her not-so-tiny tyke was the size of a bell pepper or maybe a banana. That last one didn't make much sense, but then again, her brain hadn't exactly been up for a whole lot of critical analysis lately.

Her time with Dr. Li had been uneventfully standard, and she'd parted with her next appointment scheduled, along with instructions on when to take her glucose drink in relation to her exam. The medical assistant offered Anna a choice of fruit punch or orange flavor for the drink, with far too much enthusiasm given what the situation warranted. But, hey, Anna got it. Pregnancy gave women next to no choices most of the time, so it made sense the staff would get excited over the things they could control that might make the experience more palatable for their patients.

As far as Anna was concerned, *palatable* went out the window as soon as she entered the waiting room. The fallen look on the receptionist's face was only the first of several disappointed expressions Anna had to endure throughout her visit once the staff realized she hadn't brought Iron with her.

It was like being a celebrity by proxy. The still-contractually-valued understudy to the star people had *actually* paid to see.

Several weeks ago, she could have claimed to have never seen hope flee from a collective group of people so fast. Since then, she'd been regrettably enlightened.

Anna's phone chirped in her pocket, and she fished the thing out once she got into the elevator.

Rose: Here! I'm parked next to the blue minivan. Let me know when you're done.

Rose had insisted on at least giving her a ride to and from her OB appointment. Originally, Rose's offer included going in as Anna's exam room buddy as well, which Anna had kindly refused, but she wasn't really in a position to say no to a ride. She didn't think she could drive herself anyway. Her Subaru still sat parked at her cabin where she'd left it weeks ago.

Iron had been the last one to drive it when he'd taken her out for ice cream on that early spring day, and she couldn't bear the thought of going in there. Seeing the driver's seat adjusted to his brawny frame, the mirrors angled into a position that only his barbarian form could access, would gut her all over again.

Anna tapped out a quick *on my way* and hastened her steps, eager to run from the hollow feeling that had clung to her skin beneath the remorseful stares of the medical staff.

She'd hoped time would make whatever distance that separated her from Iron seem less . . . distant. It did no such fucking thing.

He was gone. Left without a trace, except for a few bleak instructions to his brothers that condensed the entirety of her and Iron's soul-deep connection into what others, who were very much not him, could provide for her and her baby in the future.

Which was precisely the biggest load of bullshit she'd ever been mired in.

She didn't need a contingency plan. She needed *him* and his unsinkable form sitting in that waiting room, holding her hand, and making grown men think twice about commenting on her marital state.

She needed to remember what his fierce intensity looked like etched across his face as he made her fall apart in his arms.

She needed *Iron*. And he was gone.

The car door closed, and Rose handed over the snack bag of meticulously portioned and obstetrician-approved-within-reason chocolate-covered espresso beans. Anna popped her new favorite indulgence into her mouth, but the treat tasted like ash on her tongue.

Rose pulled out of the parking lot. "What's the good word?"

Anna set her latest ultrasound photo up on the dashboard. "Baby's doing exactly what baby should be doing, I've gained another five pounds, and my doctor asked whether I had given any thought to a birth plan."

"Have you?"

"The plan is to give birth. As far as my shitty HMO and I are concerned, my healthcare providers are in charge of the rest."

Rose's warm hand gave hers a squeeze. "You know we're all here for you when you're ready."

The last thing Anna needed was guilt mingling with her snack's bittersweetness, but there it was, nonetheless.

"I know. I'm just . . . not, I guess, because *he* was supposed to be part of my birth plan. He was supposed to be with me filling out paperwork, making me laugh through the pain, and bringing me extra pairs of those cozy socks with the grippy things on the bottom in case I have to walk around a lot to get my water to break. *He* was my birth plan, Rose. He was my person, and he's not here."

Anna pushed down the familiar pain that burned behind her

chest whenever she thought about it lest it turn into another full-blown breakdown. "I miss him, and I don't know whether he's okay or not. I don't know whether he's even alive, or if he is, whether he's hurt or upset or regretful or anything. I just don't *know*. I hate not knowing, and I feel like if we really had this eternal soul bond connection or whatever, shouldn't I know *something*? Shouldn't I feel something in here if he wasn't alive anymore?" Anna tapped her chest but couldn't bring herself to look Rose in the eye.

Her friend didn't say anything. What could she say, really? Anna had heard it all before, and it wasn't like Rose and the others didn't get it. Oh, they got it, all right, and that was another source of her gnawing grief.

His family had lost one of their own as well, but where Iron's loss in her life was one of immense emptiness on her part, his disappearance for them was coated in something far more sinister: betrayal, made worse by the fact that his lone parting note asked them not to understand his actions but to look after Anna instead.

The forced shift in the priorities of a family that wasn't hers sat as well with her as the sludge in her coffee pot she'd forgotten to clean out from a few days ago.

"How's Titan? Did he and the others come up with any solutions yet?"

Rose blew out a breath and clicked on the SUV's blinker as she maneuvered into a left-only lane. "Stuck and frustrated like usual. He and Brass are back to combing the archives in the den's library in case there's something they missed, but Titan can only stay down there for so long before he gets twitchy. He swears the mountain knows Iron's gone, that the whole place feels different, like the minerals miss him or something. It seems everyone's developed a much shorter fuse with exponentially longer lighters to wave at each other. I've never seen them all fight so much."

"All of them?"

"Not all. Chrome decided to take it out on his computers. He destroyed half a bay of them one night in frustration before Rhode grabbed him by the neck and forced him to go out on patrol with him. Bronze is working with the lycans to do everything to make sure Iron isn't still local. They're organizing lots of hunting parties, but it's tough with their limitations around metal. Neela's been trying to tap into her demon charmer side to see whether there are any concentrated pockets of them in the area, but that's been a head-scratcher, too. It's like they all up and vanished, which is eerie and unusual. And Tung won't come out of his room unless he's dragged out. He's taking it the hardest, I'd say. Titan says he blames himself for not seeing Iron's plans ahead of time."

The SUV rumbled up Anna's gravel drive, throwing her thoughts into further turmoil. "This wasn't what he wanted."

"No," Rose agreed. "But it's what we've got to deal with right now."

Anna grabbed her ultrasound photo and headed into the house. After she waved goodbye to Rose and shut the door, she threw the lock and squeezed her eyes shut in frustration at how far apart Iron's family had been hurled.

They were too far away for even dreams to reach.

ANNA HAD JUST FINISHED PLACING her online grocery order when another alert popped up on her phone's screen. It was a text message from a name she hadn't seen in months.

Travis: Hey, Anna. Got some news. You free to talk for a few?

Travis, or The Asshole, as she'd renamed him in her contacts, lit up her phone's background, blocking out the wallpaper she'd just put up of her baby's latest ultrasound photo.

An alarming concern prickled within her chest.

The last time she'd spoken to him had been when he was backing out of her driveway and she was hollering at him for running his piece of shit cyber truck over the only patch of proper grass her property had that far into the woods.

It had been blessed silence since then, and all of a sudden, he was throwing out a *Hey, Anna* as if he were checking in with her on what to add to the grocery order?

Should she respond? Ignore it? Pretend that she'd changed her phone number?

But then she realized he could see that she'd read the message.

Shit.

She should ignore him. Take whatever peace she could still find in her quiet cabin and burrow into it where her past couldn't find her.

Anna had started to turn her phone off when it began ringing, and to her abject horror, her thumb had accidentally accepted the call.

Motherfucker!

"Hey, Anna. Long time, no chat." Travis's oily voice slid back into her world like a snake through tall grass.

"What do you want?"

"Ouch. Look, I guess I deserve that."

Irritation tightened her jaw. "You deserve a lot of things, none of which I'm willing to do hard time for. I'm too pregnant for prison." *At the moment,* she amended in her mind.

"That's actually what I wanted to talk to you about. Not the prison thing, though."

Miracle of miracles, the man can listen when he wants to.

"You've got to be, what, six months along now? Seven?"

"Five," she gritted out, "though I'm not surprised you're not exactly up to speed with human gestational cycles. You kind of need to act like a human being before you're considered part of the population."

He groaned. "Don't do this."

"Do what, talk? Correct you on your blatantly offensive disregard for the life I'm carrying? A life that you helped make?"

"*Fight.* I don't want to fight. I just want to talk."

"You want to *talk*," she said flatly. *That* had all her Spidey senses on high alert. The only time Travis ever wanted to talk was when there was a microphone involved.

"Yes, talk." An awkward heaviness thumped between them. "I miss you, okay?"

The confession nearly knocked her out of her chair, not because she couldn't imagine his stupid mouth ever forming the words but because that was the exact phrase she'd hoped to hear from him right after they'd initially split. Back then, she'd wanted something, *anything*, to show that she'd made the wrong decision, that she and Travis still had a future that didn't involve a three-thousand-mile divide. That she and her baby would truly be missed in some way by the man she gave six years of her life to, along with a not-insignificant amount of money.

But now, what all those words did for her was trigger an army of tightly honed defenses.

"You had six years and five months to miss me. Why start now? What's the catch?" And there most certainly would be a catch. She knew it as surely as the dark chocolate bar in her desk drawer was exactly seventy-two percent cacao.

Travis made a repugnant groan, reminding her more and more of the snake she knew him to be. "Fine. Just so you know, I didn't want to do it this way."

"Do *what*?"

"I'd like joint custody of the baby."

The floor nearly fell away beneath her. "Absolutely not. No way."

"It's kind of not your decision. Hence the phrase *joint* custody."

Oh, Anna was seeing red. Bloody crimson bolts of the stuff. "You walked out on us. You don't get to walk back in. We're not a set of car keys you left on the counter, asshole. We had an agreement. It was in the deed *you* signed over to me. I get the house, you get to live your bro-tastic life in California without a child to pay for."

"If you remember, all I did was sign over full ownership of the property to you. I never actually signed anything pertaining to my paternity or parental rights."

There it was. The other shoe hovering above her head, big, bold, and smelly as all hell. "Explain."

And explain he did, in all the gloating glee he could shove through a cellular connection. "I just landed a very lucrative contract, one that any family court judge couldn't ignore even if they wanted to. The money would ensure not only my financial stability as a parent but the financial welfare of my child."

My child. He said the words as though he'd been the one carrying the thing and heaving into a porcelain peehole for months on end.

"My personal empowerment business has recently taken a new interest in the family care sector. My podcast, while successful, didn't really take off until I began having more guests related to family management and welfare. When I informed my colleagues of your condition, they advised that it would position me in a more profitable light if I could portray myself as a family man. It would make me more approachable with listeners and experts and would give me angles to talk about that would increase the markets I could target."

"Are you fucking serious right now? You want to be a dad for a goddamn publicity stunt?"

"Not publicity, *profit*. Longevity. Generational wealth.

Legacy. Progeny. Jesus Christ, Anna, I thought you of all people would understand what it would mean for a child to not have to struggle their way through life."

"You understand *nothing* about me."

"Oh no?" She could hardly work up a response before he asked, "How's your business going these days?"

Shock stole the breath from her lungs. "It's fine."

"Then why does your online booking calendar show so many openings? It would be an easy thing to point out to a family court judge, especially when the child's father expresses concerns for how the mother's business can perform with so few clients."

Humiliation scraped daggers down her throat. "You have *no right* to stalk me like that and snoop through my practice's website."

"It's the Internet, Anna. I'm not looking at anything anyone else wouldn't."

New wells of hurt coated her eyes in liquid shame. He knew as well as she did how hard she worked to grow her virtual nutrition practice and all the hurdles she was still jumping through to make it happen. But these kinds of things took time. Trust, positive reviews, and referrals grew over years. She hadn't become a nutritionist so she could hack the latest search engine optimization practices for her site. It was a long game as much as it was a rewarding one. Anna had always shared that with him, and now he was using it against her? "Why would you do that?"

"Because money talks and bullshit walks. It's nothing personal."

"It's entirely personal."

"Look, I'll make sure you're provided for, too. I wouldn't abandon you, Anna."

Except you did. And so did Iron.

"Life doesn't need to be as hard for our child as it's been for you. I've grown a lot, and I'd like to make sure the baby can reap the benefits of that. If anything, I'm learning so much about parenthood, fatherhood, and family in general. Even if we're not together, you can't deny that it would be best for the kid to have financial stability. And you know the courts always do their best to try and keep the parents in the kid's life, even if the adults are separated. Kind of the best of all worlds, if you ask me. You get some money for a change, and we all get a happy little family. It's a win-win."

"Disrespectfully, fuck you."

Anna hung up on him before she found her phone hurled halfway down the mountain. The threats laced in Travis's voice shouldn't have hurt her the way they had, but her skin had grown far thinner in recent weeks, literally and figuratively. When she tried to summon a cone of safety around her shoulders by wrapping herself in her comforter, all she got was the ghost of Iron's warmth pressing down on her. It was a hollow, empty shell, no longer strong enough to offer the protection she needed, but still taunting in its presence regardless.

He'd left her. The reasons didn't matter because they wouldn't change the result. But the pain left behind didn't give a shit. It was there, hot and heavy, beating her down with its insistence that no, Anna, you cannot do this on your own. See how much it hurts? How foolish you are for thinking you even could.

She didn't try to sniff her way out of the tears that needed to fall, because what was the fucking point? Instead, she turned off her phone and chucked it into her nightstand drawer. It landed with a *thunk*, shaking her little reading lamp and the glasses case standing sentinel next to it.

The case, forgotten but not really, housed the new purple glasses Iron had gotten to replace her shoddy pair. She hadn't brought herself to wear them since the day he left.

Now, she was grateful for the decision. She couldn't bear the thought of seeing the lie she had become reflected back at her in her paltry bathroom mirror.

The one depicting the version of her that Iron had sworn was more than enough.

CHAPTER 32

Iron allowed himself one last memory of Anna's smile before he buried it beneath the shards of his broken heart and attacked. He swung his ax high, sending an arc of blue flames clear through the mystic in front of him. The crackling sizzle and scream were the fuel that kept Iron's legs pumping, his arms slashing. If he kept moving, kept chopping down the forest of charmers like so much overgrowth, he'd crowd out the billowing need to drop to his feet and grieve.

He ducked to the left, dodging a blow from an elite charmer, then swung back around and bashed his flaming mace into the side of the bastard's head. Blood sprayed, then atomized within his fire. Iron was just about to swing his ax again when a booming command froze every charmer around him.

"Hold! He is mine."

The crowd parted enough for Cyro to charge forward, bone swords swinging. Iron erupted and lunged for the demon ruler. With a mighty swing, Iron's mace connected with Cyro's shoulder, sending him crashing into a nearby boulder. Iron was getting ready to charge again, but a green light flared from Cyro's chest and punched out on a tether to hit Iron squarely in his. He grunted, then roared as he was dragged toward the boulder like some animal on a lead. He tried to dig his heels in, but the pull was too strong. Cyro's fist met Iron's face when they collided. Bone crunched. Pain exploded behind his eyes. He stumbled back on his ass to the sound of taunting laughter.

It was all too much, yet not enough. The hits did nothing to fill the void of despair that blossomed like a chasm within his chest. All they did was annoy the fuck out of him. This wasn't a warrior or anyone close to a worthy opponent. Cyro was simply the queen of the hive who'd grown fat on his drones. The true blow had already been dealt by Iron's hand. He'd made it up here, hadn't he? Left his whole life behind so those he loved could keep on living? Lost it all, including Anna and her child, for the sake of the realm?

And this piece of shit thought he could steal Iron's focus away from what truly mattered?

Rage morphed into blind fury as Iron took in the smug bloodied grin painting Cyro's face. It was a mockery of not only him but his brothers, the mates, Anna, and every soul they had ever saved. It flew in the face of all the emotions Iron had witnessed during his time among the mortals, every smile and sob that were as much a part of him as they were the human condition.

Iron threw his hands behind him, whipped his legs over-head, and vaulted backward so his feet were on the ground again. The flames of his and his brothers' fire barricading the Empyrean cast a hellish hue on the scene before him. Thick, soupy orange mist choked the landscape while monstrous warriors as far as the eye could see surrounded themselves in dark magic capable of destroying not only any life imaginable but any souls as well.

This was what Cyro brought to the Empyrean's doors and what he'd turn the highest realm of Heaven into. A barren wasteland with nothing but death, destruction, and eternal darkness.

And Iron was only one man. One sentinel. Against an army.

But he could still fly.

Iron took to the skies and, instead of firing his flames at Cyro, spun in the air and rained sheets of flames down on the front line of charmers. Many had shields up, but many didn't, and he smiled as the sickening screams of engulfed demons rose around him, registering on Cyro's smug-as-fuck face.

Black blood and dark fury coated the demon ruler's visage, and Iron drank that shit up. "That was the wrong move," Cyro warned.

"Was it? Because it looked really efficient."

Cyro got to his feet, sank into a crouch, and crossed his bone swords in an X over his chest. Dark magic swirled about the blades, then arced through the air. Iron threw his flames out but couldn't turn in time to block the blow entirely. His body twisted in midair while his wings took the brunt of the force, seizing them into stillness. Iron plummeted to the ground. Blood filled his mouth with the shock of the impact. When he tried to rise, the weight of his wings, now limp and useless, pulled him back down.

Cyro stalked toward him, grace and swagger filling every movement. "Poor downed little bird." Then he tapped the tips of his swords together. The sound was like a beast's canines sharpening each other.

Iron went to hurl his ax, but he'd lost the damn thing somewhere in the fall. Off toward his right, a charmer skulked forward, toed at something on the ground, and quickly slammed down its glowing shield, crushing the thing. Iron saw a burst of blue fire spread out beneath the shield's rim, then extinguish on a hiss.

His ax.

Fuck.

Iron shot to his feet and spat blood on the ground. His equilibrium was barely hanging on. He still had his mace, thank the mages, and he swung it like the wild savage he'd become. Cyro threw up a blade just in time, but the force of Iron's strike was too strong to withstand one-handed. One bone sword clamored to the ground. The demon ruler staggered, then recovered by gripping the tip of the remaining sword in one gloved hand while steadying the handle with the other. Iron poured every ounce of strength he had into the strike and was renewed when his efforts finally forced Cyro to take a step back.

A surge of satisfaction emboldened Iron's muscles, and he pushed harder, hoping for one more inch to throw the bastard off-balance.

"Enough of this." Cyro gritted his teeth and ducked out of the way, avoiding the head of the mace and sending Iron to the ground with the force of the feint. Startled but not stymied, Iron rose to his hands and knees, furious. The asshole was playing with him, letting him flounder and bob like a goddamn lure on a hook. Meanwhile, the press of charmers around him was churning, growing increasingly impatient with their lack of orders.

Already, his strength was waning. His muscles screamed in protest as he turned over, but he'd been far too slow.

Cyro jammed his glowing bone blade into Iron's thigh and pushed past his armor, past his femur and tendons and muscle, until the tip popped clean through to the other side. Then an added striking force of dark magic shot into the weapon, dragging it deeper through Iron, finding an anchor in the ground beneath.

Iron roared and reached for the hilt, determined to pry it free, but when he grabbed it, the enchantment coating the weapon singed his hands with acid, which had already begun to eat away at his leg.

His vision dimmed at the corners. He tried to call upon his fire, but the pain drowned out his ability to focus.

Cyro stood next to Iron's head and leaned his forearm over his knee. The relic at the bastard's throat swung like a pendulum counting down the minutes until that army would be unleashed on the Empyrean. It was a taunting affront, and they both knew it.

"This has been a long time coming, *Daegan*. You fought well. But well isn't good enough against me. You know that."

Iron pursed his lips and spat blood all over Cyro's chin. It was a weak parting shot, but it was all he had available.

Cyro smiled, letting the tracks of gore paint his features into a gruesome battle mask, and returned the favor, twisting the blade in Iron's leg as a reward for his efforts. Breath ripped from him, and the chaos around him flickered in and out of focus.

When he tried to sharpen his gaze once more, Cyro turned to face his minions like a king holding court. "My children, I do believe we are late for an appointment." Then he cocked his head back at Iron and grinned. "Give my regards to the rest of the sentinels. You shall see them soon enough."

The swiping arc of Cyro's long arm toward the Empyrean's gates was the battle charge that had made up so many of Iron's nightmares. Swarms of charmers fell upon the barricade with those damn enchanted shields chipping away and snuffing out the protective fires that had been erected so long ago. Anywhere a shield touched the sentinels' celestial magic, the flames fizzled out and died down. Blood mixed with bile in Iron's gut as entire rungs, now cleared of their wards, were being hacked to pieces and sawed through.

Iron let his head fall on the stone supporting him and couldn't even feel the pain of the acid ripping through his leg. He just lay there, frozen, helpless.

Whether it was the pain or despair that forced his eyes

closed, he didn't know, but when the darkness stole him from his agony, the first thing it showed him was Anna, all smiley and sunny and wearing the new glasses he had given her.

Horror gripped him more tightly as he recalled her beauty, her heart, and the beating heart of her child. All perfect. All gone.

The truth of his realization dragged him further down into his pain, even as the victorious shouts grew louder beyond him.

"She was perfect," he gasped around a mouthful of blood. "She and her child. They were perfect together. Perfect for . . ."

A sharp tug at a burgeoning thought pulled him away from the unconsciousness he so greedily sought. It was just a kernel, an immature seed of something, but the thing grew weightier the longer he latched on to it.

Mother. Child. The bond is always there, no matter how far apart they are.

He thought of the bond that brought him there, of his connection to the Empyrean that had stretched wider than anything could, despite the pervasive weakness of the link.

It had always been there. *Would* always be there. Calling the child home. The message just needed a vessel.

Iron's eyes flew open, and he called forth the shard of the relic that had been absorbed into his armor and kept safe against his heart. Cyro still hovered near him, but his attention was diverted, held by the massacre at the gates. Working quickly, Iron palmed the shard and then, with his good leg, hooked the toe of his boot behind Cyro's ankle and yanked him down. The demon tumbled forward, landing on top of him. The impact jostled the blade in Iron's leg, spiking his pain and clouding his vision further.

But he didn't need his vision.

He held Cyro by the neck and growled, "If you're going to come for a sentinel, you better fucking kill him."

Shard in hand, Iron swiped the remaining relic dangling

from Cyro's throat and summoned every ounce of fading strength into his muscles. Blue flames balled around the pair of relics in his fist. Then he pushed his power out so hard and fast, commanding his fire to carry the relics toward the Empyrean's gates.

The long-forgotten pieces of the gates connected with their source, finally returning home. Fueled by Iron's celestial powers, the gates exploded with magic and light. A fireball of Empyrean energy burst forth, incinerating every charmer on contact who had been attacking the gates and blowing Cyro off Iron. There was no time for any of those demons to scream, only die in a blazing blue inferno.

But a foreign sound of terror exploded through the mist around him. Cyro was on his hands and knees, trying to scramble toward the ashen remains of the charmer contingent that had just fallen. "No! *No!*"

"Yes, motherfucker." Iron reached out and grabbed Cyro by the ankle. The meager wisps of his fire were just enough to bond with the celestial power pouring off the gates. He pulled it all toward himself, every last ounce, using his body like a beacon. The connection was a thunderclap of power that left him and Cyro twitching and gasping, but for different reasons. The demon ruler writhed in Iron's grip, bucking and bending to avoid the oppressive light any way he could.

But it was no use. Iron had seen this show before and knew how it ended.

Cyro, the creator and ruler of all demon charmers, gasped and shuttered as he twitched beneath the light's onslaught. Blue flames curled up his body before the thing disintegrated into a puddle of ash at Iron's feet. Across the misty acres cowering in the Empyrean's shadows, more cries from charmers rang out, until the battlefield settled into a deathly silence.

The air buzzed around Iron, culminating in a jarring pop. His impaled leg twitched, and he sighed as Cyro's dark magic that had fastened Iron to the ground steadily faded away. Relief kissed his temple like a cold towel to fevered skin, but he couldn't lie there and soak it all in. Not yet. Able to touch the bone sword once more, Iron bit down on the handle of his mace and screamed as he yanked the weapon free of his thigh.

The dizzying pain was a new fresh hell. He groaned and rolled over to his side, grateful for the hard ground to cradle him instead of the grave he'd envisioned a breath ago.

Cyro was dead. Actually dead. Along with his armies of charmers.

It was an unfathomable reality to behold, and Iron would have let himself sink into it further were it not for the sizzling crackles of the compromised gates winking down at him.

He took a deep breath and let the reality of what he was witnessing soothe his rattled nerves.

He was staring at the gates of the Empyrean, which no longer needed to remain sealed.

Iron tried to stand on one leg, hoping like hell the celestial light from the Empyrean's gates would speed his healing along at, say, Superman-level speed. No dice. While the acid burns had stopped actively chewing his flesh to pieces, there was no hope for using his mutilated leg until it healed more.

His wings, on the other hand . . .

Iron forced himself up onto his good knee and tried to spread his wings wide. Like old friends stiff with arthritis but still up for a good time, they creakily stretched out on either side of him. Now free of Cyro's magic and mostly restored, they lifted him from the ground and carried him toward the one door he never thought he'd see again. He didn't know how much time he'd spent staring at the monumental structure. A minute? A handful of seconds? Whatever it was, it didn't matter. He was finally home.

Iron descended upon the center of the gates, gripped two of the rungs on either side of the port's main fastener, and, using his good leg as leverage, pulsed his power into the central locking mechanism. A muted resonance swept through his core, and he used his feeble strength to pull the gates wide open.

If the raspy breaths wheezing from him were anything worth collecting, the light that poured out would have stolen all of them.

But he was too exhausted to catch the show. It didn't even feel like anything worth tuning in for, not when a far-more-pressing bone-deep weariness sat on his shoulders and insisted he sleep.

Just . . . sleep.

If I can sleep, I can dream. Maybe I'll see . . .

With his eternal charge finally completed, Iron surveyed the battlefield as he drifted to the ground. Good and empty, as it should be. Flat on his back, he was content to let the Empyrean's light get to work on healing the parts of him that could be physically stitched up. But a hollow ache kept knocking at him behind his ribs that had nothing to do with the painful bone, muscle, and sinew regrowth he was in store for.

He'd destroyed Cyro. Wiped out the charmers. Opened the gates to a home that he and his brothers had long been sealed out of.

He was finally fucking *home*, and down to the very essence of his soul, he knew there was zero truth to that statement.

His heart, his true home, had been in a comfortable modest mountain cabin with questionable plumbing, rich charm, and a woman he'd loved more than the spark lighting his soul.

He *loved* Anna. Fuck, he loved her, and she was gone.

A trembling sensation stirred within his chest, but he choked it back. Later, he would find a time to properly grieve and care for the few memories he had of her. Mages *dammit*, but there were so precious few of them.

And then another memory alighted itself upon his mind. One from only a few moments ago.

Helpless to leave that particular scab alone, Iron sat up and looked out at the battlefield. The very *empty* battlefield. He scanned as far toward the horizons as his celestial senses would go, and when they all came back just as vacant as when he'd sent them out, Iron dropped his head into his hands and yanked at his hair for all his damn foolishness.

There was no severed arm of Anna's winking back at him from the battlefield, and there never had been. It had vanished along with Cyro and the rest of the prick's dark magic.

It had all been an illusion meant to trap and coerce Iron into battle, and it had worked.

Which also meant that Anna had never been dead at all and was still very much alive.

Alive and waiting for him to come home.

And with the full healing light of the Empyrean beating down and returning his powers to him, nothing was stopping him from doing just that.

CHAPTER 33

The quaint red-brick office building at the edge of Aurora proper had a lot of things going for it, except for its unfortunate proximity to the town's looming courthouse. Whether that was by design, Anna didn't know, but it increased the intimidation factor by ten thousand percent. It was the epitome of psychological manipulation for anyone who'd found themselves regrettably yanked into the mire that was the justice system.

A pleasant sign announcing that she'd arrived at the family law offices of Rogers and Wahl, Esq., stood out among the small well-manicured lawn. The neatly dotted rows of pansies that bracketed the signposts and walkway leading to the front entrance might as well have been emergency lights on a runway ramp signaling danger for any misstep, whether sure-footed or otherwise.

She *sooo* did not want to be here, and yet like the recurring theme of her thirties, she found herself with no choice.

Anna adjusted the file folder of notes tucked beneath her arm and eyed the courthouse that stood stories above the little law office. With its prominent bell tower and cold authoritarian block lettering, there was no hiding what it truly meant.

There be dragons.

She immediately marked it as the Bad Place. The place she'd have to go to convince total strangers that, despite not having the shiniest or most abundant stack of pennies in her piggy bank, her handful of dingy copper-crusted pennies still mattered and she'd somehow turn them into whatever she could to support her baby.

But first, she'd likely have to turn over a sizable portion of those pennies to an attorney in order to represent herself before said dragons.

Anna met the receptionist with a cheerful smile she didn't feel. "Hi, I'm Anna Malone. I have an appointment with Ms. Wahl at ten thirty."

"Malone, yes. Perfect. Please have a seat. We'll be right with you. Would you like anything while you wait?"

Oh, let's see . . . The ability to take what I'm about to pay you guys and redirect it back toward my budgeted hospital costs for when I actually have this kid.

A refund of the only available time I've had to myself instead of spending it pulling every document, bank statement, and pseudo-tangible proof that I won't be a terrible mother for your perusal.

A Diet Coke and happy dreams.

And the man I can't stop thinking about.

"Nope. I'm good."

Her terseness followed her as she took a seat in the waiting room, clutching her manila folder to her chest as though its meager confines were a plate of armor capable of shielding her from anything Travis could throw her way.

It had been a solid week and a half since that terrible phone call, which had provided the perfect amount of time for her to downward spiral into an abyss she was pretty sure she'd never be able to surface from again if she sank much deeper.

Rose had been the dutiful friend Anna needed, allowing her to at least unburden some of her anxiety onto someone else's shoulders regarding the whole Travis nightmare. But even that came with a reciprocal weight that had been inadvertently tossed back onto Anna's plate.

She couldn't escape the gnawing feeling that she was, in essence, an abandoned baby on someone else's doorstep. Before Iron left, he'd neatly deposited her among a family that was so freaking heartwarming and aligned, it made Anna feel like a donated secondhand jigsaw puzzle who was expected to be enjoyed and cared for despite her missing pieces.

There was heartache, and then there was heart*break*. Neither made for a lovable human for very long, and Anna feared she was quickly reaching the end of her rope as far as palatable social consumption was concerned.

Fuck, she missed him. So damn much.

A door opened. "Ms. Malone, come on in."

Francesca Wahl, Esq., was all serious kindness as she shook Anna's hand and welcomed her into her office. "Now, I've read your intake form about your former partner Travis O'Neil. You say he's located out in California now. Is that correct?"

"Yes, that's correct."

"And he's seeking joint custody of your child once it's born."

"That's what he said over the phone."

"How often have you spoken with him since that initial phone call?"

"I haven't. It was just the one time. But he's not the type of person to make empty threats, and I'd rather have my ducks in a row and be ready."

"I understand, and I support that entirely. If you can't be proactive, being reactive is the next best thing."

Anna clenched her back teeth and wondered what the cost differential was between proactivity and reactivity in the family law circuit. She couldn't say for certain, but she'd bet her

Subaru's three good cylinders that it came with a price tag well north of equitable, given her circumstances.

But again, unfortunately, she was *not* spoiled for choice.

Ms. Wahl set her glasses down on the desk and steepled her fingers, and Anna tried not to be jealous over the fact that the woman's glasses were clearly optional. "As I'm sure you'd been made aware when you booked this consultation, our firm tries to do everything we can to mediate and reach an agreement with both parties first. Family court is not a fun place, Ms. Malone, and we do our best to stay out of it whenever possible."

Is that why you require a method of payment to be placed on file for a freaking complimentary consultation?

"I can imagine."

"Before we discuss things further, do you think Mr. O'Neil would be open to mediation?"

"I think he would be open to whatever earns him the most money."

God, she was tired, as evidenced by her snarky insistence showing up to play in lieu of her common sense. In every possible way a pregnant woman could be tired, Anna was tired. Mentally, her mind was a fog of client appointments, missed grocery orders, and painful memories of Iron that refused to release their grip. Physically, the baby had pretty much taken over any vital functions and was now running the show. That meant extreme exhaustion at random hours of the day—usually during client calls—and a frustrating discomfort doing everything else, from fitting in a car's passenger seat to standing up from the toilet.

It was taking everything in her not to pick herself up out of that chair, find a horizontal surface, and hope that sleep would finally steal her away from reality and deliver her back into the dream world where there was only her and Iron.

Anna handed over her file and let the attorney peruse the prospects of what amounted to a meager defense against Travis once he no doubt armed himself with whatever heavy legal ammunition California could provide.

And the bitch didn't even put her definitely optional glasses back on to do it.

Anna was going through the motions, *mm-hmming* and nodding where appropriate as Ms. Wahl tapped out the stake of Anna's future into her computer, when the room fell silent.

"Is this the same Travis O'Neil you've cited in your complaint?" Ms. Wahl swung her computer screen around to show Anna, and the floor nearly fell away from the room.

A formal portrait of Travis's smug face accompanied no fewer than a dozen media articles all with titles featuring *podcast host*, *MLM company*, and *consumer fraud* in various arrangements.

"What the hell?" Anna scooted as close as her belly would allow to make sense of the words staring back at her. While Anna read on, Ms. Wahl quietly closed the notes and slid Anna's files back across the desk.

"It seems the umbrella company under which he's been operating his podcast and other business ventures has been charged with running an illegal pyramid scheme. It says here that, 'Travis O'Neil, host of *Bros, Babies, and Nixing Those Maybes,* a podcast designed to help expectant families and those with young children optimize all of the must-dos to cut out all those might-dos and simplify the early baby years, is one of several people being indicted for consumer fraud. O'Neil, along with many others named in the lawsuit, is accused of recruiting people to sell courses and lectures aimed at helping young families. However, those recruited by O'Neil have claimed in the filing that they were made to buy egregious quantities of course materials at regular intervals, regardless of how many they sold, with the promise of receiving bonuses or certain compensation once they'd reached eligibility. At the time of this filing, claimants have yet to receive any payment, with some having

gone into severe debt in order to meet the distribution require-
ments for payout.'"

"Holy shit." Anna's mind was reeling, just straight up spinning like a toy top with no guardrails. Had that asshole really
done all that?

"Ms. Malone, I think it's fair to say that, given the current
charges against him, any lawsuit he might bring forth wouldn't
hold much water with a judge." Then she stood and held out her
hand. Anna accepted it gladly. "But do call if things change and
he gets in touch with you, though I can't imagine that happening." She wrinkled her nose. "An MLM? Really? I thought all
those went out of style when we turned over a new century.
Guess I was wrong. Anyway, good luck."

On lighter feet, Anna walked out of the law office, not
knowing what to do or where to go. Technically, she'd won, but
without any of the logic or actual defenses usually employed in
such legal battles.

She kept waiting for the joy to hit her, but all that kept
swimming to the surface was the lingering malaise of her
circumstances.

Nothing had changed. Anna was right back where she
started. Alone. Lost. And now even more confused.

"Anna."

A voice she thought she'd never hear again pulled her
thoughts from their murky depths. A pickup truck she hadn't
seen in over a month sat in the parking lot. Iron stood in front
of it, his bicolored eyes gleaming and his body braced against
the vehicle in all its proud strength, like the monolith of her
memories that could never be torn down.

He was here. In front of her. Alive.

Iron.

Not caring whether or not he was real, she ran to him as fast
as her ballet flats would carry her. Like no time had passed at

all, he swept her into his arms, confirming her hope. *It's really him.*

Gangly limbs, nonaerodynamic belly, ugly tears. Whatever she had, he held in an embrace that infused strength into a body that hadn't known how to hold its own since he'd taken himself away from her.

"How are you back? What? Why?" Anna's sniffles were less than ladylike, but they were met in kind by the sweet murmurings he whispered into her ear. Each word took on a twinge of desperation and longing, pulling out the most unattractive sigh from her ragged lungs.

"My Anna. My love. Mages, I never thought I'd see you again." The confession was deliciously gruff and grizzly as he cupped the back of her head and carried her, dangling feet and all, over to the passenger side of his truck where there was less risk of an audience.

"You need to start talking because I am having a freaking day, and the last thing I need is to be sent into early labor when I've still got four months to go." Tears stung her eyes as she looked upon a face she feared would only ever live in her memories. "Is this real? Are you really back?"

He smiled and kissed her softly. Every frazzled nerve that had been going haywire since the moment she'd seen him finally sank in relief.

Once he'd tucked her securely into the passenger seat of his truck—with the seat blessedly already pushed all the way back—he knelt before her in the open doorway and anchored his palms against her thighs, as if he needed just as much support from her as she did from him. "It's done. It's all done. Cyro's gone. I killed him, and the moment I did, the rest of the charmers followed suit." Then a lightness she'd never seen before brightened his beautiful brown and hazel eyes. "I opened the gates."

Anna stilled, knowing full well what that meant. Iron and the other sentinels could finally go home.

"Stop," he said forcefully, squeezing her thighs again. "I know what you're thinking."

"How do you know what I'm thinking?"

"Because I know you. My entire being knows you. It was the reason I was able to come back at all, instead of offering myself up on a gruesome battlefield."

"What do you mean?"

"Cyro fucking tricked me, and I fell for it. He made me think you were dead so I wouldn't have anything to fight for. It almost worked, too, until it didn't." The corner of his mouth ticked up, and some of that cocky charm she'd missed so much touched his lips. "I remembered the glasses I gave you, how I insisted you needed to see your life clearly because everything I saw in you was the one home I had to make damn sure I came back to. I remembered how beautiful you looked clutching your ultrasound photo and how there were some connections not even Cyro was strong enough to sever. It helped me finally see through the mirage of his bullshit and remember what I was really fighting for."

Anna sifted her fingers through his thick hair, smiling at the way the sun lifted the bits of red to greet her. God, she'd forgotten about this. His hair, the color. The sharpness of this detail had already faded from her memory, and she was so grateful to have it back. "You were gone for so long."

He leaned into her touch. "Time works differently outside the mortal realm. It felt like an hour to me. And then, when I came back, I had some errands to run before I could see you."

Her back stiffened. She was unsure whether to be curious or offended that she wasn't his first stop while she was going mad with grief over him. "Errands?"

A bit of mischief flashed in his eyes. And mirth. "I took Titan and Chrome on a little trip out to California after Titan shared what you'd told Rose about a certain phone call with Travis."

"Oh no. What did you do?"

"Nothing I didn't mind handling in person. Turns out, when you shake a palm tree, all sorts of shit falls out of it, including evidence of undocumented earnings and below-board investment dealings under the guise of *infotainment* and *being a newspreneur*, whatever the fuck that means, as if that didn't require one to be held accountable for their shady business practices. After that, we left a few choice tips with the right people, and I came back to find you as fast as I could."

"I told Rose about Travis's phone call only because it seemed like the right thing to do after she'd spent so much time chauffeuring me around and making sure I saw the sun regularly. I never meant for it to turn into a huge thing."

Iron lifted his hands to the sides of her ribs and pulled her as close as the tight space would allow. "You're family. You're *my* family, and that's what this family does. Secrets go out the window when it comes to taking care of each other." His fingers drifted over her rounded abdomen. "This is my family. My home. My heart. Not the Empyrean. When I was up there, after I pried open the gates, I didn't even enter, because I no longer recognized myself as having a home base that didn't include you at the center of it. I love you, Anna. My soul, my body, all of it is nothing if I don't have you to return to each day." Then a startling blush crept up his cheeks, and he looked away quickly before returning his soft gaze to hers. "I want to care for you, to keep your heart . . . and your child, if you'll let me."

A tender pang tapped out a wonderful rhythm beneath her breast. She thought about letting this man dangle on the hook a bit longer while she ran some *errands* of her own, but she was just as powerless to stop the onslaught of her feelings as he was.

She kissed him fully, tenderly. "Then I guess you have us both, because I love you, too." Eager happiness chased away the last vestiges of the morning's fear and trepidation, but one final thought still managed to dig its heels in. "Wait! What about Titan and everyone else? Are they all returning to the Empyrean?"

Iron scoffed. "Are you kidding? And miss out on the opportunity to become aunts and uncles?" He shook his head as if Anna had just swallowed a boatload of crazy pills. And maybe she had, because she wasn't hating any of it, even though the result had been the exact opposite of what the angels had been fighting for all along. Then he explained further. "I thought they might have had a harder decision to make originally, but turns out, it was a no-brainer. Our lives and loves are here. Plus, the moment I showed Rhode and the others the larger property plans I'd been working on for the homestead, it was unanimously decided."

She laughed and settled her arms around his shoulders. "A celestial compound?"

"Damn right. Bronze is already looking at what's involved in getting a water slide installed for one of the pools."

"*One* of the pools? How many are you planning on having?"

"As many as we want. Zoning kind of goes out the window when you've got a team of angels who can move metal and earth around to ensure there's no water table or preserved wetlands issues."

"You're absolutely—"

"Crazy?"

"I was going to say mine. And I can't wait for me and my little bell pepper to go home with you. To your family."

"Sounds fucking perfect."

EPILOGUE

Five Months Later

Anna fidgeted in her deceptively comfortable Adirondack chair, trying to reposition the pillow beneath her lower back. It was far too easy to fall asleep in those things and, apparently, her entire right side, and her daughter, knew it as well.

Olive's little rosebud mouth stretched wide on a yawn, and Anna's body tensed as if she were playing a giant game of freeze tag.

Please go back to sleep. Please go back to sleep.

As if already realizing the importance of listening to one's mother at that early age, all the muscles in the baby's tiny cherubic face scrunched up, then relaxed as her little body molded back into the crook of Anna's arm.

Anna held her breath for a moment. Once it was clear the barely twenty-minute nap had been given approval by the CEO to continue, she breathed a sigh of relief and tried to resume her own rest, but the happy sight stretching out over the field before her was far more interesting than chasing the undisturbed sleep that would come later. (Iron always made sure of that last part.)

For the past month, she'd been content to take in the pleasure of her soul bond putting stakes in the ground and marking out where he and his brothers would install the utilities for their new homestead.

Damn, did her angel look good in a hard hat. Though, admittedly, not strictly necessary for an immortal with metallic armor at the ready, Iron indulged her regardless, despite making his disdain for the thing well known. Something he insisted harkened back to their first-ever text conversation.

Such a good man, that one.

Summoned by the pull of her thoughts, or so she liked to think, he handed a clipboard to Steel and made his way to where she and Olive were sitting beneath the shade of a pop-up tent. He swept a hand over his daughter's little auburn-haired crown first, dropping a kiss there, then delivered the same to Anna.

Sigh . . .

There were some things Anna would never get tired of seeing, and the sight of Iron bestowing such tenderness on their sleeping daughter was one that still made her heart clench and flutter about her new little family like a lovesick mama bird.

"She sleeping okay?" Iron lifted the pitcher of half lemonade, half iced tea sitting on the small table next to them and topped off her glass.

"Yup. Had a bit of a scare for a second there that this nap would only last twenty minutes, but she settled back down, thankfully."

Iron purloined a sip from her drink before handing it to her. "I'll take her in a few minutes if you'd like."

"I'm good for right now. The milk coma seems to be holding,

and I'm enjoying how studious you and the others are out there. The whole lot of you with your little pencils behind your ears and all your hard hats tipping together whenever you need to argue about something . . . It's my new favorite show."

"Oh yeah? Want me to get you some popcorn?"

"Kettle corn. Or maybe the white cheddar kind."

He chuckled softly. "I thought you weren't pregnant anymore."

"And your motherfucking point, my love?"

"No point to be made. Only that one, I love you; two, I'm team white cheddar all day, and three"—he leaned down low and kissed her, effectively stealing her fire with a sweep of his delicious tongue—"I fucking loved you pregnant, as much as love you now. As long as I get to feed you and Olive, I'm happy."

"*I'm* the one feeding Olive."

"And I'm the one who gets to watch." He waggled his eyebrows like the lech he most certainly wasn't and offered up a choice grunt when she poked him in the shin with her sandaled foot. Then he caught the thing and gave it a tender squeeze before settling it back down.

"How are things coming along with the site?" Anna asked before taking a sip of her drink. Mmm, sugar.

His features lit up and drifted into a new sort of dreaminess, one only caused by the immense pride and rewarding struggle of throwing oneself into a project of the soul.

Their homestead.

After Olive was born, Anna's tiny cabin became a flutter of activity, all meticulously planned and primped by the wonderful family she could no longer imagine her life without. Those first few days, Iron would hardly put Olive down, even going so far as to sleep in a recliner with her nestled snugly on his chest. It took far more convincing than Anna thought it would to have him hand the baby over so she could feed her, and even that was done under his watchful worried eye with a notepad in hand as he timed each feeding and got in super close to ensure she was latching on properly.

Eventually, after the first seventy-two hours of Olive using Iron's beard as her new favorite bedtime stuffed animal and a pediatrician's insistence that she was growing just fine, Iron eased up a touch and let the barrage of aunts and uncles flutter their favors onto the little darling.

The beard snuggling remained, though.

When the three of them had finally reemerged from their little cocoon with somewhat of a sleep schedule established, Iron got right to work on building the property of his dreams.

Which, in turn, would be the property of *their* dreams.

What had originally begun as a separate home for Neela had Rhode had morphed into a sanctuary for them all. Contrary to what Iron had originally thought, the lure of returning to the Empyrean had faded swiftly for each of the sentinels. Once the ability to travel between realms had been reestablished, more questions poured through the gate as well. Iron's time away, for one. No one really had an explanation for how much time would pass in the mortal realm if the angels left, even for a short time. Then there was the question of Neela, who was as much demon-born as she was Empyrean-born. The celestial seraph's power that had been infused into her inception was the main reason they suspected she'd lived through Cyro's destruction unscathed, and Rhode wasn't willing to chance whether the charmer part of her would be able to pass through the Empyrean's gates on a hunch.

It wasn't like Anna could blame him. They all loved Neela to pieces and couldn't imagine taking the risk just to satisfy a curiosity.

The overall discussion about returning had been brief, with every angel voting whole-heartedly to remain in the mortal realm, with one stipulation: they'd no longer reside below-ground. Doing so had been a necessity, a sign of their past and their celestial limitations. If they wanted to start a new life in this world, they needed to embrace the light and live among it.

It had been Iron's secret dream, and watching it realized on his face every day filled Anna's heart to bursting.

"Good," Iron said, pointing to some stakes at the far west end of the property's edge. "We finally worked out the nontech options for Bronze and Clara's home, and the general utilities will be going in soon. Steel's working on digging a new well, and Titan's arranging for building materials to arrive tomorrow morning." Iron mimicked clapping his hands together in eagerness but knew better than to actually clap and wake up Olive. Then he shrugged out of his flannel and tossed it on the chair next to Anna.

Her eyes grew wide at the sight of his new T-shirt, and she had to cover Olive's exposed ear as she whisper-shouted, "No. You. Didn't."

Before he could answer, a caravan of SUVs pulled up at the site, and a whole host of fruit platters, sandwiches, salads, chips, cookies, and—dear god, was that guacamole?—was held high on the shoulders of literal giants as the rest of their family joined them under the tent.

"Molly made fresh tortilla chips!" Drea's braid swung in a rhythm that matched her exuberance.

"Of course I did. Otherwise, what's the point?"

"The point is to find the nearest suitable food object with the right weight resistance to support boatloads of guac." Drea waved a chip in the air in demonstration and scooped a healthy portion into her mouth. The moan of delight that rumbled out of her could have saved Iron and the others some demolition work if it hadn't been cut short by a swallow. "Oh my god. Amazing."

Brass came over and kissed Molly's cheek. "Yes she is."

"I've got the schedule!" Neela wandered over and flashed a detailed piece of paper that said *Olive Us Taking Turns* scribbled at the top, encircled with cutesy hearts and smiley faces.

"What's this?" Anna asked.

"Our schedule for who gets to hold Olive when. After she wakes up, of course. However, if she sleeps much longer, it'll bleed into Tammy's time, and she got upset before when Rose got to hold her for longer. Something about being the older twin. I don't know."

Titan grunted softly when Rose slammed a bag of groceries into his stomach. Then she stormed over. "Are we really going to play the birthright game? Because it doesn't matter!"

Tammy took a box of cookies out of Tung's hands. "Then why did you get so annoyed the last time I got to feed her before you?"

"Because you didn't burp her right and she spit up all over me when it was my turn to take her right after you."

"Guys, there's no need to argue about this." Bronze stepped forward, hands outstretched between the women as though he were about to referee a fight. "We all know who Olive's favorite is, and it has everything to do with my awesome stroller sessions. Kid's a speed demon. I can tell you that right now."

The last of the car doors slammed, and Chrome sauntered over to the group, gripping several bags of diapers and wipes. Anna was about to wave when the bags hit the ground and a look of marked menace slashed across Chrome's face. Then he lifted his sunglasses off and slowly handed them to Drea, who'd run over to help with the bags.

Silver flames danced through his irises.

Uh-oh.

He gestured with his chin toward Iron, who had cleared all the women out of the way and moved to the side of the tent. "That shit for real?"

Iron pulled the sides of his T-shirt wide, accentuating the

hard pads of his chest. "Wouldn't wear it if I didn't mean it. You got something to say about it?"

"Oh, you bet I do."

Bridget pulled up a chair next to Anna and leaned toward her. "What's happening?"

Anna couldn't say anything. Her throat was frozen in anticipation. So she just pointed to the front of Iron's shirt.

There, in bold pink letters, his chest proudly proclaimed, *New dad. Free hugs. Today only.*

Chrome kicked out his heels like a bull, stirring up a cloud of dust to match the tension. "You ready for this, motherfucker?"

Iron rolled his shoulders back and threw his arms wide. "Bring it."

Anna's heart leaped into her throat as Chrome charged at her soul bond. The two met in a clash of back-slapping and bro squeezing that lasted the entire length of Drea devouring not one but two full-loaded tortilla chips.

A resounding peal of laughter rose up from their tiny tent. Anna couldn't help herself. She barked out her joy until her chest hurt from the exertion. Olive startled awake and protested just long enough for Neela to sweep her into her arms to steal her time with the baby before Tammy had resumed her composure from her laughing fit.

One by one, each angel lined up and did their best to out-hug the brother before them. Some, like Bronze, went with running starts while others, like Titan and Tungsten, simply embraced Iron and cupped him behind the neck in a gesture of joyful tenderness.

It went on like that through the rest of the sunny afternoon, with hugs shifting into quiet conversations, a rather heated debate on stroller shock absorbency, and fun-filled games of Frisbee and capture the flag.

They were all there. Together, protected, safe, and happy.

It was truly the perfect family.

Anna couldn't have dreamed of anything less.

CAN WE KEEP IN TOUCH? Are you curious to see what happens when Iron has a special surprise planned for Olive's first birthday party, but everyone, including his brothers, have seemed to conspire against him? Claim your BONUS EPILOGUE when you sign up to my newsletter to see how far Iron's willing to go to impress Anna and his daughter (hint: pink nail polish and barrettes might be involved) when literally everything starts to go wrong. Enjoy!

ARE you not quite ready to say goodbye to the angels just yet? I have a special collection on my Patreon where you can read EXCLUSIVE INTERVIEWS I've conducted with each angel. And let me tell you, when I finally get to sit down with these boys one on one, you never know what'll come out of their mouths. Dive into these EXCLUSIVE INTERVIEWS to hear all the heartwarming and sometimes juicy tidbits that can only be revealed beyond the books!

THANK you so much for reading *Angel's Smoke!* If you loved seeing Iron and Anna's relationship grow, let your friends know. Help other readers fall in love with this couple, and all those hunky angels, by leaving a review.

SCAN the first QR code to start reading the BONUS EPILOGUE today!

AND IF YOU'D like to access the EXCLUSIVE COLLECTION OF ANGEL INTERVIEWS, scan the second QR code to dive right in!

ACKNOWLEDGMENTS

Despite being an avid words person, I find myself at a huge loss for them when it comes to this book and, more specifically, this series. So, I'll keep this short.

A massive hug and my undying gratitude goes to Ben for being my hype guy with each new angel that dropped into my head. I couldn't have written any of these books without you. (And you also made sure I had a steady supply of snacks, which, to be fair, helped a lot as well. You're the best.)

To every reader who loved these characters and this series, I hope these books loved you back just as hard. You deserve it.

ABOUT THE AUTHOR

Aimee Robinson is a lover of romance novels in all forms. Her absolute favorites, though, are the ones that offer a little bit of something *extra*: time travel, guardian angels, good old-fashioned meddlesome grandmothers with a supernatural secret to hide, you name it.

She believes romance novels should transport you from the humdrum to the swoonworthy, preferably while being curled up on the couch with chocolate and tea (or a martini . . . or both!). Aimee's overactive imagination lends itself to fun tales with emotional adventures, sexy snark, and happily ever afters.

When not writing or reading, Aimee enjoys spending time with her husband and keeping up with her two young sons.